Caskets Full

Caskets Full

Rick Maydak

Dreaming Big Publications

Caskets Full
Copyright © 2018 Rick Maydak

Content Editor: Aaron Hwang
Copy Editor: Kestra Matson
Assistant Editor: London Koffler
Editor-in-Chief: Kristi King-Morgan
Formatter: Kristi King-Morgan
Cover Design: Macario Hernandez

ISBN- 978-1-947381-12-4

Dreaming Big Publications
www.dreamingbigpublications.com

Chapter One

My father once said,

"You can pick your friends...

"And you can pick your nose...

"But you can't pick your friend's nose."

Sage advice. Smart man.

I don't remember much of him, other than musk and whiskey. Tanned, sundried skin. Thick lines upon his cheeks and dark sunken eyes, but otherwise a face I have lost. The finer details are not there. I do not remember much since the war.

I do remember a coppery taste, a ringing in my ears. The smell of saltwater and brine. Sand under my nails. However, I do not remember him. Nor my mother. Not that well. Only glimpses, a flash here or there.

But I do remember my love. Her I will never forget.

It is mere moments before dawn, before the sun crests above the skyscrapers and caresses my tomb, that she comes to me. It is always the same: at first I get mere glimpses of her scarlet hair, shining like red tulips tickled with morning dew. The sun creeps through the strands, exploding her follicles in a grand fireworks display. Her green eyes shimmer in the morning light, sparkling like an aurora. She bites her lip, smiles, flirting with me, laughing at me.

I miss her. It is at these moments, tucked in tightly in my bunk, deep down in my living grave, next to dead bones, spider hollows, and discarded pizza boxes that she creeps back into my life, stalking me, haunting me.

It has been so long now that I can no longer hear her voice. My mind can no longer grasp the light octave that once sent me to my knees. That soft way she would say my name, the way she could calm my rage with each word. I suppose I was always a violent man, a killer, a lunatic. She kept that creature at bay, calmed the beast within, and tamed the Frankenstein that was I.

It is during these early morning hours that she sneaks back into my life. I try so hard not to think of her. Of what became of her. Did she marry? Did she have children of her own? Did they grow and give her a sea of grandchildren?

Was her husband a kind man? Did he hold her tight on winter nights? Did he twirl her hair amongst his fingertips, as I once did? Did she ever think of me when he made love to her, lost in a memory, a cheating heart and soul if not in body? Did she remember the way I held her, the way my arms felt, strong, powerful, yet kind while wrapped so tightly around her gentle waist?

Did she ever think of me as she aged? Did she look for me around corners, amongst shoppers at the mall, amongst the empty, lost faces of the city bus?

Did she live a long life? Did she die painlessly, amidst the dark of the night, her last breath a soft kiss to an empty room? Did her children hold her hand as she passed? Or did she suffer at the hands of cancer? Did she die slow, her life force drained day after day until the devil disease ultimately came to collect? Did she die alone? Oh God, did she die alone, forgotten in an empty hospital room, the only witness to her passing bedpans and beeping machines?

I try so hard to pretend; pretend that I forget what she looked like. Most days I am successful. However, it is during these early morning hours when I awake suddenly that I see her, her soft freckled face burning into my brain, branding my heart never to forget.

And as I mourn her, I wonder, did she mourn me? Did she sob as they lowered my empty, red-white-and-blue-draped box into the earth? Did her heart pound and skip a beat as the guns fired during that lonely morning? Did she claw at the dirt, angry with the God who took me too soon?

Or did she forget me? Was it easier that way? To pretend that I did not exist, that we never had been. Did she bury my memory deep within her heart, only to have it break free at a moment's notice, when the world beckoned with emotional triggers, moments of stimuli that brought me back to her? Back to life, resurrected from the dead. Those moments where she too went back to the ocean, could hear it hiss and burst as the moon lit a pathway to heaven across the waters. Did she remember lying in the sand, her head rested upon my chest, my heart thundering as she stared up into the darkness, the night teeming with summer stars? Did I haunt her as she haunts me?

The day will not reset these mornings. There is no escape for me. No mountain of cigarettes or vats of black coffee can help my head. My eyes burn the most on these days. The air always feels the coldest, my tomb never so lonely. Cotton never speaks on these mornings. I have never asked him if he has glimpsed these moments; he has never mentioned it nor do I wish to bring it up. These mornings hurt the most. If she could see me now. See what I have become. How she would hate me.

I imagine she is up there now, looking down on me, disappointed. I know I have let her down. In the name of God? Is that what this is? Death in the name of God? Sanctioned madness from the ultimate forgiver?

I stare at Cotton's coffin and I scowl. I spit on his grave and he says not a word.

I say, "Speak, old man," but he remains silent. It is as if he is not there at all, as if the box is empty.

I think of what we have done, all that we have accomplished. We carry out our mission like good little soldiers, the finest mercenaries, violent missionaries of the cross. This granted power is a burden. A necessary burden to carry out the Lord's grand plan. This plan is confusing to me—I am not evolved enough to understand. However, I cannot help but think of a quote I once heard, from someone I have long forgotten, who said, "Power corrupts, and absolute power corrupts absolutely."

At this thought, Cotton clears his throat. And I am no longer alone. There is a new name. Another victim. Another demon to slay.

Chapter Two

The man with the burlap sack over his head said, "Please...please let me go." Where his mouth should be a miniscule lake of saliva formed through the threads. He sat upon the dusty, cracked concrete floor, hands tied tightly behind his back. Garbage ties pulled tight upon his wrists. "Why are you doing this?"

The room smelled of burnt vegetation, pollen, and spores. The air felt damp, heavy, and humid like a swamp. Overhead a few light bulbs dangled from long lines; they buzzed and snapped, not making a clean connection, offering a little light for mere seconds, then they were off again. Faulty wiring.

I squatted down, hands upon my knees, knees that burned with fatigue. I leaned in close. I could smell fear mixed with egg salad upon his breath. Hot, sour air squeezed through the strands. "You know damn well why I'm doing this. Did you actually think you'd get away with your crimes? Your sins? I know everything."

The sack shook back and forth in disagreement. The rope I tied about his neck was coming loose. "You've got the wrong guy. I've done nothing!"

I reached forward and clutched the top of the sack. I ripped it off and tossed it over my shoulder. It landed with a wet smack, soaked through.

His bloodshot eyes were wild, pupils dilated wide. His curly black hair had turned into a sweaty, oily mess. His olive skin glistened in the moonlight that filtered through the warehouse's windows, windows twenty feet above our heads. I was not sure what he saw, but one look at my face and he screamed.

"Get away from me! Get away!"

I stood up and went over to his desk. Behind us a sea of flowers, vines, and roots loomed.

"I know I'm hard to look at. Been told that before. But I think that perhaps the Bella Donna I gave you is starting to kick in."

He tried to stand but his legs shook like a baby giraffe learning to walk. He fell backwards against the wall, then to the floor in a cloud of dust and pottery dirt.

Upon his desk, I grasped a strange looking root. The root looked like a demonic little man, frozen in stance by an angry God. It was about two feet long; the root split at the torso and formed two withered legs. A thick stump protruded outward from the top, looking like the head of a decayed corpse. Two dangling, scraggly arms reached at ninety-degree angles to the left and to the right, fingers flipping off the world. I carried the root over to him.

"This is a mandrake, is it not? Is it true when you rip these from the ground they scream like children?"

The man said nothing; he looked at me with swollen, red eyes. He started to breathe rapidly, struggling further with each breath.

I said, "You know, you've got quite a collection here. Different nightshades... this blue flower here, if I'm not mistaken, is Wolfsbane. And over here you've got some Wake Robin, Corn Cockle, and back there upon that far table you've got some White Snakeroot. Plus..." I went over to his desk, placed down the mandrake, and picked up a petri dish full of seeds, each about the size of a ladybug, shiny and red. "These look like Crab's Eye seeds. You've got a regular cache of nature's best arsenal. Weapons of natural destruction. An entire warehouse full!"

I tossed some of the seeds at him; he recoiled against the wall. His teeth chattered; he shivered and backed up against the rust-colored brick. His white button-down shirt was soaked through. Earth and pollen stained his black slacks.

I noticed that I too had soaked through. My black t-shirt was ruined. Pit stains mixed with deodorant; chalk colored armpits. July had not been kind. So humid you could cut the air with a blunt razor.

"You see I've done my research. I read quite a bit. I have all the time in the world. When you have as much time as I have, you might as well read... What I don't understand though..." I walked slowly over to the desk and picked up the demonic root, "... is this mandrake here. This thing is not that poisonous. Not really. At least not as much as some of the other shit you have. Might cause severe diarrhea, some minor delusions, but that's about it."

I leaned in and shook the mandrake in his face; he closed his eyes. "P...p... please... get that thing away from me..."

I stood back up and cracked my neck to the left. I held the mandrake like a baby boy, cradling the root in my arms. "You don't pretend this thing is like your kid or something, do you? Or your pet or something?

You freak. These things are disgusting looking. Downright terrifying." I tossed it onto his desk; the left arm broke off and fell to the floor. I pointed at the cowering man before me, shaking my finger at him. "You know, Hitler used to carry one of those root babies around. Thought it was good luck. Guess it wasn't."

He huddled against the wall. Despite the blaring heat, he shivered from the toxins. He clasped his arms with his hands, rubbing his skin in a vain attempt to get warm. "Are...y...y... you a Nazi?"

"Am I a what? You called me a what?!" With my steel tipped boots, I kicked him in the face. The sound of teeth crunching against bone echoed throughout the warehouse. His head smacked the wall with a crack; a bloodstain the size of a soccer ball formed amongst the brick. "You think because I'm bald, I'm a skinhead?! You have the audacity to call me that, you freak?!"

Blood poured from his nose. "B...b... but you have that swastika tattoo... below your eye." Thick, oily tears oozed from his eyes.

Is that what you think this is? A swastika? No, you idiot. It's a cross!" I leaned in close; the sickly stench of his dirty blood wafted towards my face. "See?!"

Hands held firmly behind his back he could not wipe the blood clean. He craned his neck to the side and did his best to wipe his nose on his white sleeve. It streaked the fabric with bright red blood mixed with mucus. A disgusting mosaic of red and brown.

"Then...why...is...it....it... upside down?"

I smacked his face with my hand. His skin was wet; it felt like soggy cardboard. "I find it an insult to wear a crucifix. I'm not fit to wear it that way. I fashion myself after St. Peter. They crucified him too you know. I doubt most people know that." I stood back up and picked up the mandrake's broken arm. "He was crucified upside down. He didn't feel he was worthy to die in the same manner as his Lord." I tossed the twisted branch towards him; he scuffled away from the wall as if I had thrown a bloody limb. He backpedaled across the room in a trembling crab walk, difficult with bound hands. His arms shook as he attempted to hold himself up.

I continued, "St. Peter was a liar. He lied three times to the Roman Sentry. Still, God forgave him. You see, this is my only hope. That I too will be forgiven."

His arms gave out, tired, bound wrists unable to support his weight. He collapsed to the floor, a broken mess of bone and flesh. I could tell that he was shutting down. A long spittle of drool hung from his lip. He took deep, weighted breaths. He wheezed each time, his lungs full of phlegm. Lips trembling, he said, "Tell me…why… why have you done this to me? I am a botanist. I've done nothing."

"Oh, I wouldn't say you've done nothing; in fact, you've accomplished quite a lot. I know everything about you. I know what you are, what exists within your flesh."

Outside, the moon must have disappeared behind dark clouds; the warehouse plunged into darkness. The light bulbs flickered overhead, flashing in the black with each successful connection, the room now lost in a rave like strobe light. Outside, the wind roared. The walls shook as air drafts clawed their way in from the outside. A storm was brewing. Off in the distance, beyond the walls, I could hear the Boston Harbor bell buoys knock around the water, pinging away. The sea was getting rough out there, along the docks. Something was coming.

I said, "I know that you stalk women. I know you have a penchant for blondes. I know that you go to that gym in Downtown Crossing—you sit on your exercise bike and don't even pedal. You stare at your magazine but you're not reading. You're looking for your next doll to play with. Before you poison them with these roots and berries."

"No, you've got it all wrong! You've got the wrong man!"

"Oh, I've got the right man alright. I know everything about you. Your name is Christopher Lindor. You grew up in Hingham, Massachusetts, in a cape style house with three bedrooms by the bay. In high school, the girls made fun of you. You never could get a date. You never went to a dance, no prom for you." I marveled at the blue color of the Wolfsbane flowers. Beautiful. I continued, "By day you are a professor at MIT. By night, you stalk women and murder them with toxins and poisons. You see I know everything about you. I have dreamt of you. And once I dream, He takes over. He knows everything about you. You see, He has named you. You have made the list. It is not good to make the list. Because then I'll come for you."

I was not sure if he heard me at all. His eyes rolled back in his head. Mucus poured from his nose like a molasses waterfall. He was starting to shut down. He barely moved his lips as he said, "Who….? Who's named me?"

"Why God of course. God has named you." A pair of dirt-encrusted gloves sat on his desk. I put them on and clasped the Wolfsbane's roots. I pulled the plant from the pot and crunched the flowers up into a ball. Then I took some of the remaining Crab's Eye berries and stuffed them inside. A tiny eggroll of toxicity. "You know, I wonder what happens if you ingest this much Wolfsbane all at once. Let's find out, shall we?" Lightning cracked the sky sending shadows of roots and vines dancing across the walls. Outside the warehouse distant thunder roared across the water.

In one last attempt to move, Christopher Lindor's body convulsed as if having a heart attack. Limbs dead, nerves severed, despite all his efforts, he moved maybe an inch across the stained floor. I knelt down and held my face mere inches from his. I wanted to make sure he heard these last words.

"Back to hell demon. You will not harm another innocent. Hades welcomes you."

I stuffed the toxic eggroll onto his tongue and then held his mouth shut with my right hand. With my left, I clasped and pinched his nose. Mucus poured out like thick maple syrup.

His head shook like it was going to explode.

I was thankful to have the gloves.

Chapter Three

The Sunday morning edition of the Boston Globe, dated July 9th, 2005, second page, had an intriguing article about the tragic death of a Clarendon Street health club worker. The article states that on the previous Friday morning, while a throng of sweaty commuters stood by, a bullet shot clean through Mr. Charles Stratton's abdomen. Turns out that Mr. Charles Stratton, the store manager, was handing out free bottled water outside the door of the health club to the many suits that passed by on their way to and from the commuter rail to work. The day was hot to say the least, one of those miserable summer mornings where the humidity makes the whole city seem to stick together like discarded popsicle sticks. The type of day where the sweet smell of fermented garbage overpowers the streets, wafting up from the back alleys and sewers, a stew of bubbling and boiling bacteria. Classic Boston summer heatwave.

Six months later another news story broke about Mr. Charles Stratton. An abandoned child, he had relocated to Boston from West Virginia two decades before. Seemingly irrelevant at first, as one read the article it was apparent that the writer's intent was to establish a motive, a background, to explain Mr. Stratton's suffering, confusion, and delusions. Turns out that Mr. Stratton had laced the water he was handing out with a chemical that caused intestinal bleeding. No deaths, but as city health officials claimed, had Mr. Stratton been able to continue his macabre lemonade stand for a few more weeks, he could have killed hundreds. The paper estimated that approximately one thousand three hundred commuters had so eagerly ingested the tainted water. There was no mention of the gunman who culled Mr. Charles Stratton from society. Folklore spread throughout the office buildings of Back Bay. Just who was this man? And how did he know? Or was this just karma paying back Mr. Charles Stratton for his deeds?

December 21st, 1995, the Westport Examiner reported upon the premature death of Marie Ladich, a nurse practitioner and avid visitor of Horseneck Beach. A lover of the South Coast, she had often told her friends that Westport was the best-kept secret in the entire state of Massachusetts. Many revered her; hundreds attended her funeral. Ms. Ladich was assassinated execution style in the back of her head. Her family deemed it best to keep the casket closed. A large chunk of bone had cleared clean through her skull, giving her what looked like a third eye socket upon her forehead. Rumor has it a young man, desperately in love with Ms. Ladich, forced his way through the funeral home. He carried half a bottle of wine tightly at his side, his eyes were bloodshot and wild as he sauntered into the room. Apparently, he ripped open the lid to get one last look at his beloved, only, at the sight of her contorted body, to throw up all over her corpse. What no one realized at the time was that Ms. Marie Ladich had killed three patients with an overdose of morphine. Later, as discovered in her diary, the media learned that she felt sorry for these people and their suffering, and was only aiding in their passing from this life. The diary goes on to read about how the power of having someone's life in her hands was intoxicating, and that she could not help the horrible things she had done.

This I understand very well.

In 1997, a jackhammer, in broad daylight, ripped a construction worker in half, yet no one witnessed the crime. His entrails spilt upon the pavement like bloodied snakes after a St. Patrick rampage. Upon further investigation, the media learned he was an escaped convict who had murdered three women.

In 1985 in Taunton, Massachusetts, a Toyota hatchback crushed an elderly man on his way to church. Hans Fredrick was a model churchgoer; he had served as usher for twenty years. He left behind a wife and seventeen grandchildren. What no one knew or ever found out was that he was a Nazi. He himself had pushed the button on the Auschwitz gas chamber upon many occasions. This secret goes with him to the grave. Not even his wife knows.

I know.

You have seen my handiwork. Evidence of my existence has graced the newspapers for sixty years. Yet none of you have noticed the pattern.

Chapter Four

I read a novel once by a Dr. Frederick Steinberg who thought he offered a brilliant alternative theory to time. As human beings, we tend to think of things in linear form. Life to us is a straight line. It has a beginning, the moment doctors rip us out of the warm, icky cavern of our mothers and bring us, freezing, into the cold, sterile hospital world, and it has an end, the moment when our hearts stop beating one last thunderous time as our bowels release our last meal into our shorts.

I just hope when I go I fill up on chili first.

Dr. Steinberg however thought differently than most other scholars. He proposed that the timeline in and of itself did not truly exist. While we perceive to go down a straight path, where our pasts become hazy, dark memories that fade into oblivion with time, this only occurs in our mind's eye. In fact, he proposed, each moment along that line of perception exists forever and never ends. The only thing that moves past any individual event is our own minds.

I for one found this theory fascinating. What it meant was that we never cease to exist. It meant that when we die only our mind perceives death as a new event, when in fact, everything we have ever done in our lives is continuing on forever. Think about it for a moment. Think of all the fabulous memories. Summer at Cape Cod. The time you hit your first home run, or kissed your first girl or boy, all occurring, forever and ever into infinity. It is a wild concept. Of course, there is a dark side to the theory. I cannot help to think of all those drunken sorority girls going down on random guys in the back alley behind the frat house. According to Dr. Steinberg, they are still going down on them.

I read Dr. Steinberg's book in 1965. The problem is, I have not read it yet as I stand here in the morning light, the salty briny smell of the ocean flooding my nostrils and clearing my sinuses. They have packed me into a coast guard landing craft. I'm six deep in this taxi to hell, my rifle held tight against my chest as I stare at the back of a soldier's helmet. His name is Michael Crabtree. I met him in boot camp. He hails from Austin, Texas. He is eighteen years old. I am eighteen years old. Last night we played cards at base camp in Portsmouth, England. This morning, we received the code word "Neptune". I cleaned my weapon, boarded a jeep, and found myself loaded into this sardine can. Now I wait to die.

Michael Crabtree and I are much alike. Like me, the army drafted him. Like me, he is fond of his country and proud to serve. His parents, Michael Senior and Paige Ellen Crabtree are quite proud of their boy. My parents are proud of me. We both graduated high school last year. He was an honor student. I was not. He was on the football team, played quarterback. I was on the football team, played defensive end. He has a girlfriend back home. I have a wife. Her name is Jennifer. We were married in secret last fall. My parents do not know and neither do hers. I miss her terribly.

She has wild red hair and tastes of strawberries. Freckles kiss her cheeks. Her eyes are the color of pine trees… no, more like the color of the grass in the late fall, swelling from the post-summer rains.

Michael Crabtree is my best friend. In ten minutes, I will watch his head explode.

The sea is rough. Our boat bounces through the frigid waters, tossed to and fro about the channel. The air is thick with moisture as a stinging mist pelts our skin like buckshot. The center of my stomach feels empty, as if I have not eaten in days. I threw up before boarding. I made sure no one noticed. I pretended I had to use the latrine. I threw up in the toilet, adding my unprocessed breakfast to the processed dinners in the hole below.

I close my eyes; my insides churn. It feels as if I have two tiny, clay-like demons inside my abdomen. I imagine that they have miniscule claws, the size of pins, at the tips of each finger. I can see them clearly in my head, ripping away at my insides, giggling and laughing. They are the color of concrete. No, more like mud, a dark brown mud that reminds me of dog shit. I can almost hear them in my head, laughing, chortling away.

Time to die, Bobby boy, time to die!

I hear shouts around me as our sergeant shouts out orders that no one can hear. The roar of the ocean is deafening. Our boat bounces high upon a wave, practically knocking us into the water. Freezing water pelts my skin as we land with a crash. My legs buckle and I slump in place, held up by the shoulders of the two men standing next to me.

The man on my right is Charlie Wilson. I met him a month ago. He is a devout Catholic. Out of the corner of my eye, I can see him chanting something under his breath. I envy him. He has hope. He has prayer. I have nothing. I gave up on church. Seemed like mindless bullshit to me. But it sure would be useful now. What is that old saying? There are no atheists in foxholes? I think that applies to Operation Overlord as well.

It is June 6th, 1944. When we set out from England, the sky was clear. I would later learn that Eisenhower chose to launch due to the improved weather conditions. It had rained for days. Now, as we close in on the shore, the sky has taken on an ashen color, mixed with black streaks that I know only can be smoke from cannon fire and the charred remains of those who landed on Omaha first.

The boat lurches again as a plane roars overhead. My throat fills with acid as my heart thunders in my chest. I hear a soldier a few rows back start to cry. The men around him offer encouraging words of bullshit. Charlie starts chanting faster. We are all of the same brood. Poor boys from the Midwest. If we do not die here, it will probably be in the steel mills, coalmines, or slaughterhouses. Some of the boys can barely read. I, as I mentioned, can read. I enjoy it immensely.

As the plane engine trails off in the distance, the sea becomes eerily calm.

I hear Charlie whisper. "I hear it now," he says, so soft that only he and I can hear.

I watch as Michael's helmet starts to shake. I can feel it too, the pounding artillery sound, like bass drums of the Gods. The echo fills the ocean as the pounding vibration rattles our bones.

I hear a high-pitched scream, no... more a whistle-like sound, careen through the air towards our boat. About a hundred yards to my right I watch the sky explode in a cloud of ash as an artillery shell pops. A plume of ocean water rises like a hydra into the sky, snaking in all directions. Our boat lurches to the left from the blast. Charlie falls against me, still muttering under his breath. For a split moment, as my head thunders from the echo, my eyes make contact with his. He is not there. His eyes look listless and dead, the color of rusted steel.

I say, "Charlie, wake up, man. What the hell is wrong with you?"

But Charlie does not hear me. I do not hear me. All I hear is this awful ringing rattling about my head, ping ponging back and forth. His teeth are chattering. I watch as his left eye rolls back in his head and I know that something is wrong. Blood pours from his mouth like a tipped paint can. He slumps in his stance. His chin hits his chest as his dog tags spin in the air. Time and space seem to slow down to crawl around me as I watch him gasp his last breath, like a struggling fish out of water. As he collapses to the floor the men around me scream at the sight. A three-pronged piece of shrapnel pierced his helmet, as if Poseidon himself lurched from the depths and speared him like a humpback whale. Charlie Wilson shakes a last time, shits his shorts, and leaves this world. He is the first of us to die.

The air explodes in a sea of sulfur as another artillery shell lands to our left. I watch in horror and clutch my rifle as the boat next to us explodes into an orgy of limbs, guts, and dark, black oil-like blood. The ringing in my ears does nothing to muffle the screams of the men half-alive, their limbs melted to the metal floor of their landing craft, a soup of intestines and nerve endings. Their boat roars off to the left, no one at the helm, exploding into a Viking funeral pyre.

A plane screams overhead towards the horizon that is only now coming into focus. I can see the ridgeline now, a hazy black line amongst the smoke. Every other second the ridgeline lights up with tiny fireworks, miniscule Christmas-light-sized pops that, after a few moments, I realize is mounted machine gun fire.

The throttle is pushed down hard and the boat lurches forward. Like a roller coaster to hell, we bounce over the waves, the mist of the ocean covering our faces in a cold, wet slosh. I am thankful for it. For it hides my tears.

I had always imagined what death would be like. I guess I never had imagined that I would get a warning first. I had always hoped that I would go in my sleep, or suddenly. Maybe in a car crash. Something that took me by surprise. But to know it is coming, to know it is stalking you, only minutes, maybe seconds away, is sheer terror.

I watch as the men around me make the sign of the cross. Michael Crabtree starts chanting the Lord's Prayer. I look down at Charlie's corpse. I notice that his bloodied head, the back now caved in like a rotting gourd, is resting on my boots. I cannot move, lest I stand on his back, I am stuck in my stance. I look up at the sky and see a black smoke careen towards us like the devil's fog. I slowly nudge his dead head off my boot and push him away. No one seems to notice. Too consumed with unavoidable fate. Death is coming. He stands behind the metal door in front of us. It is only a matter of time before it lowers and we storm out into his onslaught. He stalks the ridgeline, laughing at us, mocking us.

It is then that I hear the first ping, the sound of bullets careening off the front of our craft.

Our sergeant yells, "Get ready, men!" He stands at the back, a caricature of war, wet, bushy moustache and rough skin. He chews on his soggy, unlit cigar, safe behind his shield of soon to be dead boys.

The pinging sound gets louder as I hear the shouts and screams of men from other boats that have reached the shoreline. The ridge stands before us, shrouded in a cloud of thick, black smoke. It is like staring into a firestorm. I see the inferno light up as machine gun fire rains down towards us, smacking the front of our boat and pelting the water, creating a slapping sound.

Over the edge of the craft, I can see off to my right, boats that have reached the shore a mere thirty seconds before us. It only registers in my mind in a brief flash. I see the doors coming down into the water as the men fall like dominoes, cut down in the machine gun fire. I watch as those in the back crawl over the dead like swarming rats, eager to dive down into the cold, briny water, as if it somehow offers cover from the ripping metal rained down from the angry God upon the hillside.

Off amongst the smoke and smell of gunpowder I make out what appears to be large, steel constructions, in the shape of X's upon the red stained beach.

My head lurches backwards as a sharp knife-like pain shoots up my spine, careening up my neck towards the base of my brain. An artillery shell explodes a few feet in front of our boat, sending the nose-diving downwards like a submarine. The boat pulls the men in the front under first; they drown like mice as those behind them push down on their struggling bodies to keep themselves from going under. Those on the back of the ship are catapulted into the air into a sea of bullets that spray their bodies like buckshot. They hit the water with a smack as the life ebbs out of them, food for sharks.

Along with Michael Crabtree, I am catapulted, flying into the ocean at the head of the ship. The water, heated from the explosion, is boiling like a cauldron. My skin burns as I scream.

I hold on tight to my gun as if it somehow will offer me protection from the machine guns upon the hill. I sink down into the water as I watch bullets rip through the dark green sea in slow motion. Time seems to crawl as my ears ring. I hear nothing but this awful ringing. Something grabs my feet and pulls down hard. The saltwater burns my wild eyes. Michael sinks before me, struggling with his pack. I watch as he drops his rifle; it sinks towards the floor like a depth charge. As Michael looks upwards towards the ocean ceiling, his head explodes like a squashed plum.

There are bodies all around me, sinking down towards the depths, the devil collecting his quarry. With my left foot I try to push off my right boot but it will not give; it is tied too tight. I know if I do not get to the surface soon my lungs will explode from the pressure. But I am terrified that if I attempt a breath, my head will be shot clear through with molten steel.

I know fear, true, real fear, more real than anything ever in my entire life. When I look back now and think about the things that used to scare me—speaking in front of a class, asking a girl out—it all seems so trivial, so pointless. I realize at that moment that most of us are nothing more than parasites, sucking on society and life's tit as if we deserve an inheritance that we had no help in building or creating. Pointless, meaningless fucking lives of going to work, reading the newspaper, drinking beer, and then doing it all fucking over again. But God what I would give for it at this moment as I feel the cold of the ocean freeze my bones.

Knowing that I will drown if I don't reach the surface soon I drop my gun and with both arms swim to the top. The water has grown dark and murky. I can taste the coppery blood upon my lips as I hold my mouth shut tight, terrified that if I release for even a second, I will drown in an instant. I hear the muted sound of machine gun fire, screams, and explosions above my head. As I clear the surface of the ocean, I witness hell upon earth.

Entrails cover the beach; blood and guts. Collapsed dead men upon dead men stack upon the shore, a skeletal highway that only the grim reaper would enjoy. The smell of gunpowder overpowers my nostrils, mixed with the foul stench of raw meat, blood, and death. The air pounds with gunfire as the artillery upon the hill seems to have no end. Wave after wave of soldier, someone's father, son, brother, and lover collapses on the shore, dominoes that lead back to Hades.

I gasp in horror. Then I feel it. I feel a hot, lancing sensation in my stomach. The sea around me seems to bubble and boil. Suddenly I feel like I have to throw up as a pool of crimson surrounds me. I reach down into the cold water and feel the hot, gushing sensation of my insides contributing to the cesspool of chum.

Suddenly I grow tired as my mind grows foggy, hazy. The smoky ridgeline goes blurry as my legs, treading water, suddenly feel like heavy, dead tree limbs that I cannot control. My heart begins to pound in my head, the only thing I hear. Gone is the machine gun fire, the artillery blasts, the ringing in my ears. All I hear is my own heartbeat, thudding like a bass drum, slower and slower.

I sink.

I sink down towards the depths. Down past the floating, bullet-ridden bodies of my comrades.

I grow cold, the farther I sink. The light of the surface grows darker, as I descend. Every few moments the surface lights up with another explosion.

But not after a while.

After a while, I see nothing but darkness, the farther I sink. I begin to wonder if I will touch the ocean floor. I sink for what seems like eternity, in the black, in the ink, the oily ooze, the tar pit of the ocean.

It is then that I realize that I was close to the shore. It does not make sense I would still be sinking.

But then again, I have never died before.

Chapter Five

My feet felt heavy in my steel tipped boots. The brick passed slowly under my feet. My shoulders felt burdened by my backpack. A solid week's haul of canned goods from the food bank. My mind felt clear despite the bourbon and whiskey. When you have lived as long as I have, you develop a tolerance to alcohol. No matter how much I engulf, clarity remains. The curse of a tolerance accumulated across decades.

The wind was cold, one of those winter nights where every star shone out against the black tar backdrop of space, a million pinholes through the canvas that lies over all of us, hiding us from the true reality beyond. But I could not see the stars. I had to imagine what they looked like. Here in the city, the stars are hard to come by. Too much light. The gleaming, glass and steel office towers of the financial district hovered behind my head, lighting my way as I walked down an alley into the North End.

The smell of pasta sauce, garlic and fresh fish filled the frigid night air. I salivated like a dog, but the canned goods would have to do. No nice restaurant would accept me. I'm not welcome. Nor do I have the money. When you are in my line of work, money is hard to come by. You have to make do with what you have.

I looked up and squinted. Dehydration stung at my eyes like pins and needles. I still see the world in a hazy shade of red, as if I am looking through lava glasses. It has been like this as long as I can remember, ever since I woke up. It makes going to the movies or watching television pointless, like watching everything wearing 3-D glasses that don't work. I suppose I have gotten used to it over time. I find that you get used to most things... except for the passing of time. I have never gotten used to that.

It was getting late. I do not wear a watch but I have gotten used to the passing of hours. It has become my curse. Most people long for time to slow down, they worry about their lives passing too quickly, caught up in their own stress, jobs, family, affairs, and bullshit. Quests for power. Greed. It is these same people though who curse the clock. They swear at the mirror when they begin to notice wrinkles below their blackened eyes. They curse at white strands of hair. They are afraid that time is passing them by, too quickly; they never have enough. Me, I've got all the time in the world. I have it in spades. I loathe it. It's been too long.

I have been here too long.

I stole a pair of headphones and an iPod from some punk college kid I culled a year back. He raped his girlfriend. Got her pregnant. When he found out about it, he tried to abort the kid by knocking her down the stairs. The kid lived but came out pretty messed up. Needless to say, he made the list.

His iPod was full of punk rock songs. At first, I wasn't sure. I had enjoyed the birth of the genre but hated what it had become. But this kid had good taste, despite the horror he had wreaked upon the world. I played the tunes at the highest setting as I walked, blasting the fast power chords and grating voice of a band called Nothington. There is something about the longing behind the gruff voice that always drags me in. It was my soundtrack as I trekked slowly through the alleys of the North End, towards my home.

The North End is Boston's Italian district. It was there that old Boston congregated. You'll find Paul Revere's house nestled amongst the bricks, restaurants, cafes, and pastry shops. A walk down Hanover Street will take you to the Old North Church, made famous in the story of Paul Revere. America was born here, for better or for worse. Personally, I don't carry a flag. Not anymore. Not now that I have gained the knowledge of a greater perspective.

The streets of the neighborhood resembled narrow corridors. The buildings were made of stucco and brick; all attached together, a twisted and cluttered mess of fire escapes, windows, and smokestacks on either side of the road. The neighborhood really was a time warp to old Italy. More European than American in many respects.

I made the turn down an alley and stared down the darkened corridor. The light of the city faded behind the last turn; the alley was pitch-black save for a band of moonlight that crept down between the smokestacks of the apartments on either side. The moonlight illuminated a path amongst the brick; it faded into darkness down the alley, a hazy, milky mixture of black and reds. The sweet, inviting smell of the pastry shops, the salivating stench of garlic was long gone. The stink of fermented garbage, rotten meat, and piss surrounded me, engulfing me. I have made this turn before. I have been in this city too long not to know the dangerous places. This is, was, and always will be a dangerous place, but it is a straight-line home. And I can handle myself.

I took the iPod out of the inside pocket of my overcoat and turned off the sound. I took off the leather headphones and felt the cold bite of the night nip at my ears. With a sigh of relief, I took off the backpack and popped the headphones inside. I slung the backpack over my right shoulder and felt it bite into my skin again. The cans were heavy. I reached into my overcoat and pulled out my cigarettes. Camels. I fished out my lighter and it caught as usual. Old reliable. I took a deep drag and felt the hot smoke cake my insides. I breathed deeply as the nicotine filled my lungs.

I noticed I only had five cigarettes left and it dawned on me that I forgot to pick up another pack. Not that I could afford it. I've seen many things over the decades, but the one thing that has perplexed me more than anything else is how much the price of cigarettes has gone up. No good fucking politicians trying to tell me how to live. I want cancer, motherfuckers. It would finally be a ticket off this Goddamn rock. Instead, I have to pay eight fifty because your heart is bleeding for all us addicts.

I heard a scuffling sound at the end of the alley, not like rats huddling in the night, but more like the soft footsteps of sneakers that do not want to be heard. A soft, deep whisper follows it. Then a chuckle. I heard what sounded like a beer bottle crashing into a dumpster, somewhere out there in the black, then the sound of shattering glass. Then I heard a wheezy, labored breath and I smiled. This would be good exercise.

I took two steps forward and spotted the dumpster, just off to my right, making love to the grimy brick wall. As I tossed my cigarette in, I caught a whiff of paint thinner and regretted my decision. The dark, seemingly empty cavern of the dumpster ignited in an inferno of oily rags, discarded pastry boxes, and prophylactics. I stepped back from the heat. The alley exploded in a sea of orange. My pupils squeezed closed as my focus came into attention.

Three men stood before me. A fat man who resembled the human blob stood in the middle. A Red Sox hat turned sideways upon his oversized, pancake ears. He wore torn jeans and a leather jacket that was too tight against his man tits. To his right was a skinny, perverted looking shrimp. He had stubble about his chin and wore a thick, gold chain around his neck that dangled against his wool coat. His pants were too tight, black leather like some wannabe rock star. On the other side of the fat man was a short, stubby man with an alcoholic nose. He wore torn jeans and a red ski jacket. He smelled like the paint thinner.

The fat one in the middle said, "Wrong turn, old man." He grinned like the Cheshire Cat, all teeth and no gums. The punk with the gold chain smiled, all gums and no teeth.

I took out another cigarette and lit it up with my zippo. Old reliable caught as usual and the warm smoke filled my lungs. I smiled at the taste of hot ash in my mouth. I said, "For who exactly?" and returned his grin.

The fat one said, "Give us your wallet, motherfucker." The skinny punk frowned at me, as if he actually thought he was intimidating. He pointed at me as he said, "Yeah, you motherfucker. Listen to what he says and hand it over."

I surveyed the three of them and my heart filled with joy. The stubby one with the alcoholic nose would not be a problem. He swayed in his stance; could barely stand up. The skinny one would probably snap like balsa wood. The fat guy, well, he could be a problem.

"And if I don't?"

The fat guy pulled a switchblade knife from his coat pocket and flicked open the blade. "Then we cut you. You don't want to be cut, tough guy, do you?"

I took a drag of my cigarette and blew a smoke ring at them. "Well, I could use a shave."

The skinny punk's bloodshot eyes grew large. The white of his eyes glistened in the firelight. "He's making fun of you, Randy! Cut 'em! Cut 'em!"

The important thing is to make them make the first move. Get on the defensive, let them lunge first, make sure they miss, and then beat the crap out of them. Randy would miss. Guaranteed. He looked like he would have trouble simply walking with those Christmas ham thighs of his. "Yeah," I said, "Come on, cut me! Come on, you fat fucking pig, cut me!" I seized the opportunity. I flicked my cigarette at him.

Randy rushed me in what appeared to be slow motion. Not because my world somehow slowed down around me, but, rather, simply because his thighs were stuck together like blubber and this was as fast as he could move. It was a labored, struggling rush, kind of like when a running back loses his first step and is way past his prime. Like watching Shaquille O'Neal run down the basketball court towards the tail end of his career. Fucking sad.

He lunged with the knife; I ducked to the left and with my right arm, I grabbed his forearm and snapped it back upward towards his face, breaking it in two places. You could hear it crack; the snapping bone echoed down the alley like a baseball bat splintering from a ninety mile per hour fastball. He screamed like a girl, a shrill sound that amazed me as it came from somewhere down in the depths of this over bloated meat sack. He fell to the ground like a drunken manatee. He writhed at my feet, holding his arm against his chest, slobbering, blubbering, and crying like an infant.

The skinny punk yelled, "Randy!" and rushed me. He was much faster than his obese friend, but no track star. He tried to punch me; his fist grazed my ear as I ducked under and spun around him. I felt slow, weighed down by my backpack. I took it off my shoulders and tossed it to the ground. I heard the cans smack the brick and regretted it. I did not want to dent any. They needed to keep.

The stubby drunk with the alcoholic nose jumped on my back like a chimpanzee. I fell to my knees and ducked my head; he careened over my shoulders into this friend. They fell backwards against the dumpster, a burning hot oven from the fire that raged within.

The skinny one screamed as the side of his face melted against the heat, a fried egg upon a dumpster skillet. He pried himself loose and slumped down, sat Indian-style—oh wait, sorry, crisscross fucking applesauce—and screamed while holding his head in his hands. The fire behind him grew in intensity. The alley burned a fiery crimson. Sirens would be coming soon. The North End fires draw attention. Too much fear of leaping flames. An entire row of houses could go up at once, a tinderbox of brittle wood and brick.

The stubby one with the alcoholic nose backed up against the brick wall next to the dumpster. To his left, the dumpster burned. To his right there were four plastic trashcans that smelled of discarded diapers and Chinese take-out, as if one could tell the difference. I could tell he was scared, the way his legs rattled. I took out another cigarette and lit it up, then moved in close. Dammit, I was almost out. Why is it every time I get in a scuffle, I chain smoke?

"You know, you and your boys there…" I paused for a moment to point to his two friends, who writhed upon the urine soaked broken brick, "…aren't on my list. So I can't kill you. Not yet."

His head shook; his lips drooled as he belted out in a slobbery prayer, "Please, please don't kill me! Please. I meant no harm. I was just out with the guys, you know? Please."

I shook my head in disgust as the guy pissed his pants in front of me. A warm trickle fell from his left pant leg; steam formed and careened towards the heavens.

I took a drag and blew smoke in his face. I grinned; I could not contain my joy. "I know that you rape and pillage at night. And I know that you paint houses by day. I can smell the paint thinner all over you. I thought at first the smell was coming from the dumpster, that's why the damn thing ignited like a tailgate party, but maybe it was you I smelled." I took another drag and grinned as the taste of tar filled my mouth. "You know, paint thinner is really flammable. You really should change after you get off work."

"Please no. Please no, dear God no!"

"Oh, he's here. In fact, I work for him. Nice feller I suppose but I never met him. I hope to soon. I really do. It's culling scum like you that'll get me there." I was three seconds away from lighting this pervert on fire when I remembered. I heard Cotton's voice in my head. He made sure I remembered. He always makes sure I remember.

He is not on the list.

Fuck, I thought as I rolled the cigarette between my fingers. *He should be.*

He is not on the list.

I grimaced at the thought of letting these punks go. Behind me, I heard what sounded like the whimpered cry of a beaten dog echo softly amongst the alley walls. The skinny punk rocked in his seat. He held his head in his hand, sobbing, like a teenage girl recently dumped by her college boyfriend. Out of the corner of my eye, I saw that the fat whale had passed out from the pain.

He is not on the list.

I gritted my teeth and rolled my eyes. "Fine!" I yelled towards the end of the alley. "Give them time and they will be!"

The dark did not respond.

I would have plenty of time to argue with Cotton soon.

I turned my attention back to the cowering alcoholic. "Get the fuck out of here." I pointed my cigarette at him. "And if I ever find you in this alley again I will eradicate you, do you understand me?"

He said nothing, just nodded; his urine-soaked stain grew bigger.

"You come around the North End again, I so much as see you eating a slice of pizza up in this neighborhood, and I'll follow you back to whatever hole you crawled out of and murder you in your sleep. Do you understand?"

He nodded again, his eyes, listless, catatonic, almost dead. I scared the soul right out of 'em.

"Now get the fuck out of here and take your two friends with you."

I picked up my backpack, slung it over my shoulder, and headed out the end of the alley. As I headed toward Copp's Hill, I could hear him try to no avail to wake up the fat whale. It would be no use; he was long gone, passed out upon the brick.

The walk up Copp's Hill is always a difficult one. My knees burned, as they always burn; I could feel my joints clicking and clacking like two raw bones rubbed together. The Old North Church loomed behind my head. The ghost of Paul Revere entered my mind as the frigid wind nipped at my ears like a harlot. I imagined the two lanterns held high in the steeple like two demonic eyes watching my every move.

The alley now a distant memory, the night was quiet, more silent than usual. The sound of the wind muffled the dull roar of the city as it whistled through the alleys, belched forth, breath from the underworld. I came to the entrance of the old burying ground, and with much effort, struggled up the concrete steps, my legs wobbling beneath me. With my right hand, I grasped the wrought iron gate and pulled myself up onto the recently shoveled brick walk. Tombstones jutted up from the snow banks to greet me, my old familiar friends.

I nodded to Father Newman's stone as I walked past. The sound of my steel tipped boots clacked on the brick; it sounded as if I was knocking on the door to hell. In a sense, I was.

"Good day, Father," I whispered to his stone. I smiled and imagined him up in the tower, holding the lanterns high. "I hope your arms aren't tired."

He did not answer back. Sometimes he does, but not tonight. Even when he does, it is very hard to hear him. Poor ole bastard. Doomed to hold those lanterns forever.

The Charles River, a bright white frozen ribbon, glistened in the darkness before me. The burying ground has a great view across to Charlestown. The lights of the brownstones flickered off the river, giving it a rhythmic, almost snake-like movement to it as I walked down the path.

I passed Prince Hall's spire and nodded at the old black man, the father of black Freemasonry. "Good day, Prince," I said. He too is silent tonight.

As I crested the hill, I saw my destination, my home. The Mather tomb, a square brick box about four feet tall, five feet deep, five feet wide. Where Cotton is seldom quiet.

I started digging out the base around the tomb in the early seventies. After over twenty years of quiet, tireless work, I was able to construct my underground lair almost entirely out of site. Over the years, save one punk kid whom I scared shitless, no one ever noticed that the Mather nameplate could move. Heavy, sure, but anyone who goes the gym occasionally should be able to move it. Most people stare at the gravestones and take pictures, little else. However, over the past two decades, the number of folk who visit the burying ground has dwindled a bit. People seemed to have lost interest in history. Most would rather watch movies, play video games, or go to football games. Distractions are the name of the game these days.

I dug it out with a spoon. Took me forever. Did it after three in the morning when the streets are dead. New York may be the city that never sleeps, but Boston slumbers. Hell, even the subway shuts down at midnight around here.

I knelt down, my knees burning like acid. I dug my fingers behind the edges of the nameplate and took a moment to catch my breath before I gave it a strong tug. It stuck at first, as it always does. The tug sent a pain spidering through my shoulders like a lightening. I grunted and spat upon the ground and gave it another shot, tugging with all my might. It came free and sent me back pedaling on the snow. I hit a patch of ice and fell to my knees, soaking my jeans. I clutched the nameplate tight. I did not want to crack it.

I looked around quickly to see if anyone was watching. The night wind howled. I heard the tree branches crack and groan, protesting the ice that burdened their feeble limbs. The streetlights flickered as the snow fell, now in buckets, fast like a swarm of bees, twirling in the air.

The street was empty. The lights in the nearby brownstones were dormant. Just me, a hundred or so tombstones, and fifty or so dead bodies. More than half are missing. Few folks know that. Grave robbers.

First, I tossed my backpack into the hole. I heard it land with a thump. I sat the nameplate down next to the hole, making sure it was close enough to grasp. I crawled inside the brick box, legs first, as I held onto the top of the tomb with my hands. I felt the absence of earth. No matter how many times I had done this, my heart fluttered, panicked that I might fall. I spun myself around slowly. With my right arm, I clasped the top of the tomb across my left shoulder and turned my torso about, careful not to slip. The top of the tomb was slippery and cold to the touch. As I successfully spun around, my feet found the ladder. I leaned out of the opening, the only thing visible in the graveyard my ugly, bald-headed mug, sticking out the side of the Mather Tomb.

I chuckled to myself at the thought. If anyone saw me, it would be madness.

I pulled the nameplate across the entrance, then, with the two leather straps I had epoxied to the back, pulling it shut, clean against the opening.

Pure darkness.

I stood upon the apex, trying not to fall, feet prone upon the top of the ladder.

Pitch black. The smell of earth, damp and dust. The smell of the underworld.

With my trusty zippo, I lit a lantern that hung to my left. It illuminated the tomb and my way down. Exposed dirt, roots, and rock surrounded me.

The drop is only about twelve feet, but deep enough that if I ever fell and did not mean to, I could snap fibula or two. I descended the wooden ladder, carrying the lantern with me.

My room is not much. Despite twelve feet deep, I only dug it about fifteen feet across. I ran into Cotton's casket and decided to stop. I only ever found one. No Increase Mather, Cotton's father. Who knows where the old bastard is. Not here.

I have a solitary table with one chair, my bunk a sleeping bag next to Cotton's casket. I have a radio that runs on batteries. I ran a wire up through the dirt, at the base of the tomb, to act as an antenna. In twenty years, no one has noticed. While the earth acts as a dampener, I only play it at night, late, while the city sleeps. In the corner, there is a wooden chest that I built from scrap lumber that holds what few clothes I have. Mostly sweatpants and a few pairs of torn jeans.

A copper pipe runs down out of the ceiling along the back wall, down to eye level. It too runs up to the base of the tomb. It is my fresh air, and, when necessary, my cigarette smoke's escape hatch. A sudden snowstorm can be a bit problematic. If I don't clear the opening, I can run out of air.

I leaned down and picked up my backpack. I sat upon my only chair and took out a can of peaches. I used my most valuable appliance, my hand-wound can opener, and opened an evening snack. Despite giving me shit in the alley, for some reason Cotton was quiet.

Not wanting to wake him, I enjoyed my peaches in silence, gulping each one down, a soggy, sloppy mess. I tossed the can in the corner amongst countless other empties and carried the lantern over to the sleeping bag. An iron hook dangled above it. I hung the lantern, took off my coat, and crawled into my sleeping bag. I turned off the light as the black took over.

It is peaceful sleeping in a tomb, as long as you don't mind the cold and the occasional earthworm slithering across your forehead when you least expect it. It is quiet down here in the dark. It is where I belong. I do not know why I keep waking up each day but I do.

I blame Cotton. Sonovabitch always has another job for me.

Chapter Six

Endless stars fill my mind. Red stars, like the stars you see if you push down real hard on your eyeballs with your thumbs. Around me, I hear the ocean hiss and burst. I'm face down in the wet sand. My head pounds with shattering artillery fire echoing from deep within my mind. A salty taste teases my lips as I inhale a gulp of briny seawater. I choke and feel the acid in my stomach rush towards my mouth. I pull myself to my knees; the ocean crashes behind me. Frigid ice water careens up my pant legs and I shudder. I pull my arms tight to my chest. I rub my hands up and down my skin. My skin feels numb from the ocean. I'm freezing. Where am I?

The taste in my mouth turns from salt to copper. With my knuckles, I rub the saltwater from my eyes, eyes that sting with pain. As the beach comes into focus, I realize the source of the copper taste. Blood stains the beach. Pink sand surrounds me. This can't be.

A helmet washes up next to me, the top cracked open, blown open. No head inside. I pick it up and flip it over to see the inside encrusted with bits of brain and skull burned into the hard plastic.

I struggle to my feet, my knees knocking with fatigue. I turn to see a red ocean, crimson—a cauldron of dead men. Boys. What is left of them. Limbs, dog tags, pieces of clothing, a jacket here, a shoe there. All floating towards me, swirling around as if some wicked witch created an ultimate stew of death. All dead. All dead. I should be dead, too. Yet for some reason I breathe.

The sky is gray, the ashen color from battle remains. How long has it been? I cup my ear and listen for gunfire. Out there, the battle must rage on. But I hear nothing. Nothing but the sound of the ocean. Bursting and thrashing. And that goddamn ringing in my head. An endless siren. An air raid between my ears.

My clothes are torn, stained red with blood. My jacket is long gone, probably lost out at sea. My shirt, once a dark green, is now a muddy brown, ripped open across the mid-section. My dog tags stick to my chest. I shiver, the wind crisp on my wet skin. I feel a bead of water, too thick, mixed with blood, the blood of my friends, slither its way down my neck.

The beach is empty. I blink my eyes as more comes into focus. There is a hill in front of me, large dunes with grass sprouting high.

I remember very little of what happened. How did I wash up on the beach? My last memory was sinking into the darkness. I did not expect to wake up. At least not here. I should be dead. I should have woken up somewhere else. But where? Should I have known? Who does? I suppose those of us with great faith have absolute clarity about what will happen when our time comes. And if anyone ever tells you that, do not believe them for a fucking second. No one knows. Pick a religion. People all have their theories. Who is correct?

Do we really truly know? How could anyone? As children, our parents teach us what to believe. Depends on your family's lineage. The roulette wheel of birth comes with assigned God and savior.

The only thing most humans all seem to agree on is that this is not it. The world we live in is just one stop on the commuter train. Only thing is, we have no knowledge of where the next stop is and no fucking clue where we got on. We just know we got on. We all got on. But we do not remember. Hell, we don't even remember what we did two weeks ago. What we had for lunch. What happened at three thirty, two Wednesdays back. We forget. It is in our programming. And thank God for it. Can you imagine remembering everything like it was two minutes ago? We would all drink Drano if that were the case. We need to forget.

It heals us.

I do not know what to expect when we die, and I don't know now as I stand here upon the beach. One thing I know for sure: I'm not dead. That much I know. I should not be here. Did God save me? Or something else? The wind feels cool upon my back.

A path leads up the dune. My knees kill me; my bare feet sting. My skin burns from the cold. But somehow, I'm still here. I'm alive. In one piece. One giant mound of shivering flesh. But alone. Vulnerable and lost. No shoes, torn ragged clothes. Where am I? Where was I? Was Omaha beach yesterday? Was it two weeks ago? Longer? The state of the ocean, the frothy, foamy broth of blood, guts and bone tells me that not too much time has passed. But was it hours, days, or weeks? No gun. I have no gun. Shit, I have no gun. I'm exposed. If this is still France, France is enemy territory. God knows what is on the other side of that dune. I look left then right. No bayonets. No knives. Nothing but a few helmets and tattered blood-stained clothing. Nothing I can use.

The sky is hazy, gray and choked with ash; it is impossible to tell what time of day it is. I guess it would be early morning as the sky seems brightest above the dunes; that must be east.

The path is sand, mixed with rocks and twigs that crunch too loudly as I walk. The ocean bursts behind me, hissing and moaning, belching out a bad meal of dead soldiers onto the shore. I hold my head low as I crest the hill. I don't want to get sniped. Slowly, I creep through the sand. The air smells of salt and rotten meat. My eyes dart back and forth; the wind howls behind me. I have to be as silent as a ghost.

What would I find? What would be there? A Nazi post? A garrison of deranged lunatics waiting to slay me with lead? Slowly, the horizon comes into focus. Thank God. No one. Instead, I'm standing on the outskirts of a tiny French Village. From the looks of it about thirty tiny houses, little boxes made of stone and brick. The streets appear empty, deserted. Silence. The only sound that of the ocean crashing back behind me.

I creep up slowly to the nearest house, a bungalow style, pastel blue, close to the path. Small, it looks to be no more than four rooms. Outside there is a clothesline that runs from a nail above the backdoor to a post about twenty feet out. A woman's Sunday dress, a girl's pink blouse, a man's black slacks and blue button-down shirt dangle from the line. Without too much guilt or remorse, like a common criminal I pull down the pants and shirt, my eyes locked on the periphery, checking to see if anyone is watching. As I rip them down, I fall to the ground; the grass is high around me. Too high. As if no one had tended to the yard in some time. I can hide as long as I stay low.

There in the tall grass I strip naked. I have to get rid of the sick feel of my wet clothes against my skin. As I strip down, I marvel how I have not a single scratch on me. Not one bruise. As if I have been born again. A brand new baby in grown man form. Cock, balls, and all. Everything intact. Not a single scar. No signs of battle. As if I have worked a desk job my entire young life.

The pants are a bit loose. Careful not to make too much noise, I rip the corner of my wet shirt into a thin band. Using it as a belt, I synch the pants tight against my waist. The shirt fits better. Whoever this guy was, he was bigger than I am, but not in the chest. The only thing I need now is shoes.

On my hands and knees, I stalk through the tall grass like a lion up to the back door. The door is solid oak with a vertical window running down the middle. I pull myself up against the back wall of the house and look down the horizon. To my left, nothing but grass, sand, and the tops of the dunes leading down towards the shore. To my right, the back of another stone house. Past that one, another house with too tall, uncut grass.

I close my eyes and listen. Any sound would do, something to give me my bearings. Anything to let me know what I am up against.

But I hear nothing. Nothing other than the hiss and burst of the ocean down the other side of the dunes.

The air is cleaner up here; however, the dominating smell of salt water prevails.

I peek in the window. A wooden table. Four wooden chairs. No signs of life. A thick layer of dust lies upon the table. A bowl of cereal sits there, milk curdled, the oats churning about in mold and mildew. Perhaps someone left mid meal.

It is deserted.

To my surprise, I find the door to be unlocked. I jiggle the handle; it turns with ease. I swing the door open and tiptoe into the house.

Next to the dining room is a small kitchen, just large enough for a tiny homemaker to prepare home cooked meals. A pot, full of still water, sits on the toothpaste colored stove; dust floats at the surface of the water. I listen for sounds but hear nothing other than the quiet ticking of a grandfather clock that stands against the corner wall to the left. The golden pendulum swings gently, as if unware of the collapsing world.

I tiptoe into the living room and find it empty. Open magazines are strewn across the floor; several wooden chairs are tossed about. A large, wooden radio sits underneath the front window. A thick layer of dust about an inch thick coats the top.

As I turn the corner towards a bedroom, a sickly smell meets me. It is the smell of rotten meat. Of hamburger left out to long. Of pizza left in a hot car for a week. It is the smell of maggots. Of death. Of decay. Of the destroyer at work, taking back once given flesh.

There in the tiny room are the decaying bodies of the couple who lived in the house. Both shot in their bed. A picture of them droops above the headboard; crooked, as if knocked sideways. Otherwise, there is no sign of struggle. Just the two bodies next to each other, hands at their sides. Their decomposed faces stare at me, their eyes open wide with shock. Perhaps they were surprised in the middle of the night, woke for mere seconds before the SS put a bullet in their skulls. Whoever pulled the trigger was a good shot. Got 'em right between the eyes.

I pull my new shirt over my nose. The stench is unbearable. I notice at the foot of the bed a pair of socks and shoes. I pick them up, cross myself, shut the door behind me, and venture back out in the living room.

I feel bad about stealing a dead man's shoes. Those poor bastards. Shot dead in their home. A man's house ought to be his castle. The one place on earth where he is always safe from the evil that runs rampant in this world. This world left unchecked, without a guardian, a floating rock, lost in space, left for dead by its creator. Forgotten. Those two there in the bed. Another pair in a long list of forgotten souls. Left to fend for themselves against a marauding, never ending, and never forgiving source of evil. Now, it is the Nazi's turn. However, there were those that came before, and there would be those that would come again. The Persians. The Mongols. The Huns. Every generation has its source of evil run amok, aimed to destroy us all.

The history books glorify the battles. Those that fell. In the Army, they feed us propaganda. They feed us bullshit. We are warriors they tell us. We are soldiers of God. We are to free the world from tyranny. They romance it up. Glorify war. Glorify death and carnage into something more than what it is.

But it is murder. It is all murder. It does not matter for what cause, or what reason, or how many men are running around in armor, wearing flags or shouting slogans. It is all murder.

And these two here were murdered. Here war shows its ultimate ugly face. The battlefield shows the carnage, to be sure. The stories of the greatest battles will fill the history books for ages.

Meanwhile, these two rot here in their bedroom. Long forgotten, while the greatest battle of all time rages onward.

It does not matter for what reason, for which flag, for which ideology, or for which God—not to a maggot. A maggot eats regardless.

A maggot's belly is full.

These awful thoughts enter my head as I put on the dead man's socks and shoes. The socks feel warm on my feet. The shoes are about a size too big but they will do. Hell, man, this was war; I'll just have to rough it.

The shoes want to slip off my feet as I walk back into the kitchen. I need to find a knife. Something, anything to defend myself. The kitchen drawers are all painted white, the handles a black iron. I pull the first one open. Towels. Then the second one: empty. Third try: a drawer of knives. Thank God. I smile as I take out the carving blade and tuck it into my pants, the blade up towards my stomach, gently touching. The metal is cold against my skin. I untuck my shirt, letting it fall down over the blade, concealing it.

I walk back into the living room amongst the gentle ticking of the grandfather clock. There out the front window, not a single car, not a single person. The sky is black now. Off in the distance I hear the dull roar of what is either thunder or artillery.

I stare at the bedroom door—those poor people; the memory of their contorted faces, their decaying bodies, burns a permanent image into my gray matter.

One thing I know, if there is a God, He seems not to give two shits towards matters such as this. Such as war. He has allowed this. Generation after generation. Perhaps He even enjoys it. Makes for good entertainment. A night out at the box office for Him. If there is one certainty to humankind's future, where we go from here, until the world ends in a rain of fire, is that there will be war. There will always be war.

To war is to be human. To be human is to go to war. Why? Find the flavor of the week; there is always a reason from some maniac, whether by birth, election, or force. The world is full of maniacs; that is a certainty. It just becomes a crying shame when one of these lunatics comes to power.

Do not give power to the insane. It is like giving guns to the homeless. Bad fucking idea.

I creak open the door and venture down the street, armed with only the blade hidden under my shirt.

The cobblestone street is full of broken glass. My new shoes crush the shards as I walk. I hunch over and walk slowly; I have to be careful. Could be snipers anywhere. I hold my head low, as if it will somehow offer protection against even the worst shot. Out here on the street, I am a sitting duck.

I pass a blue house on the left. Blood splatters the front glass. At the yellow house next to it, the door is shattered by an axe. The one after it, a red bungalow with slate shingles, has busted windows. The one after is burnt to the ground, a mound of charcoal colored wood and ash. A rusted tricycle sits amongst the broken boards.

Whatever happened here, happened. Thankfully, there is no one left in the town. They are gone. Either to heaven, hell, oblivion, or a concentration camp. All dead or gone. It appears that I have the whole town to myself. A kid in a candy store? Not quite.

I hear a roar above as a bomber flies overhead. My flight instincts overwhelm, I kick open the door to the red bungalow and hide in the foyer. I spin around to see if I am alone. The couch, a pea green concoction of felt is overturned. A child's toy truck nestles against my oversized shoes. I hear nothing but the click of a clock in another room. I smell the same stench of rotten meat as before. I dare not explore this house. I cannot bear to see another body. This is enough death to last a lifetime.

The rumbling roar of the bomber fades as it disappears into the ashen sky. Is it one of ours? I guess I will never know.

Despite the stench, a new sensation overwhelms my gut. The sensation of hunger. Starvation takes me; my stomach pangs with desire.

The kitchen looks to be just off the living room, just like the other house. Unfortunately, that is where the smell is coming from.

I decide to leave the house to find a market, a restaurant, a tavern, anything.

The streets are empty. This little French town is nothing more than a ghost town. All gone, no one left.

I walk slowly down the street until the end; it dead-ends into a crossing street. Splintered, destroyed trees line the street to the right. The trees to the left look soaked with the salt of the ocean, the bark covered in a white film. Safer this way. Or so I presume. I take the left.

The sky is darkening further now, as the rumbling sound comes closer. No bomber this time. This is thunder. The wind picks up as the sky opens, pelting my brand new dry clothes with frigid rain.

I just got dry. Shit. I need to find some place. Some place safe. The wind howls around me as the rain hits me on all sides.

There, a bar. Perhaps the Nazis left some food behind, or at the very least, a keg or two. God knows I need a drink.

Hail the size of turnips starts to fall, pelting my skin as the sky screams with lightning that sizzles from cloud to cloud as the Gods go bowling. I dart across the street in the rain, covering my head from the stinging buckshot raining down, over to the bar's wooden door. I turn the handle and, to my surprise, it opens with ease. Doesn't anyone lock anything in this town?

I slam the door behind me, my back resting against the door as I breathe heavily. My lungs hurt from all the ash I took in at Omaha. As I hold my eyes shut I can feel my heart race, thundering in my head, beating fast, the sound mixing with the sound of thunder from outside.

Suddenly I hear the gravely sound of someone clearing his or her throat.

My heart revs up to a million miles an hour as I open my eyes, my fingers ready to rip the blade from my pants. My instinct tells me to leap, to attack, to flay.

I open my eyes and see a man dressed in a white apron and black-buttoned white dress shirt standing behind the bar. He is cleaning a glass with a white rag. He is bald, the light of the bar reflecting down across his head, which shines like a chrome bumper. There are about five wooden tables, all empty. A fire burns in the corner. The bar, mahogany, is about ten feet long with only four stools. Dark green paint mixed with faded photographs covers the walls. The room smells strange, musty, a wet camel smell.

The man grins at me, his eyes a steel gray. He appears in his late forties, early fifties. Overweight, he looks to be no more than five-foot-two. He has bad acne, bad skin. He nods, acknowledging my existence, and says, "Take a seat." He points at one of the bar stools before him. "Go on, don't be shy."

The blade feels cold against my exposed skin.

He removes the rag from the glass, throws it over his shoulder, places a pint glass down below a tap, and pours a pint. The beer is amber in color, the bubbles, inviting. He places it upon the bar, in front of a lonely stool.

"Sit. Have a drink."

He grins at me, exposing red gums, the color of chum. His teeth look too small in his mouth, tiny pebbles. He points again to the glass.

"Please, have a drink. I've been expecting you."

Chapter Seven

My all-time favorite song has to be "Canary in a Coalmine" by the Police. Sting's lyrics could never ring more true than they did in that song. It is a euphemism for how one ought to live his or her life. Early coalmines did not feature ventilation systems, so miners would routinely bring a caged canary into new coal seams. Canaries are especially sensitive to methane and carbon monoxide, which made them ideal for detecting any dangerous gas build-ups. As long as the canary kept singing, the miners knew their air supply was safe. A dead canary meant get your ass out of there as fast as you can.

We ought to live our lives like those canaries. People do not realize how caged they really are. Trapped in their own lives, oblivious to how long their timeline is or is not. Most people think it is sad when they find out that a friend, loved one, or celebrity comes down with a terminal illness.

I disagree. Rather, I personally feel that it is a blessing. For it is only then that people start living like that canary. They understand how precious each moment is. When every minute of your day ticks away, the hand of the clock your signal of demise, you begin to appreciate every single last second of air that fills your lungs.

Before your brain synapses spasm into goo.

Before you shit your pants one last time.

Before your nerve endings burn out when your brain has lost its will.

Before your soul evacuates your carcass, leaving behind a worm ridden sack of decaying flesh.

You have finality. You have closure. You make amends. You say your peace.

You accept your fate.

It has been determined. And unlike others, you get to know in advance. You get a sneak preview. You watch the trailer of your own third act. The last volume in your own personal trilogy. Youth, adulthood, and then death. As I said, worm food. You become a maggot's breakfast. You become one with the earth.

Ashes to ashes, sperm to sewage.

If only we all knew our last chapter. What freedom we would have. Would you get up at six o'clock in the morning to commute an hour plus to serve your asshole of a boss? For whatever it is you waste your life doing?

Work. More work.

Rework.

More rework.

Over and over. Repeat.

Would you waste your time crying over the missed field goal that sailed wide left, leaving your favorite football team three points from a perfect season and a shot at the national title game?

Would you worry about counting calories?

About your wardrobe?

About how you are the only one of your friends without a Prada handbag?

After an enough time, and enough contemplation, you should come to the only logical conclusion. These concerns, these worries, these anxieties, are meaningless.

If you knew you were going to die next Tuesday at four thirty in the afternoon would bother stopping for that red light? Would you care enough to go to work? To diet? To hit the gym? To wipe your ass?

You are not a savage, are you?

We ought to live like those canaries. Seconds away from death, or perhaps hours, or days, or years. They do not know. We do not know when our time comes. Is death standing around the corner waiting for you in the terminal, watching you get on the plane? Is he behind the wheel of a drunken driver's car at two o'clock in the morning the night of Halloween? Is he masquerading as a deranged knife-wielding madman at your local mall?

When will Death find you?

The only thing I know for sure is that he is not looking for me.

When you wake up with an earthworm trying to burrow its way into your nose, it is time to reexamine your life. When you feel the sickly sensation of a spider clawing away inside your ear, it is time to have a drink. When you find yourself lying deep underground in a pre-revolutionary crypt, talking to the pile of dead bones next to you, it's time to check yourself in.

Find the asylum, sign here, and accept your straight jacket. Or re-enlist with the army. For if you find yourself in this situation, it is obvious that you fucked up somewhere along the line.

However, when the bones talk back, that is when things start to get really weird.

If you do not know who Cotton Mather is, you probably fell asleep during high school history class. However, considering America's sad state of education, perhaps I should at least offer up a tidbit that might jog the recesses of your mind. Perhaps there is a buried memory, lost amongst countless hours of television shows, video games, and endless nights spent on the tablet.

Cotton Mather was a preacher in Boston during colonial times. Famous for many writings on Puritan theology and ideology, he is most famous for his role in the Salem Witch trials, and witch hunting in general. Often given a bad rap, famous for adding fire and brimstone to the subject of witchcraft, Cotton today would tell you those were the best days of his life.

However, his current predicament, his penance, is a direct result of those particular days. Helping me. Interpreting my dreams. In another state. In Limbo as they say.

He said, "New Englanders are a people of God," as I pulled the earthworm from my nose. It felt a lot like pulling gooey, viscous, flu-ridden snot out, only this one was wiggling on its own.

"The problem is, they settled in the Devil's country..." His voice sounded like a far-off whisper. "The Devil took acceptation to this."

"So you told me," I tossed the worm into the corner. It found some loose dirt upon the frigid floor and gently burrowed away. The frozen ground was cold on my feet; the icy burn crept through the threads of my wool socks. I wrapped my blanket around tight and took a seat at my table. My tomb was mostly dark; the only light from two candles that I had placed upon Cotton's rotted casket. The smell of earth and damp was everywhere.

"The Devil is now making one attempt more upon us; an attempt more difficult, more surprising, and more snarled with unintelligible circumstances than any that we have hitherto encountered."

With my hand-held can opener, I opened a can of pinto beans. I drank the slimy broth. It tasted terrible; the beans were starting to go rotten. Should have checked the expiration date. The liquid ran down my stubbly chin. I shuddered; gross. I said, "So you told me last week."

Cotton wheezed, then continued, "An attempt so critical, that if we get well through, we shall soon enjoy halcyon days with all the vultures of hell trodden under our feet."

I laughed a hearty laugh as the beans slid down my throat. I did not bother to chew, I devoured them whole. My stomach panged. At this point, I would eat anything. "I'm still waiting for those halcyon days there, buddy. I've heard this speech of yours before; middle school history class. You gave it centuries ago, you old bat. All you do is repeat yourself. Over and over. Broken fuckin' record."

"The time is near. The time is upon us. We have almost filled our quota. The Gateman will let you pass soon. And I'll be free to rest eternally."

I wiped my chin with my blanket. "Bullshit, Cotton. We're no closer now than where we were a decade ago and you know it."

With my lighter, I fired up a heat canister, one of those kinds you see at cheap buffets that keep the food lukewarm for hours. I emptied some of my bottled water into my only pot, tossed in a bag, placed it on my wire rack that sat upon the table, then placed the canister beneath it and began to make some hobo coffee. I stared at the water, waiting seemingly forever for it to boil as Cotton mulled his thoughts. Finally, he said, "Do you remember last night's dream?"

I shook my head and closed my eyes. I saw flashes of blond hair, little else. "No. Not really. Just a face. No name. No reason."

"That is alright, my son. As usual I have remembered for you. Her name is Jane Theroux. An executive at a mutual fund company. She is quite well off. She has used her position of power to belittle others."

"And that puts her on the list? Tell me something new. Every executive in the history of business has gone on a power trip or too. They're all like that. Capitalism they call it. We can't wipe them all out. You sure about this Cotton?"

"The holy God permits the Devil to hook wicked scholars from time to time. Who are we to judge his orders of execution? We must obey the Gateman."

"Fine. Tell me more." The pot began to boil.

"At age eleven, Ms. Theroux drowned her cat in her parents' pool just to get their attention. At age sixteen, she fornicated with forty-seven percent of the varsity football team. At age eighteen, she had her first abortion. She cheated her way through high school, then college, by having carnal relations with her male teaching assistants, not to mention two females. Through the use of sex, she worked her way up to a management position at her company."

"So a sex maniac. Hardly worth death. We don't kill porn stars, why this one?" I poured the coffee into my only mug, one of those Looney Tunes coffee mugs—Tasmanian Devil.

"She is personally responsible for three hundred and fifty employees losing their jobs. The decision was hers and hers alone. She works her staff round the clock to make up for the lack of resources so her unit still appears productive and capable. All the while she barely works at all, and mostly from the confines of her own luxury apartment when she does."

"Sounds like a real mean-spirited bitch." I took a sip. The coffee was awful.

"One of the men who lost his job lost his house. His wife left him because she viewed him as a failure. In a fit of rage and disgust, he murdered her, then his six-month-old child, both by shooting them in the head before turning the gun upon his own temple."

"Awful."

Cotton's voice rose in anger as the fire and brimstone of the old man shook his dead bones, "SHE MURDERED THAT FAMILY THROUGH HER GREED. SHE IS ON THE LIST. NOW DO YOUR DUTY." The candles upon his casket shook and shivered.

I winced through another sip. "What about the guy? Has he been punished?"

"HE WRITHES IN HELLFIRE. However, he needs a bunkmate. A demon lives within the flesh of Ms. Theroux. A demon born of her own doing, her own creation, her own vocation. ERADICATE HER AND SEND HER TO THE PIT."

I tossed the coffee upon the ground. Horrible, wretched hobo coffee. I watched as the steam floated in the candlelight.

"Alright. Fine. I'll scope it out."

♦♦♦♦♦

Not before long, I found myself pounding a few pints behind the bar of a place called Bukowski's. Named after the great writer himself, the bar prided itself in the works of the craft. Various beer mugs and steins adorned the wall in honor of the beer club's favorite dead authors. A huge oil canvas of Bukowski hung in the back above two pub tables. I told the bartender my favorite Bukowski novel was *Ham on Rye*.

He had no clue to what I was saying.

The bar resided in the first floor of a parking garage in Boston's Back Bay neighborhood. The Mass pike, I-90, roared just outside the window, tunneled under Boylston Street. The large office towers of Back Bay, The Prudential Center tower, and the John Hancock Tower, or as I call it, the glittering razorblade, were just outside the doors. The bar smelled of spilt beer and pine sol.

To say I needed a drink is an understatement. I always needed to pound a couple before the kill.

I spent the afternoon with Cotton, debriefing as much as I could about this Jane Theroux. Her face burned in my mind, the only thing I remembered from last night's dream. She was not particularly attractive, no blemishes, no acne, but a rat like nose with two beady, cauldron-black eyes below perfectly manicured eyebrows. The kind of broad you pass by in the bar without noticing. As if she is not there. Yet somehow, sex has become her weapon of choice. Her method of getting ahead. I suppose there are always takers when free pussy is readily available.

One of the reasons I liked coming to this pub was that it always had a great beer selection. I was drinking a rare Dortmunder-style lager from a brewery called Great Lakes, out of Cleveland, Ohio. A strange beer to find in a downtown Boston bar. The beer tasted fresh, almost straight out of the vat. When you have lived as long as I have, you need to try new beers, even if it costs a little more. The staples get old.

The only issue I have is the cost. Paying for a premium beer is difficult for someone who does not have a job.

For years, I worked in the food service industry. It worked well in the seventies and eighties before the rules got tighter. It got harder and harder to pass without proof that you are alive. I have a fake ID, easy enough to obtain if you know the right people, but with a social security number of a dead man, it is hard to find gainful employment. All this new technology is making things more difficult.

I did odd jobs for years. I mowed lawns in the 'burbs. I used to ride the redline down to Quincy to find yard work. I worked for a loan shark for a while. That lasted until he wanted me to off some poor bastard.

And I don't kill people not on the list.

These days I sustain myself off the money I find on the people I kill. I resisted for years. Didn't seem right. I felt like a common thug. A parasite, sucking the funds off the evil dead that I would eradicate.

Over time, though, it became a necessity. I had no choice. I need to eat. And drink.

In my zest for death, I tried starvation. Despite a hunger I could not control, I could not lose a pound. I once starved myself for a ten-day period. I did not drink food or water. My mouth felt like the desert. I got these awful blisters on my lips. But I did not lose a single pound.

And the hunger remained.

When it dawned on me that I could not partake in a silent suicide through fasting, I knew I had to eat. When I could no longer find gainful employment, I had no choice but to fish through the wallets or purses of list victims.

Victims. Bullshit, they are not victims. They are demon-possessed.

They are evil incarnate.

They are witches.

And as Cotton will be the first to tell you, this is a witch hunt.

These are the things that entered my head as I tried to avoid the subject at hand.

I took one last sip and licked my lips.

The clock on the wall said it was time.

Chapter Eight

Jane Theroux's alarm clock goes off at seven o'clock every single morning. She prefers to wake to the same song every day. Her song of choice is always the same country ballad about a jilted woman. I do not recognize the singer's voice, but that does not surprise me. Keeping up with the times is something that is difficult to do when you sleep in the ground. Not to mention, I am not much of a country fan. Never was. All sounds the same to me. Uneducated. I know it isn't true, but I cannot get past it. I'm a prick, I know.

By seven thirty-three each morning, Jane has shit, showered, and ventured to a small coffee table by her window. She will enjoy her ample Boston skyline view while she sips on her morning cappuccino. She has a fancy cappuccino maker that anticipates her awakening. Thank God for technology.

She looks the same each morning: towel wrapped tightly around her tits, another wrapped about her head like a turban. I have never understood how women do that. One of humankind's greatest mysteries for sure.

Her eyes are always bloodshot. Dark pools form underneath each socket. She always looks like she has gone twelve rounds with a prizefighter.

She is typically hung over from yet another wine binge, her nightly ritual. Most mornings, despite her promiscuity, she awakes alone, her only companion her too-fat tabby cat. Someone should have put that cat down years ago. The cat is so old it can barely stand up, not to mention it smells like road kill.

By eight o'clock, her face is usually so caked up with concealer and makeup that the dark blotches under her eyes fade into a sort of a simmering, beige soup. It reminds me of French onion soup. French onion soup with a layer of burnt Swiss cheese.

By nine o'clock, she will arrive at work a mere six blocks away.

By ten o'clock, she will have destroyed the souls of at least six people.

By eleven o'clock, she will have flirted with her boss, demeaned a subordinate, and lambasted the bathroom janitor.

At noon, she will go to lunch across the street and pay twelve dollars for a salad and eight bucks for a glass of red wine.

By one o'clock, she is usually checked out for the day even though her carcass sits at her desk, pretending to read a document.

If there are no meetings scheduled in the afternoon, she will go to the gym and sit on an exercise bike reading business magazines without pedaling. She finds it important to stay up on the latest buzzwords and lingo.

She possesses no real knowledge. She possesses no real skills other than her mouth, which she uses primarily in two ways. The first, as a great speaker. By keeping up with business trends and lingo that she learns from her stationary bike-a-thons, she is on top of her game in almost every setting. The second use, well, you can figure that out from what Cotton told us. She is an expert at that as well.

She has had the practice.

I know these things because I have tailed her for weeks. She is a creature of routine, and that routine varies little. The only time it varies is in the hours between eight and midnight when anything goes at the wine bar.

She's not averse to taking on two cigar stinking, sweaty, wrinkled businessmen all at once in the wine bar bathroom. The key to landing her? Wear an expensive suit and a nice watch. Any other back-story will do.

It has been so long I have even contemplated it myself. Then I'll remember my shaved head and black cross tattoo; no way in hell could I pull it off.

Last week I snuck into her loft townhouse in the middle of the night. Getting past the doorman was easy. All I had to do was light a bag of shit around the corner. He was attracted like a moth to a porch light. Do not ask me where I got the shit.

The lock was easy. After decades of practice, I find getting into places to be quite effortless. Getting out is sometimes harder, if only because I do not want to be seen. I've been lucky over the years. The police have chased me many times. Luckily for me, I know the alleys well. It is easy to lose them. Most don't run well if you get my drift. And by the off chance the Police do pinch me in, Cotton has his ways. Odd how no one can remember my face.

Her loft apartment was on the top floor, the fourth floor of the building. There were only two rooms, the main room a giant basketball court size of a room that acts as a living room, family room, winery, and kitchen all at once. The ceilings were about twenty feet high; loft style. On the horizontal side, the entire wall was made of glass. A view of the Back Bay skyline shimmered in the not too far distance. The night I entered, the Old John Hancock Tower's spire was colored blue. No storms expected on the horizon. A full moon shown down across the city as not a cloud covered the sky. Snow covered the streets and parked cars below. The light of the moon and the streetlamps from the street below offered enough to see clearly in the dark apartment.

The back wall was brick, brick in color that resembled blood mixed with crushed rust particles. The floors were a dark hardwood, shiny and smooth, not a scratch on them. I imagined them slippery to anyone in their socks. My steel tipped boots sank rather easily into them, as if they gave way to tiny springs underneath. I felt as if I was walking on the parquet of the Boston Garden.

Stainless steel appliances glittered from the wall next to the bedroom, the second room. A marble-topped kitchen counter with bar stools stood in front of it. An empty wine glass, wine bottle, and a few slices of uneaten cheese laid upon the counter. The room smelled of apple spice. There next to the cheese, a candle recently blown out. The wax was still in liquid form. I pinched the wick; it was still warm.

By my entering the room, Cotton has entered the room. That is all it takes. And Cotton remains. He stays and watches, everywhere I go. One of the benefits of Limbo I guess. Being everywhere at once.

You see, I know all the morning habits of Jane Theroux because Cotton is still there, ever since that night. He watches. He always watches. I broke into her office building and the same thing occurred.

Cotton is quite an ally, even if he is a preachy sonovabitch. He feeds me information.

I tiptoed through her kitchen, then gently creaked open her bedroom door. A crack of light lead across the hardwood floor towards her wooden sleigh bed. Had she woken up, she would have seen my dark, bald silhouette standing there silently in the moonlight, breathing a tad heavily. But she did not wake up.

I watched her sleep for twenty minutes, contemplating the kill.

She slumbered in her silk pajamas and silk sheets, the lavender colored comforter pulled up tight around her cheeks, her blond hair tangled about her head, down across her forehead, covering her eyes. I recall how cold the room felt that night; I remember marveling at how I could see her breath in the air.

Her eyes fluttered in her sleep, dreaming of God knows what. Power and glory, I can only assume. I'll never know. Her chest expanded slowly, the mountain of covers rising and falling.

I could not kill her. I couldn't decide how. I had my blade with me but thought gutting her would be too messy.

I could have put a bullet through her head. But that would ruin the sheets. Shit, what if the cat eats her?

Usually I'm not concerned with these things.

Truthfully, coming clean, the real reason was I couldn't kill her in her sleep. I could have waked her but something about it did not feel right. It felt too evil. I felt like a common thug. A true serial killer.

I'm not a monster.

I would just have to kill her later.

And now that day has come.

◆◆◆◆◆

I followed Jane Theroux since she left the gym. It was one of those sit on the bike not peddling like a stooge magazine reading events of hers. Despite not breaking a sweat, as not a single bead of her own stink expelled itself from her pores, she decided to shower.

After caking herself with makeup, she put on a black dinner dress cut low about the shoulders, strapped on a pearl necklace and wrapped up in a fur coat. She then hit the streets on the way to her favorite wine bar. Another night of anticipated conquest.

She was meeting friends tonight. Or so she thought.

They would never see her. They would never see her again.

No one would ever see her again.

The Boston winter sky was dark, a black charcoal as dense clouds forced their way down amongst the skyscrapers. The salt-soaked pavement passed quickly beneath my feet. The wind gusts bit at my ears. It must have been ten below with the wind chill. Jane was about twenty feet in front of me, bundled up tightly in her fur coat, her gate forced, walking fast against the wall of wind. I had a hard time keeping up. The city smelled of burnt Italian sausage and roasted nuts. Despite the cold, the street vendors were out in full force.

I fumbled through the folds of my coat. With my right hand, I found my gun's handle. I held it tight; it felt frigid in these conditions.

At the next intersection, Jane took a hard left. She cut through a row of townhouses to get to Newbury Street.

For those of you have never been to Boston, Newbury Street is a living, vibrant testament to man's greed. Boutiques cascade up and down both sides of the street. It costs more for a lamp here than some people's entire yearly rent. Excess rampant. Wealth, greed, gluttony, they've got it all. Trophy wife grand central. You should see it in the summer, teeming with cleavage, Prada, and high heels.

I increased my pace as she reached the intersection. Turning left, she disappeared around the corner behind the brick wall of a corner brownstone. I had to hustle; she was too quick. I took the turn, and she was gone.

This was something new for me. I must have been slipping in my old but not aging way.

Fuck.

I lost her. Now what?

To my right there was a narrow alley no more than four feet across between the townhouse on the corner and the start of the row houses. From the corner of my eye, I caught a glimpse.

I saw blonde hair.

I saw a black and white fur coat.

I saw my quarry squatting in the alley with her black laced panties up around her ankles.

I saw steam rise from the hot urine she sprayed all over the concrete like some alley dog.

I saw my opportunity.

A gust of wind kicked up the snow plowed up against the edge of the street, creating a twirling wall of white mist that hung behind my head as I slid into the alley, shoulders practically touching both alley walls, my black coat blocking any light coming in from the street.

From her vantage point, I can only imagine she saw nothing but a sinister bald head and my black tattoo of a crucifix under my left eye against alabaster skin. I grinned; the snow twirled above my head.

She shouted, "Get the fuck away from me, you pervert!" The last bit of her stinking urine trickled down the side of her leg. Her knees knocked together. Her back was against the brick wall, one hand holding her Prada bag, the other struggling to rip her panties northward. "I don't have anything you want!"

I could not help but grin as I felt blood rush to my face. I could feel my skin flush as my heart raced in anticipation. "Oh, but you do have something, my dear." I bit my lip and stared at her.

She pulled her panties up, and then shoved her skirt down as she started to back up in the alley. Her bag caught on a rusty metal pipe that stuck out of the alley wall. Instead of letting it go, with the opportunity there to run, she instead pulled on the bag, but it caught, refusing to let go. Too many important things inside. She wouldn't want to lose them.

She screamed, "Leave me the fuck alone!" Her black eyes were wide with fear and shock. Her face was as pale as the snow that twirled in the air above my head. There was only one way out, and that was behind her.

She screamed down the alley, "Help me, anyone, help me!" Her shrill call for help fell on deaf ears as the roar of the city drowned out her feeble cry.

She pulled on her bag one more time, then decided to let go. She turned to run; the heel of her right shoe snapped off, sending her flailing against the wall. Two of her expensive red nails broke off as she clutched the brick, steadying herself.

An idea came to me. The pipe had a rotted, brittle base. It was barely holding onto the wall. With a good tug, I ripped it free. I clutched it like a shortened baseball bat and held it high above my shoulders, as if I were waiting for a fastball. My form was perfect. Elbow up. Time for a dinger.

As she gained her footing, I crashed the pipe down as hard as I could on her kneecaps. She screamed so loud my eyes hurt from the sonic blast. She collapsed to the ground like scaffolding toppling over. As she fell, her skirt hiked up, exposing shattered knees. Instantly they turned purple, swollen like grapefruits. Blood started to bleed through the skin of her kneecaps like an open wound through gauze. Tears fill her eyes as snot poured from her nose. Sobbing, she asked me to leave her be.

"Please, don't hurt me anymore. Get it over with. It's okay. You can have me."

She hiked up her skirt and while her right hand massaged her busted knees, her left hand pulled her panties, still soaked with urine, back down her ghost-white legs.

I asked, "What makes you think I want that?" I stood above her, the pipe held tightly in my right hand, rested against my leg. I cocked my head to the side, grinning. "Is it because you think I look desperate? Do you think that I find you attractive?"

Sobbing, she looked up at me, her lips trembling. "Well isn't it? You're going to rape me and kill me, aren't you?"

I leaned in close to her, my face a mere foot away. I could smell her fear upon her breath. That and wine mixed with expensive lipstick. Cherry. "Oh, I'm going to kill you alright, but I'm not going to rape you."

Her lips trembled, shaking, wriggling like my bunkmate earthworm friends. Tears cascaded down her chin. "But why? Why?"

I put the pipe down between my feet, resting it upon the concrete. The wind howled down the alley, sending with it a burst of snow. Putting my hands upon my knees, I rocked in stance as I leaned in like a catcher steadying for a pitch. Several snowflakes pockmarked themselves across her porcelain face. Her face was so ghostly white I could see her blue veins bubble up from underneath her skin, skin that appeared almost translucent in the minimal light.

"God has asked for you," I said. "You have sinned. You have mortgaged your soul for a life of power and greed. You have raped this world of all that it offers. Now your debt is due. God is foreclosing on you."

Tears poured from her eyes as she screamed.

"No, please, God no!"

Her scream echoed off the alley walls, sounding like a tortured cat. For a moment, I thought about her fat tabby and how the thing would probably starve to death.

I felt bad for the cat.

I stood back up and clutched the pipe. Holding it high above my head, I brought it down on her face in a single motion. The pipe crunched into her skull, shattering it like pottery. Her face mashed up like a cheap, dollar

73

store Halloween mask. Urine trickled down her leg as her dead hand firmly held her black lace panties.

I got one last unwanted waft of urine and closed my eyes.

Another rotten soul culled from the world.

Another demon eradicated.

Another witch executed.

Yet I felt sad. All I could think about was the damn cat.

Chapter Nine

The beer tastes strange, almost wine-like. Like how I imagine mead tasted back at the dawn of civilization. It tastes full of berries, twigs, grain, grass, and a hint of dog shit. I imagine that perhaps a Sumerian might have enjoyed this about three thousand years before Christ, as he gulped down ounce after ounce of this sludge prior to the hunt. A warm tingle fills my veins as the alcohol meanders through my body. This is no ordinary beer; the alcohol content seems higher than normal. It is awful. Yet somehow wonderful at the same time.

As I slosh the putrid, yet strangely inviting liquid around my gums, I take in a closer look at the man before me. He is short, squat, almost toad-like, with diminutive, stubby, goat-like legs. He is wearing a white dress shirt. Sweat stains his collar with dirty minerals that have soaked into the fibers. He is wearing black suspenders that hold up his pants, pants that loosely cup his fat thighs and ass. He wears three rings on his right hand; the gold from the bands, identical in nature, glimmer from the corner fireplace's ample light. As I stare at the bands, I notice that his fingers look like sausages: pulpy, filled with purple veins. I take another sip and wait for the man to say something. The room smells like a hyena's asshole.

He rocks back and forth on his heels, clasping his hands together upon his belly. His face is flush, red, as if he wears rouge about his cheeks. Bald, his head glimmers like a shiny pot. He smiles a mouth full of gummy pebbles.

I hear a roar echo in from outside as a bomber passes overhead. The bar rattles as the plane buzzes the town. I am still in shock; my chest feels empty. None of this makes sense. I should be dead.

The man says, "Yes, you should be dead. You took two bullets to your chest, one through the shoulder, and a fourth through your left thigh. One of the bullets that pierced your chest ripped your heart in half."

The emptiness in my chest turns into a cavern. My mind starts to collapse like an imploding star. My skin tingles with nervous anticipation. "How... how do you know this?"

He smiles a gummy smile, "Oh Robert, Robert, Robert. I know all about you, Robert Turner."

I clench my teeth and take a slow sip of beer. Again, awful. Like drinking grass mixed with salt water. But then that aftertaste... somehow... is satisfying. My lips tremble. "How do you know my name? Impossible." I want to run but feel too tired to move.

"Oh, I know more than your name, Bobby. I know that you were born in Canton, Ohio. When you were ten years old, your parents moved to Attleboro, Massachusetts, to be near your grandparents. Your grandfather had fallen ill. Your father wanted to be near him during the last days."

He clasps his hands behind his back and begins to pace back and forth behind the bar. The wine glasses that hang overhead gently start to swing. He says, "I know that when you were drafted you didn't mind. The Army was always going to be in your future. Let us face it, you were not the sharpest knife in the drawer. It was either the Army or go to work in the factories. Let us be honest, shall we? Do you have a single talent? What exactly are your skills? You were never book smart, but nor were you technically sound at anything other than rushing the backfield. You have the skillset of an eighth-grade drop out." He smiles wide, a huge gooey grin, as if he is enjoying every second.

The emptiness in my stomach expands; I feel sick, bile rising. I notice my fingers shaking. My legs feel numb, as if my limbs have calcified, as if I am turning into a statue, starting from my feet up. Facing death had been the most horrific experience of my life. But I did not die, and now, here in this bar, I am more confused than I ever have been in all my life.

He says to me, "Don't you spend time worrying about things you cannot comprehend." His grin is strange, almost too wide now, pink fleshy gums exposed beyond normal. His forehead glistens in the light; with an ash and dust-stained bar towel, he wipes the sweat from his cheeks. Whatever is on the towel smears across his skin. He looks like a baseball catcher on a hot August afternoon. Second game of a doubleheader. Earth-tinged sweat.

I can barely move. My lips tremble as I speak. "What's happening to me? If a bullet ripped through my heart, I should be dead. I don't feel a thing."

He lifts a pint glass from behind the bar, and jerks back on the single tap. The handle of the tap is bronze in color; it appears to be a carving of a ram's head.

He takes a drink from the pint, downing half the glass in a single gulp. "You've been pulled back."

He stands there grinning at me, smacking his lips.

"Pulled back? What does that mean? Pulled back from where?"

He finishes the second half of the pint and sits the empty glass down upon the bar. Froth and foam cascade down the glass's walls. "I think you know where. Where else would someone like you go?"

I feel my heart thunder in my chest. "You mean... from Hell?"

He speaks to me the way my father used to. Condescending. "Bingo. Your common sense was always your strong suit, Bobby. Very good."

I eye the only door. It seems so far away. I take another sip and say, "But I've never believed in any of all that. Hell isn't real, only a fabrication of the human mind!" I feel my life begin to slip away. Everything I knew, gone in a moment, thrown out the door, chum for the sharks. Sharks that dwelt within me, within my own mind, shaping my beliefs, or in this case, lack thereof.

He shakes his head back in forth, grinning. "Oh Bobby, Bobby, Bobby. So much for your common sense. For it is your lack of faith that brought you there to begin with."

"You said pulled back. By whom?"

He leans backwards on the bar and folds his arms across his chest. "Why, by me of course."

I feel a shudder sear its way up my spine like liquid fire. My eyes grow dry, dehydrated like the desert. My chest feels hollow, as if something ripped my heart out. The man across from me is the most terrifying thing I have ever witnessed. All five-foot-two of him. I could squash him like a bug. If he was human. But it is obvious, that whatever he is, he is not human. He can't be. How does he know what he knows?

He seems to sense my thoughts. "I am the Gateman. I sit in between."

"In between what?"

"Your world and the next. Between heaven and hell. I believe the Catholics call it Limbo. The space in between."

"I don't believe it."

"Belief is not required when evidence is genuine. I do not require that you believe or have faith. Only that you witness."

"But why? Why did you bring me back?" I take another sip of my beer. I am drinking too quickly. I tend to do that when nervous. I have reached the bottom of my glass. I feel the alcohol flow through me. Intense, one drink feels like a keg.

He takes my glass, pulls back on the ram's head, and pours me another.

"I brought you back because your fate was undetermined. You do not belong to the Devil. You belong to God. And God has a purpose for you. I'm sending you back."

"Back?"

"Back to the world. Back to humanity. But this is no second chance for you to waste another life away. You are our indentured servant. You belong to God." He places the pint in front of me. "Drink."

I take another pull. My head starts to spin as my mouth starts to tingle. My swollen lips tremble. I struggle to speak. "I don't understand."

He clasps his hands behind his back and starts to pace again. I hear the sound of artillery shells pop outside the bar. They sound distant, but not distant enough. The war rages on. "You are not meant to understand, only to obey, or the pit will welcome you. I'll gladly toss you back in."

"I don't understand. If I've been to hell, then why don't I remember it?"

"Because I have taken that memory from you. I assure you, the terror is beyond anything you can imagine. To leave that memory in your mind would make you useless to me. One of my roles in this realm is to choose the cullers. Those that seek out and cull demon-infested minds from the world. And I have chosen you for this task. No sense sending you out there a bumbling, blabbering coward."

"A culler?"

"Yes. You will go back to earth. You will live amongst the murderers, rapists, and thieves. You must find your sponsor. Together, you will cull the world of sinners. You will send the Devil back his minions before his demons are ripe. Before their infestation can take root in the minds of innocents, and multiply like a disease."

"But how, how will I know?" I feel my limbs growing heavier still. I slouch in my seat as exhaustion weighs upon my shoulders. Out of the corner of my eye, the room seems to turn into a haze, getting darker, as if a giant shadow is encroaching, starting to swallow us.

"Your sponsor will help you. It is his task to help you through this. Your... purgatory."

The blackness inches closer. Suddenly, I feel as if I am moving backwards, further away from him, yet I still feel the stool beneath me. I think I'm going to pass out. I struggle to say, through labored breath, "But how will I find my sponsor?"

"You must go to Boston. There you will locate Copp's Hill burial ground. Listen to the gravestones. Your sponsor will find you there."

I feel my stool tip over as the fear of weightlessness grabs me. His voice starts to echo as I feel the sensation of falling. Still clutching my pint glass, I fall further and further away from him. His voice cascades towards me as if I am at the bottom of a great canyon. "Listen hard! Listen well! Finding your sponsor is your only chance of leaving that realm! You must obey God's commands or you will be sent to the pit!"

Down and down I sink, further and further down a dark corridor, falling, arms flailing, heart pounding as I careen into the black. I hear the gateman's shouts echo downward as he careens out of focus, out of sight, but seemingly in control of my mind.

"I'm sending you forward! To the time where faith slips for good! The first moments before the world dives into its secular self! The beginning of the long endless decline into fire! You will remain in this realm until you meet your quota! God demands your service! You will remain on this rock until your deeds are done! Immortality can be a curse when you're caught in between!"

The black races past me, fully enveloping me in darkness. I fall and fall, the wind rushes past me, the smell of sulfur invading my nostrils, seemingly forever, into what appears to be a bottomless pit. I see no bottom, only black.

My mind spins wildly, a web of confusion.

I have no idea what is happening to me. Reality has lost its bearings. I have no concept of what is real, of what my past is, where I have been and where I am going. The Normandy invasion—was it days ago or years? Did it ever happen at all?

My entire past comes into question. Everything I have known and cling to as my life seems suspect. Whom, what can I trust? My own instincts, usually reliable, seem unstable, useless. Helpless. I feel fucking helpless. For the first time in my life, I feel completely helpless of my situation. Only once before did I feel this way, standing upon that boat, waiting for the door to drop, as the bullets pinged and lanced all around me.

Falling and flailing, heart racing, stomach churning, blood thundering in my head—I come to the only logical conclusion. I am dying. Not dead. Not alive, but dying. I know that I must still be back there, on the beach, washed up shark chum, bleeding my life force out all over the sand. It is the only thing that makes any sense. The Gateman, the story of purgatory, it is nothing more than my own mind trying to compensate the confusion of death.

I'm going to die. I am dying.

It has to be the case. The strange taste of the beer was probably my own blood mixed with seawater cascading down my throat, drowning my insides. The ever-increasing tiredness, then haziness, then fall down this dark pit has to be my last moment. In a few moments, lightning should be flashing before my eyes as my synapses burn out one last time.

Then I'll shit my trousers there on the beach. The high tide will take me back out, turn me into a feast for the sea. I will become one with the earth. Return to the cesspool from which I crawled out.

It will be for the best. Real or not, the Gateman has one thing accurate: I am a fucking waste. No purpose whatsoever in life. No skills, no ambitions, no drive. Nothing to contribute. I am a parasite. Sucking on humanity's collective tit. Offering nothing, providing nothing, giving nothing. All I have ever done is take. It will be a fitting end.

The fall is deafening in its silence. I feel nothing now. No sound of rushing wind, nothing at all, as if I am in a vacuum.

Then suddenly I feel a sharp pain shoot up my spine as I smack hard into something. I see stars and bright light. As I wait for the stars to clear I half expect to see Lucifer himself sitting before me, stroking his hard on and laughing his ass off.

Instead, I see the base of cornstalks. A bright light pushing down, punishing my eyes. I look up in amazement. Where am I?

It appears to be high noon; the sun is directly overhead. Not a cloud in the sky, a sky an ocean blue. The smell of burnt vegetation is everywhere. The sound of humming bees echoes all around me. The air feels thicker, soggy with humidity. I have landed in a cornfield?

As I rise to my knees, I notice I still wear the oversized, baggy pants that I stole from the clothesline outside the tiny bungalow in France. I am still wearing the shirt, too, only the knife is gone, and my shoes are missing.

What the hell is happening to me?

My knees burn. I look out across the field. To my left, an endless sea of corn as far as I can see. To my right, a rural route. Down the road, about a quarter mile, is a red barn with a tobacco advertisement painted on the side, in English.

I am in America? What? How can that be?

Fear and uncertainty claw at my brain. Why am I out here? What happened?

I decide to make for the barn. I walk slowly, careful in my bare feet. I notice that my toenails are blackened like charcoal. My feet are gray in color, they look frostbitten. I can still smell the seawater on my skin; I can taste the salt of the Atlantic on my lips.

This does not make sense. How can this be?

I reach the road and look to my right. Not a single car in sight. To my left, the barn comes clearer into focus. There is a stand out front, selling corn and various other fresh vegetables. I can hear the soft moo of bored cows echo from behind the barn.

As I walk towards the barn, I step on a pebble that shoots a sharp pain up my leg. Wincing I lean over and dig it out of my foot. A chunk of skin tears loose. In disgust, I throw it into the cornstalks.

The sun is hot. It must be summer. Late summer. No breeze. The constant buzzing of bees serenades the air.

As I approach the stand, an overpowering hunger pangs at my stomach so hard that I almost double over. The stand, which is essentially a wooden box suspended by three sets of double legs sits in front of the barn.

Not a soul in sight.

I reach for an apple. As I am about to raise it to my lips, I hear a voice.

"You going to pay for that, my son?"

A man comes out from around the side of the barn. He is wearing dusty overalls and steel-toed work boots. His face is red and rough, as if he has been in the sun too long, all his life. He has a thick beard that needs tending. He is holding a machete in his right hand. The rusty blade is so long it almost touches the ground.

Nodding, I reach for my pocket. "Yes, yes... I..."

My pockets are empty.

My face must have given it away. As I put the apple back down on the table, he waves the machete in the air, back and forth, as if it represented him shaking his head in disagreement. "No, no, that's alright, son. I can tell you're very hungry. If you don't have the money that's all right. Who am I to turn away a man in need?"

"God, thank you, sir," I say as I devour the apple. The sweet juice of the fruit flows from my mouth, streaking my chin. "You have no idea what I've been through."

He leans on the side of the barn and places the machete against the wood paneling. "Try me, son."

I shake my head back and forth. "No, that's alright. You wouldn't believe me if I told you." No way. This guy will think I'm crazy. Although crazy would make sense. Only insanity could explain all of this.

He grunts, then snorts, then pulls out a pipe from his pocket. He packs the pipe gently before firing it up. He grins at me as he takes a puff. The smoke billows upwards into the summer heat. I notice several of his teeth are missing. The ones that are still there are as brown as the earth. "Anything I can do for you, son?"

I crunch down the rest of the apple, and then hold the core in my hand, unsure of what to do with it. I toss it behind my head; I never have been one for manners. I say, "You can tell me where I am."

He sucks on his pipe and bites down on the end. "What are you, son, some kind of alien? Them saucer people drop you down out there in the field?"

I shake my head and with my left thumb and forefinger push down on my eyes. My head stings. What the hell is this guy talking about? It seems like he really has had some legit experience with "saucer people." "Let's just say it was a rough night. Now where the hell am I?"

"Kansas."

Something that looks like a car crests the horizon. What the hell? I have never seen anything like this in my entire life. It has wheels—but what?

My heart races. What is this steel contraption coming towards me? Stuttering, I turn back to him, I notice his grin as he puffs on the pipe. "When?" I ask.

"What the hell do you mean when? It's July, my boy."

"I mean what year?"

He laughs as he dumps the pipe to the ground, tapping the back so all the tobacco will fall out. "You on something, son? You must be kidding me."

I watch as the car, or what looks like a car, races past. I see the silhouette of the driver staring straight ahead. The car rumbles by then disappears into the distance. Drumbeats pound in my head. "Just tell me when, okay? Humor me, will you?"

His face grows solemn. "1965," he says.

Then my mind explodes.

Chapter Ten

In 1938, I married my high school girlfriend. We eloped to New Jersey and got married by the justice of the peace. There were two witnesses. One was not wearing pants. It was more than an interesting night. The courtroom was a desolate place, full of vagrants and weirdoes. But we didn't mind. We spent the weekend walking the Jersey shore. We made love in the sand and slept on the beach, out under the stars.

As I laid on my back, tangles of her red hair fell upon my chest. It was one of those warm summer nights where the air was a hot, welcoming breath that kept you warm throughout the night. I will never forget that one night in particular.

It was our first time.

There was something so free, so pure about that night. The way we did not have a care in the world. The future, the past—nothing mattered except where we were. Little did I know how fleeting things would be. Looking back now, I remember that night with more clarity than anything that has occurred since Omaha beach. My life seems like a giant blur. The years have all started to blend together. When you sleep in a crypt, you turn yourself off from the outside world. When your profession is to hunt down and murder demon-possessed people, you have lost touch with reality.

Reality is only a matter of perception. It exists only in the mind's eye. Without a context, the world is a jumbled mess of colors and chaos, brought together by our own individual mind's perception of the way things are, or ought to be.

We tend to get caught up in the "ought to be."

We don't notice the world for what it really is. We live a fairy tale life in our own heads. We watch television programs, commercials, and politicians that tell us how to think, how to feel, what to believe— what our reality ought to be.

But it is not reality. Not true reality.

For the world is evil. The world is the Devil's playground. Cast loose from the pits of hell, God has allowed him to run rampant on this earth. His minions are multiplying, and before they should be. Yet God sits in silence. It is as if he is missing altogether, lost somewhere out there in the universe. Cotton and I are the only troops. The last line of defense. We are vastly outnumbered. And for the life of me, I do not know why. I don't understand His motives.

God knows the end to all of our stories. Time is outside the realm of someone who sits above. It is similar to the tower guard in an ancient city. Standing hundreds of feet above the ground, the guard sees the angry horde approaching before anyone in the walled city below. He has a preview. Like God, he knows the outcome before it occurs. He knows that they are doomed.

So I do not know why God has allowed the demons to multiply. I do not know why I seem to be the only line of defense. As Cotton tells me, it is not up to us to understand, it is beyond us, but duty calls all the same.

But that night back on the Jersey shore, with the sky lit up, cascading with stars, reality had yet to rear its ugly head. My mind's eye only perceived the here and now. And that was the greatest moment of my life.

Her name was Jennifer. Her hair was the color of freshly picked red roses. Her skin was smooth like porcelain. Her eyes, green like the leaves of eucalyptus. She was my love. As I mentioned before, she tasted of strawberries.

I dream of her often. It is only my mind reaching back to that reality. That reality is still occurring, lost in time, lost in space, returning to me in the depths of slumber. My mind returns to the beach, to that time, while my body sleeps in the ground, in the cold icy earth. I smell the ocean when I sleep. I taste the saltwater on her skin. Her lips like fruit. The air, warm, blowing in hard off the ocean that crashes, hissing and bursting in front of us. The horizon, a black emptiness save the shining band of moonlight that looks like a lost, ghostly highway out across the water. The smell of salt and seaweed.

My dreams always start this way. Every single night. The problem is I can never stay there with her long. She never speaks, always asleep, cuddled in my arms, her face tight against my bare chest. There is no thought of war. I know not of reality. I have never met the Gateman. I have never met Cotton Mather. I am at peace. I am in my own personal heaven. I am where I want to be, back to a moment, however brief it might have been, that stood still in time, burning like a beacon in my heart.

Forever. Oh, I wish forever.

Then it flames out. It always flames out. And I fall back into another realm. The realm of the demonic.

This particular night, as I thrashed back and forth in my sleeping bag, the Jersey shore pulled away suddenly. I found myself in an empty church. I sat in the first pew. In front of me was an alabaster altar held up by a dark green marble slab. A gold crucifix adorned the front. Poinsettias and small trees decorated with Christmas lights sat on both sides of the altar. The back wall was a crimson curtain. Suspended from the ceiling was a large, ornately carved crucifix; Christ looked down, seemingly disappointed. 'Course, I would be disappointed too if I was strung up there like that.

A bank of dimly lit candles sat along the wall to the left of the altar, four rows, about twenty each. Their soft light filled the church with a warm glow. The crucifix shimmered in the candlelight as it swayed gently back and forth. Stained glass windows ornamented the outer walls, each one representing one of the apostles. The soft light of the moon outside penetrated, cascading a myriad of colors across the pews. I saw doubting Thomas amongst the glass and I grinned; my old friend, my kindred spirit. The church was as silent as a crypt. The air smelled of flowers and incense.

Then I heard a shriek, followed by a scuffling sound. The sound of a struggle.

I stood up and turned on my heel; my shoes squeaked like squashed mice. I stared down the pews behind me. They were empty, about twenty rows deep on both sides of a center aisle. At the back were the confessionals, doors closed, but seemingly empty.

I followed my instincts. I walked down the aisle, towards the entrance.

As I stood in the foyer I heard what sounded like a child sobbing, followed by a grunting noise. It was coming from the stairs that lead down into the church basement. I clutched the wrought iron bannister and stairs were marble, worn from centuries of footsteps. I reached a basement floor that resembled a checkerboard. There were cheap tables and folding chairs everywhere. The smell of a recent bake sale hung in the air.

The room was long and dark, illuminated only by the fire exit signs at the back. I heard the sobbing sound more clearly now. It was coming from the corner. I saw a large shadow holding a smaller shadow to the floor.

I took one last step before the larger shadow wheeled and looked at me. The shadow's eyes were a fiery crimson. I shuddered. The stench of sulfur fumed from his eye sockets, wafting like a liquid in the dark. It smelled so bad I had to suppress my gag instinct. Then I saw a shadow of horns.

The creature hissed at me as I approached. "You are not welcome here…"

The room started to get darker and darker; the darkness assaulted the corners of my eyes, oozing like oil intruding upon the world. The creature's eyes fell dormant. The shadows melted into the floor. My legs felt heavier, numb, like I was walking in wet cement. I fell to my knees. I felt a sharp pain shimmer up my spine. I bent over in an electric pain. I held my head in my hands—the worst migraine ever. I shook my head back and forth, trying to alleviate the pain. But I could not. Bent over, I grabbed my knees and put my head to the floor.

Then I woke up.

I woke up in a spasm. I tossed the sleeping bag off me in a panic, as if spiders were crawling all over my body. I often wake up, terrified that spiders have decided to feast on my flesh. For someone who wants to die, the idea of insects consuming me terrifies me to know end. I know that they will—it is only a matter of time. We are all destined to become a feast for the pests that run the earth. My only hope is that they wait until I have evacuated this carcass first. I don't want to feel it!

My lantern swung above my head. I reached up and turned the light up, fully illuminating my four-walled world. There, above my head, was a large, black spider. I shuddered and backed up against the wall. I took out old reliable and burned the hairy motherfucker alive. I swear I could hear it squeal.

I said, "See you in hell." It crackled under the heat. The spider curled up, contorted, destroyed, another skeleton of ash. The dead spider stunk like burnt hair.

Already wearing stained gray sweatpants, I stretched on a matching, yet bloodstained, sweatshirt.

It was cold down here in the earth.

I ripped my coat off the back of my only chair and rummaged through the pockets. I found my Camels and lit one up. I pulled my one rickety wooden chair over underneath the copper exhaust pipe. I took a long drag and rubbed the back of my head. I winced; that one hurt more than most.

I blew the smoke into the bottom of the pipe. Up above the tomb, the smoke disappeared into the cold Boston night.

I said, "Damn, that was a bad one." I rubbed the base of my neck. It stung. Like when you turn your head to fast and bust a nerve or two.

I heard Cotton whisper but could not make him out.

Turning to his coffin, I said, "Speak the fuck up, old man. I can't hear you."

His voice was raspy and jagged. "They seem to be getting worse. Your dreams seem to be impacting you physically."

"Don't I wish. This will go away in ten minutes. Always does. I'll never get sick. I can't willingly die. My only hope is that one of these times, one of these witches will take me out."

Cotton cleared his throat and then spoke. "But then you will have lost. You will have not filled your quota. The Gateman has to come for you. Without filling your quota, if you were to die, the Devil would welcome you into his arms. Moreover, I shall not say that you would prefer that. We have a vocation here."

"Speaking of my job, I don't think I need much help interpreting this guy's sins. I could tell what he was doing. But I didn't recognize the church." I took a drag off my cigarette. Holding the smoke in my lungs longer than I ought to, I felt my chest burn. Exhausting the smoke, I spit it into the copper tube. It careened towards the cold night air above.

Cotton said, "St. Stanislaus. Father McKay. Jonathan McKay. God has named him. Cull him from the earth."

I took another drag and nodded my head. The pain about the base of my neck was now gone, just as I thought it would be. "Yeah, yeah. I'll get to it in a minute. I need some fucking coffee first."

"I've never understood your zest for profanity."

I stood up and flicked the cigarette upon his coffin. The ash sent sparks flying about. With my iron skillet's handle, I put out the butt. "Yeah, well go fuck yourself, Cotton."

♦♦♦♦♦

St. Stanislaus is located just south of Boston in the suburb of Quincy. Quincy, located on the Redline, is a bustling, diverse burrow. One of the last stops on the Redline, it is one of a few genuine, independent small towns connected by the subway as opposed to the commuter train line. This gives Quincy a unique community. The majority are commuters into the city, young folk who have retreated from the sky scrapers in search of cheaper rent. The old timers still lament days gone by, back when the Boston sprawl had not yet raped the town, the town with much patriotic pride. For it is here that John Adams and his family had a farm. It was here that John Quincy Adams was born. A rare town that can claim the birthright of two American presidents. A town with much history. And now, thanks to the subway line, a town littered with bums. It is almost as if the homeless have given up on the city to migrate here and try their hand at panhandling outside the YMCA.

It was Friday, during rush hour. The sky was a dark gray, nondescript as the void. There were no clouds—only a dark gray haze that filled the horizon. The sun, gone beyond the hills, seemed to be a distant afterthought, as if it never existed at all. It was how I imagine the sky must have looked back when the meteor hit, wiping out the dinosaurs: gray, full of ash, blocking out the sun.

I grabbed the rail above my head and held on tight. The train bounced and jerked back and forth. The Redline juts out from the depths of the city after it clears South Boston or Southie as the locals call it. The ride from Southie down to Quincy is one of the longest on the subway line. It is here the Redline runs above ground next to the highway and the harbor on its trek towards the south shore.

The train bounced along, moving at a rapid pace. The rails screamed a high-pitched scream, higher than normal, as the air was cold, tightening the metal tracks. There were no lights on the harbor. In the distance, a black oily pond stretched in every direction.

The train was packed. Primarily young businessmen and women dressed to the part. Black ties, red ties, blue ties. Tie after tie. Ties unfurled. Ties tucked into coat pockets. Ties tied tightly, ties shoved into briefcases. The noose of the business class. A constant reminder of status and servitude.

The subway car felt like a swamp. There was barely enough room to stand at all. Sweaty, stress-filled bodies surrounded me. I couldn't move. Their disgusting bodies rubbed up against me but I could do nothing. There was a fat woman in front of me that kept rubbing her ass up against me but there was nothing I could do about it. Trapped. I felt like a cow in a slaughterhouse. Packed in tightly, waiting for my turn. A diseased Nazi death train. Next stop Auschwitz. The car smelled of sweat and B.O.

To my right was a man bundled up in a long, gray overcoat. He was wearing sunglasses despite the fact that we hadn't seen the sun in weeks. Nestled between his legs was a long white staff. It extended from the floor to just above his head. He had sandy brown hair that looked as if it had never seen a comb.

This man was blind.

I stared at this man, not afraid that he might notice. I felt sorry for him. Far be it from me to admit that anyone in the world could possibly suffer more than I. I may be trapped. Stuck here on this rock, killing people until my deeds fill my quota and quench an angry God's blood lust. But I cannot imagine what it would be like to spend my days in total darkness. The helplessness the man must have felt. To never see a sunrise or a sunset. To never see the sky on a perfect summer day. To stand next to the vast expanse of the ocean, the one place where all my fears melt away into insignificance, and not see a damn thing except blackness. Darkness. The void. A kind of living death. And here I zest for death. I would welcome it. But blindness? That truly would be hell on earth. To see absolutely nothing but the black. That is Hell. Why does that seem so familiar?

The car bounced into the Quincy Center station; the metal wheels shrieked like a banshee. The car came suddenly to a jolted stop. I fell into the woman in front of me. The wall of people started to churn like rats in a trash bag, pushing, nudging towards the exit. The blind man stood up and walked out as the crowd allowed him to leave first.

I smiled, if but for a moment. It seemed as though there was some shred of common human decency left. In all honesty, I was shocked they didn't trample him to pieces. They always dash to their cars in an attempt to leave the parking garage as soon as possible. One giant stress-filled commuter game.

Stuck behind the jockeying throng I found myself about twenty people behind the blind man who was now ascending the escalator, tipping and tapping the escalator walls with his stick. A sea of movement milled about in front of me. I made my way to the base of the escalator and waited in line. After a few moments, I was through the station and out onto the street, into the night.

The air was cold. One of those colds that causes your sack to crawl back up inside you. When your body does that, you know it is too damn cold outside.

I exited the station and passed two homeless men begging for change next to the taxi stand. The commuters kept their gaze firmly affixed to the concrete, trying best not to make eye contact. If there is not eye contact, I suppose, there is no guilt.

As I passed, I patted one of the guys on the shoulder. He was a wearing a dusty old jean jacket covered in glam metal band patches from the eighties. His hair was long, hippie long, encrusted with all kinds of filth. Missing two teeth, his smile was too gummy; his breath, putrid, like ass. "Good luck, buddy," I said as I walked by. He let out a grunt but said nothing, just stood there shivering in the night air.

I headed north along Hancock Street. The church was about six blocks down on the right. I huddled into my coat, pulling it tight. I could feel my skin burn, almost tearing from the lack of moisture in the air. It was as if God was sticking a straw up by ass, sucking out all my juices. Dehydrated from too much bourbon and beer, my skin felt like a crocodile's. My bones ached as I walked and the cold sent shivers up my spine.

About three blocks from the station, I spotted the blind man up ahead, tapping his white cane on the sidewalk, about a block up in front of me. He was at an intersection, seemingly waiting for the light to change. How he knew that the light was green was beyond me. Maybe it was a sixth sense.

Then I got my answer.

Suddenly, without warning, the blind man tossed his cane high up in the air. In a single motion, he ripped off his sunglasses, pocketed them in his coat, and caught the cane as it whipped back towards earth.

This guy was faking.

He was fucking faking blindness.

I needed to know why.

I ran up behind him as fast as I could and tapped him on the shoulder. He turned and grinned from ear to ear. I could smell whiskey on his breath.

I grabbed his shoulders with my meat hooks and spit in his face. Still grinning, he started humming. The guy seemed high, his eyes darting back and forth like a deranged lunatic. "Why," I said, "Why the hell would you fake being blind? Give me one good fucking reason!"

He laughed under his breath while grinning. His laugh was a high-pitched giggle, like a schoolgirl. A spittle of drool careened out of his mouth down onto his chin. Freak.

I wanted to hurt this man. I needed to hurt this man. "Answer me!"

Still he giggled; his eyes looked past me, as if I was not there.

"Goddammit!" Unable to control my rage I reached back, mustered up as much torque as possible, then slammed my fist into his stomach. He doubled over, collapsing to the ground like a broken card table. I saw nothing but red as hatred burned in my veins.

With my steel tipped boots, I kicked and kicked and kicked. I heard the sound of bones splintering as his ribcage shattered. He should have been sobbing but he was not, instead he giggled away like a crack addict.

"Why, dammit!"

He spit blood on the pavement and laughed, "I just don't want to stand, and that's all!" His chest heaved in and out like a maimed animal; he spit a tooth out onto the pavement. His eyes turned gray and listless. His breathing began to calm, as if a panic attack had disappeared. He breathed softly and spit more blood on the pavement. He said, "I just don't want to stand..."

I reared back my foot, ready to break his jawbone, when a voice spoke in my head.

He is not on the list.

Wheeling, I stared down the street behind me. The sidewalk was empty; a commuter bus roared off in the opposite direction. Cars whizzed by with not a care. No one looks in Boston, or Quincy for that matter. They only see what they want to see. Ignore everything else. I looked up in the sky and shouted, "Dammit, Cotton, you stay out of this! This guy is a freak!"

That may be. Nevertheless, he is not on the list. Your dreams did not name him. The Gateman has not called for his soul. Cull this man and sealed your fate is.

"Shit!"

I squatted down and put my hands on my knees. My black overcoat fell over my kneecaps, mushrooming to the concrete. With my right hand, I grabbed the man's collar, forcing him to look at me. His nose was broken, shifted to the right. His swollen left eye was turning purple. Blood streamed from his mouth. A mouth that still grinned, despite the pain. With all my heart, I wanted to end this man. But I could not. He was not

on the list, not named, and there was not a damn thing I could do about it.

"If I catch you pulling this shit again, it will be your end. Do you understand me?"

Rather than responding, he hummed. He grinned, hummed, and spit blood on the pavement.

"Fucking waste." I shoved him to the ground; his head bounced off the pavement with a crack. Giggling, he writhed and then contorted into a fetal position.

"The hell with it." I stood back up and stepped over his shaking body to cross the street.

There must have been ten cars that passed buy us and not one person stopped. Not even a honk. Nothing. My last shred of respect for humanity had left my heart. I was wrong. That single moment of hope was a lie.

These people are all parasites. Maybe they should all be on the list.

That is dangerous thinking, Robert.

I shook my head in an attempt to drown out Cotton's thoughts. "This is my mind! Stay the fuck out of it. You can help me do the Gateman's biddings but you STAY THE FUCK OUTTA MY HEAD!"

I reached into my coat pocket and fished out my cigarettes. Old reliable caught and I inhaled the first drag. I love the taste of hot ash. My lips tingled from the sensation. Damn, I love nicotine. Nicotine, caffeine, and alcohol, gimme gimme gimme.

After a few drags, I cleared the next two blocks and came to the church. Typical of New England, it was painted white with a large front door and a steeple that had a boner for the sky. Stained glass windows depicting the apostles ran up and down the side. Plastic grocery bags twirled in the night air.

I had been here before. In my dream.

Chapter Eleven

It is 1968 and I am lying in bed next to my second wife. It has been three years since I landed in the Kansas cornfield. Three years since I met the Gateman. The Normandy invasion was three years ago. Or twenty-four depending upon who you would ask. For me it has been three years, and that is all that is important. I did not go to Boston. I did not stick my head on the ground listening for the dead to talk to me. For all I know, I never was at Normandy. I have done my best to block the whole messy business out of my head. What happened to me is not possible. It is not plausible. I must have made the entire thing up. Listened to too many war stories from old timers at the bar. The only problem is, buried underneath my underwear in the top drawer of my dresser are my dog tags. They bare my name, Robert Turner. One tag is melted, unreadable. How did that get there?

I have spent the last three years trying to live a normal life. I took a job at a bowling alley in Columbus, Ohio. I am a pin monkey. There I met a slightly overweight blonde named Katherine. She is not ugly but she won't grace any magazine covers either. She has a mole underneath her nose, perfectly placed off to the right. She is pretty enough. Enough for me anyway. Her expectations are low. I fit the bill nicely. I enjoy the comfort of knowing that she's next to me. I will be the first to admit, I am afraid to be alone. This is why I agreed to marry her on such short notice. We eloped to the county courthouse. We honeymooned in Cleveland. Truthfully, more than anything, I'm afraid of the dark. I'm terrified that I'll fall back into another tunnel, only to come out the other end, staring Lucifer and his minions in the face.

I try not to think of Jennifer. Every time I see a thin redhead, I close my eyes.

That life is over.

That life never happened.

The Jersey shore is a distant memory. It is not my own. It cannot be my own. I must have seen that in a movie or something. I was not there.

Or so I tell myself.

Denial is my bedmate. Ignorance is my best friend. Alcohol helps. Each night I fall into a drunkenness that obliterates the confusion.

It is the only way. It has to be.

Tonight is the first night of the rest of my life. Tonight is the night when my life will start down a tumbling path, following the rabbit deep down into its hole, never to return. The first domino, the harbinger of death. For tonight, I have my first dream. My first vision of darkness.

As I lay next to Katherine, her back against mine, her naked ass against mine, always touching, always warm, my mind falls into the abyss. My eyes, heavy as they are, start to blink as the room goes in and out of focus.

My dresser starts to flash; the closet door seems to bend slightly to the right, as if it is slowly melting. I smell something foul, skunk-like, rotten egg-like. Sulfur. The room takes on a hazy shade of red, almost milky as it mixes with the darkness. I have the sensation of slowly spinning, as if I drank too much booze, but I know that tonight was a light night; I only hammered about seven drinks. I should not be drunk.

I'm not drunk.

I'm falling now into the black, clutching for my bed sheets but not finding them. Searching for Katherine's warm round ass I find nothing, I'm grasping at air. Falling. Falling.

I land with a thud; a sharp pain shoots through my limbs as the milky red fades, sparkling into a soft white light. I find myself sitting in a college dorm room. I am on the floor, my legs crossed. I'm rocking back and forth in my seat like a deranged crack addict. A quick assessment and I know that I am in a woman's dorm room. There are flowers on the windowsill. The bedspread has a clover pattern. There are about twenty pairs of women's shoes overflowing, belched forth, from the closet. Dresses are everywhere, as if the closet is puking out the unwanted. I sit next to a single, wooden desk, the color of sun-tanned flesh. The smell of flowery perfume dominates the night air.

The bed is not empty. I see long brown hair fall down over the side of the comforter. I see the mound beneath the sheets move up and down, slowly, as her soft breath makes a miniscule whistling noise through her nostrils.

The room is dark, but not pitch black. Outside, a streetlight pours through the window, through barren tree branches, creating a sinister shadow on the wall tangent to her bed. The shadow looks like demonic fingers, clutching, grabbing, pulling at the body beneath, but causing no harm, as it is only the tree shifting in the wind outside.

On the wall above her head is a pennant. The pennant is scarlet and gray. The words, "Cheerleading Squad" run down the middle of it. At the base, is a large "O".

I'm at Ohio State.

A bright light shines underneath her only door. I hear the sound of heavy footsteps followed by labored breathing. Suddenly there is a shadow at the door.

What happens next happens fast.

It happens hard.

It happens while I sit there, rocking in my stance.

The doorknob jiggles gently. I hear a clicking noise as the lock gives way. The door swings open suddenly and a beast enters the room. I am a large man, but this guy makes me look like an art school reject.

He stands well over six feet tall and has the shoulders of a rhinoceros. He's wearing a black sweatshirt with matching black sweatpants. Something large is pushing the fabric of his pants out in front of him.

He jumps on the edge of the bed and grabs the girl by the throat. She lets out a muffled yelp. Watching from the floor, I cannot see her face. He is mostly shadow; I cannot see him well. His jaw is chiseled granite, sharp angles that cast a comic book style shadow on the wall. Smacking her face, he pulls down her pajamas. Her long brown hair sprays in the dark.

I am rocking back in forth as I am sitting on the floor. I try to yell out but I cannot. My mouth feels funny, sloppy, as if I have no control. I try to stand but I cannot stop rocking. I'm moving back and forth as if on a pendulum, trapped in place, a dead zombie with no motor skills, but a fully conscious mind.

The girl struggles, pinned beneath his weight. Her left arm claws at the wall, fingernails breaking. Outside, the wind howls, the tree branches creaking and cracking in the night. Shadows pass fast along the wall as low, dense clouds stalk across the autumn moonlight. I sit there immobile, a statue, frozen in place, unable to move a muscle yet still rock back and forth, back and forth.

A large, dense cloud passes over the moonlight, blocking it out. The room falls into blackness, dark as ink, dark as the deepest depths of the ocean. I expect this to be my return, but to where I'm not sure. Would I wake up next to Katherine's warm ass or back on the beach, drenched in my own blood, choking on saltwater? Or worse? Would I wake up in my coffin, six feet under, scratching at the wooden lid like a trapped dog? *I'm alive down here, motherfuckers, I'm alive!*

Or.

In hell.

Suddenly a band of light filters through the window.

The room is now full of mist, coming from a realm I can only imagine. I see a shimmer of light on the bed, a reflection, something long, something shiny, something sharp. As the blade leaves the man's boot my heart thunders in my head as if I am in cardiac arrest. Swallowing, I taste only bile, as if the evil I am witnessing is transforming me, turning me into something other than human.

With a fast jerk, the man slams the blade down upon the girl's breast. Her chest makes a crunching sound as her ribcage collapses. Her arms and legs sprawl outward, like a struck crab on the beach. Hand held firmly across the girl's face, the man whispers softly.

"Shhh, my darling. It will be over soon."

Horrified, I try to yell, I try to scream, but find my lungs paralyzed.

Her eyes are wide with horror, glistening in the moonlight. All at once, as his left hand holds her mouth firmly shut, with his right he pulls the blade south towards her navel. She splits open like a piece of fruit.

I want to wake up, motherfucker, help me wake up!

The man casts his gaze towards the closet, down towards the floor, looking, searching. He finds me and stares me right in the eyes.

I can see little in the dark. I see a chiseled jaw that looks like it could crack diamonds. His hair is too long in the front; it cascades down across his forehead, falling across his left eye that burns a dark crimson underneath. His right eye is a bright, white-hot flame that seems to simmer in place, a cauldron of heat and light. A scar scampers along his right cheek, a battle scar from a drunken brawl no doubt. There is something oddly familiar about him.

He asks me, "What are you?" His voice sounds like gravel, like layered chunks of concrete put through a grinder. "What are you doing here?"

I try to yell; I try to scream but cannot. My tongue is dead in my mouth, a floppy fish out of water.

The girl struggles one last time, her limbs shaking, as her life essence leaves her body. Releasing her mouth with his hand, he turns and wheels towards me. I can hear the girl gasp a last breath before she leaves this plane and returns to wherever it is we come from.

To the dust.

To the void.

To God?

Or something else?

For if there is a God, how could a monster like this exist? How can God allow this beast in the world?

I rock in my seat. My skin tingles in anticipation.

He yells, "What are you?!" He clutches his knife in his right hand. The girl's fresh blood, bright red like a cherry cordial, drips from the blade down onto the floor. Behind him, the girl's body collapses inward, a slaughtered turkey, a chewed-up lobster, a conquered chicken breast.

He stomps towards me and kicks me clean in the mouth.

I see stars. Countless stars, as he explodes into a tornado of light. But I feel no pain, and I wake up in my bed, covered in sweat.

I scream. I scream louder than I have in my entire life.

Clutching my pillow against my naked body, I stand in the middle of the room screaming like a three-year-old child having a night terror. Sweat pours from my armpits; my skin glistens in the moonlight like a wet frog.

Katherine falls to the floor and lands with a thump. She lets out a howl; she sounds like an alley cat that got her ass cleaned in a fight. She struggles to her feet, her knees wobble. Her eyes, eyes as wide as an October moon, convey her terror. "Bobby! What the hell is wrong? What this time?"

I shake my head back and forth as fast as I can, as if it would help me erase the wicked memory. A memory that would now curse me forever. Shaking too quickly, I hurt my neck. Pins and needles shout towards the base of my head.

The images are too real. That was no ordinary dream. I was there. I smelled her perfume. I saw her die, and I smelled her death. That girl died right before my eyes and there was nothing I could do to save her. That monster is out there somewhere, I am sure of it. Somehow, I knew him. I know who the son of a bitch is but I cannot place him. He was real. He is real. I am sure of it, as I am sure that the sun will rise and fall.

Dropping her blankets to the floor, Katherine hobbles over to me in the darkness. She trips over my shoes at the foot of the bed, and then steadies herself on the dresser against the wall. Naked, her tits drooped too much to the floor, looking too much like tube socks with eight balls stuffed inside. Dangling windsocks. "Baby, are you alright?" she says to me as she opens her arms, ready to hug me.

I yell, "Don't touch me!" I back up against the window. The glass feels frigid on my ass, as if it too, like the outside world, has turned entirely into ice.

"Bobby, let me help me you, please let me help you."

"No, stay away!" That poor girl. Gutted like a stuck pig.

I notice that I am having a hard time breathing. My lungs kill, burning from the pack of cigarettes I inhaled throughout the day. I can taste the tar upon my tongue. My hands shake as if I have arthritis. I can barely control my limbs.

Katherine says, "Sit down, honey. Sit down." She reaches her hand out to mine. Still in shock from what occurred, my instincts reduced to nothingness, half-expecting to see her melt before my eyes, I take her clammy hand in mine and let her guide me to the edge of the bed. I sit down, my wet ass sticking to the sheets.

She says, "There, there…" while she rubs my back. I can feel her hand slip across my skin like a hockey puck; saturated sweat. "It was all a dream."

I shake my head in disagreement. Still clutching the pillow, I say, "It wasn't a dream. I'm not sure what it was, but it wasn't a dream."

She kisses my wet, salty shoulder. I can see her skin crawl as she wipes her lips clean. I imagine I am sweating alcohol. Too many kisses like that and she'll end up buzzed. "What was it about?"

My head starts to hurt. A sharp pain starts at the top of my spine, cascading towards my frontal lobe where it simmers like chili. Wincing, I hold the bridge of my nose with my thumb and forefinger. "Sheer horror. You don't want to know."

"Please, Bobby, please tell me. If you can't talk to your wife, then who can you talk to?"

I take a deep breath. "Okay. Okay, I'll tell you. It was about a girl. A girl up at Ohio State. A man broke into her room and held her down. He killed her. He shoved a knife into her sternum and gutted her like a farm animal. He killed her! And I had to watch. I had to watch it all. And the son of a bitch saw me. He saw me sitting there and there was nothing I could do to help her."

Katherine let out a little laugh, almost a whimper. "Oh Bobby, it was nothing to worry about. You just picked that up on the news."

The pain leaves my forehead as fast as it came. "What did you say?"

She rubs my slimy back with her hand. "I said you picked that up on the news. Two weeks ago, there was a story about some poor girl murdered up on campus. Awful story. From what they said, it was much like you described it. Poor girl didn't show up for class for days. The kids who lived on her hall started complaining about the odor coming from her room. They said it smelled like pizza left out too long. Poor kids. They had counselors up there for a few weeks. Don't you remember?"

I close my eyes, concentrating, searching, and probing my memory. Then I remember the newscast. We had fish that night. Fish sticks, that is.

"Well you should try picking up a newspaper Bobby. Or reading the news. All you do is read those silly novels of yours. It happened... oh, maybe four weeks back now."

Suddenly I remember it all. Yes. And the fish sticks were nasty. Funny what the mind will trigger.

She shakes her head, and then wipes my sweat on the blanket. "Don't you remember—we talked about it at dinner and everything? You never listen. And you never remember anything. Which reminds me, I have an appointment tomorrow. Do you remember that?"

I stand up and toss the sweat soaked pillow to the floor. It resembles a wet marshmallow—it splats as it hits the ground. "No... what? No, I don't remember." I stumble over to the dresser drawer and start to fish through my underwear. I pull out my cigarettes and my zippo lighter. A lighter I have had for seemingly forever. Old reliable. I light up a butt and take a deep drag, and then expel the smoke into the room.

"Open a damn window, you asshole, I don't want to breathe that shit. You're stinking up the room. You're not allowed to smoke in here, remember?"

"Fine, fine," I say, cracking open the window. I collapse to the floor, my back against the wall beneath the window, still naked, penis dangling between my legs, a bored serpent who could give a shit about my fears and woes. The cold night air seeps in like an angel of death, stealthily, slithery. I blow the smoke above my head. The hot embers of the cigarette waft towards the fresh oxygen that billows in from the outside. "So, what is this appointment you're talking about?"

"You never fucking listen to me!" She stands up and angrily wrenches open up the bathroom door. Slamming it, I hear her scream as I remember I had left the toilet seat up again. "Put the goddamn seat down!" I hear porcelain smack as she takes out her frustration on the lid.

I take another drag and blow some smoke rings into the middle of the room. Starting to feel better. It was all just a dream, nothing but a dream.

I flick the butt out the crack in the window into a snowdrift. I slam the window down and pull the clasp tight. I rub my face with my hands, pushing down on my eyelids. My skin feels dry, dehydrated like a camel's ass. I go over to the bathroom door and lean up against it. Putting my ear to the wooden grain, I can hear her sobbing on the toilet.

"Baby, I'm sorry. I'm really sorry. I didn't mean to hurt your feelings. I'm just having trouble remembering things is all. I can't recall anything anymore."

I can hear her sniffle behind the door. Her voice sounds sad and lonely. "That's because you drink too much. You're killing yourself with booze."

"Ah, come on baby, you know I'm okay. I have a royal liver, you know that! Besides, you drink with me most nights."

"Not anymore. And not as much as you. I have a couple. You drink three times as much as me."

"Fine, baby, if it will make you feel better, I'll promise to cut back." *Yeah right,* I think. *We'll see about that.* "Now what are you crying about, huh? Come on; stop wailing back there like some jilted teenager, what's going on? You can talk to me."

The next sound I hear is the sound of the toilet paper roll spinning wildly. Following it is a sound that sounds like semi-trucks down shifting on the highway. She is blowing her nose.

"I can't drink anymore."

"What? Why not?"

"I think I might be pregnant."

Suddenly, my tongue feels like a dead fish again.

Chapter Twelve

When you meet the Lord's regent, your life changes. What you thought was normal is no longer. Up is now down, down is now up, you see life in a different manner. The sun's rays no longer bother you as much as they used to. You're just happy to have the light land upon your face. The hot summer wind no longer makes you angry. You don't feel parched, you don't mind sweating, and you certainly do not wish it to go away. In the winter, you will find that the cold no longer bites at your face. Your wind-burned, alligator-like skin no longer creates a sense of panic. You don't mind being tired. You don't mind a sugar rush. Getting drunk no longer brings guilt or remorse. You don't mind being bored. Boredom offers serenity. Peace of mind is a cherished gift. But you also don't mind indulging in remedial entertainment. Time loses its meaning. No longer are you concerned with the linear aspects of your life.

It is all right to age, if you can. I cannot, but if you meet a regent of the Lord, and yet you still age, that will suit you just fine. Growing old no longer brings the same fear. Losing a child, friend, or parent no longer brings the same longing, the same loss. The stress of the world doesn't weigh on your shoulders the way it used to. The days' activities don't carry as much importance. For most folk, there are not enough hours in the day. Many are slaves to a routine. Wake up, hit the exercise bike, treadmill, jog, or cross fit; piss, shit, shower, shave, go to work, come home, eat dinner, play with the kids, watch some mindless sitcoms, piss, shit, shower, go back to bed. Repeat for twenty years or more. Wake up to find yourself old, wrinkled, regretful, and remorseful. For most folk, twenty years into the job begets panic. They are not who they thought they would be. They had dreams of grandeur that faded out as youth decayed. For the destroyer is always at work, plodding along, sometimes slow, sometimes fast, sending us back to the dust from which we came.

But if you meet God's regent, these fears disappear. For it is okay that you wasted your life in some nonsense profession. It is okay if you never got your dream home, dream car, dream girl. It is okay if your sports team never won the big game. It is okay because now you know. Now you have clarity. Now you have reached the absolute karma in the universe. You know. You *know*.

You know that when you die you will not disappear into nothingness. You will not fade away upon the wind, a wisp amongst the willows that dissipates over the horizon. Your time is not over. The linear aspect of your life, from the beginning, gets a permanent extension. You do not have an end. God's greatest gift is retribution, delivery from oblivion.

The only problem is, the only certainty is that you do not end. There are some uncertainties that remain. What may happen to you is forever hellfire. Your flesh seared from your body forever. You could become the main attraction of a pig roast, your body slowly turning over the spit, over and over, apple shoved into your mouth. You are not dead; you are alive, for eternity. Burning for eternity. Of course, if you have led a good life, heaven awaits.

But what exactly is heaven? As humans, we've written countless books about the underworld. Dante's *Inferno* comes to mind. The seven layers of Hades. But what is heaven? Ask anyone you know and they will tell you a different answer. My mother used to say that heaven was wherever and whenever you were happiest. I guess for me, heaven would have to be the Jersey Shore, Jennifer in my arms, a hot summer night with the waves crashing at my feet. Not a cloud in the sky. Stars as far as the eye can see. If heaven is anything but that, well, I might as well become the pig.

I, having met an honest to goodness regent of the Lord, did gain some of the clarity in which I speak. No longer do the events of the day offer me stress, other than my continued declining faith in humanity. Despite my unique gift of knowledge, people bother me. I can't help it. But other than that, in one sense, I am blessed, blessed in the fact that I care not for the future. I only care that it ends. At the same time, however, this has become my curse. As no matter how many people I kill, God does not seem satisfied. I have still not met my quota. The dreams keep coming. And Cotton keeps running his mouth.

If you meet God's regent, and that regent belittles you, taking no qualms to remind you of the failures of your life, of how utterly stupid you are, one of two things can happen. If you are feeble minded you are likely to fall inward, recoil, and spend the rest of your days in a mental hospital, seemingly forever, becoming a medical mystery, as you just don't seem to age like everyone else. A man stuck in time. You become a government cover-up. If you are like me, however, you might get pissed off.

No, I am not college educated. Yes, I can barely do basic math. Fractions confound me. Forget about calculus. No, I was never going to amount to anything other than cannon fodder. In a sense, I got what I deserved. Now that I have not died, an ignoramus I am not going to remain.

Getting a library card is easier than you think. Stealing one is even easier than that. The Boston Public Library has become my den of refuge if you will—my home away from home. Certainly, it smells much better than my home. It is also vast enough that I can hole away in some corner without the wandering eye. Without the concerned eye. Without the weariness of those who do not have upside down crosses tattooed upon their face. It is here that I conduct my research. I stay until it closes. Some nights I hide amongst the stacks, always a step ahead of the security guards. After they make their rounds, I can hide in a few places. I've scoped this building for years. Like the bathroom. I have taken many a bath in the Boston Public Library's third floor men's room sink. Need to clean up somehow. Cotton is dead and even he complains about my stench.

I was never a religious man. Having met the Gateman, you might say I experienced an overnight conversion, although the overnight cost me twenty ageless years. Since then I have spent my free time reading. Not reading nonsense, mind you, but studying up on ancient cultures and religions. If I were truly ever going to understand where it is I am heading, I would have to know where we have been. As a race. As humans. As a culture. And one thing I can tell you, we are one fucked up group of animals.

If you read a history of the world, as I have, what you really end up doing is reading a history of murder and war. For the ancients really only took the time to write down their conquests in battle; this was pretty much all they gave a shit about documenting, other than their gods. Bloodlust has usurped throne after throne throughout time, since the dawn of civilization. Violence riddles our history. It goes without saying that we needed a savior. Without one, we were destined to murder, rape, marry our sisters, and commit genocide without an afterthought. You think things are bad now? Read up on ancient history.

Next time someone on the subway pushes you, don't get angry. Be thankful that you are not living in an ancient, walled-up city under siege. Next time your favorite television show is a rerun, don't get mad. Be thankful that bubonic plague has not swollen your lips. Next time your boss gives you some shit at work, be thankful that your commander did not put you in the front row of the phalanx. Next time you get angry that your team lost, be thankful that an ignorant mob did not sacrifice your children to an angry God.

This brings me, finally, to my point. I am not a religious man. Yes, I converted. However, I am still not a religious man. In my studies, I have come to find that the name of God has caused more bloodshed than anything else has. And not necessarily the Christian God either. Any good old god will do. Take Baal for instance.

Baal was a famous Phoenician god who was worshipped in the time of the early Israelites, namely from the time of Abraham. If you are not familiar with Abraham, old Abraham lived during a time when Yahweh, who became "God" to us, was in direct competition with Baal for the hearts and minds of the people. Yahweh was able to win for many reasons and kicked Baal's ass. The story of Elijah tells us that Elijah challenged the priests of the camp into a contest to see which god was stronger. Whichever god could light a bonfire soaked in water without the use of fire would win. Old Baal couldn't do a damn thing, Yahweh lit it like it was birthday cake candle, and that was that.

But Baal did not die out. He existed in the minds of the Phoenicians for centuries, and was later the chief god of the famous antiquity city, Carthage. Carthage sat on the northern African coast and was, in the early days, a rival of early Rome. The Carthaginians got themselves into a skirmish with the inhabitants of Syracuse, a Sicilian city, and went to war. When the Syracusans marched upon Carthage, the Carthage priests became so overwrought with fear that they placed their statue of Baal over an open fire pit. They then rolled their babies and toddlers down the statue's arms into the flames. They watched as the children burned alive, the children's skin popping and charring like baby back pork ribs. The idea was to appease Baal so he would deliver them from the approaching army. Apparently, it was not good enough as, not only did Baal not show up, but the enemy also sacked the city and killed all the priests. Sound sick? This is true shit. Archeologists found the kids' bodies. It's a good thing the Romans salted the earth when they were done sacking that shithole. The hell with those sick pricks.

The story of Abraham tells us that Yahweh was also thirsty for blood. He demanded the sacrifice of Abraham's son. But God called out to poor Abraham just in time, right before he brought the knife down. Told him to bail. I guess He just wanted to see if poor old Abraham was stupid enough to do it. Turns out he was. Instead, God was happy with a slaughtered goat. Back in those days, goat slaughtering, dove halving, and sheep killing was all the rage. God craved spilt blood, or so the stories say.

I tell you this because I have no respect for religious men who pretend to be righteous. Men who pretend to know the way, masquerading behind a mask that no one can see. False prophets, fake so-called truth tellers—there has always been a history of violence towards children when it comes to religion. This is why I have no problem killing a priest. As far as I am concerned, this next motherfucker is no different from Baal's disciples. Sure, this guy may pretend to be a follower of God, but he is not. Just like those that came before, he has preyed on the innocent. He has preyed on the little ones, the children.

God has named him. Jonathan McKay. The next person on the list.

I entered the church and took in the scents. The air smelled of burning candles and incense mixed with pine cleaner. The church was empty, almost cavernous, as the wooden pews sprawled out before me like horizontal dominoes. I heard nothing but the faint murmuring of an old woman who prayed in the front row. Two sticks, or what looked like pencils, held her hair tied up in a bun. She looked like a retired librarian, apparently feeling guilty for some sin or another. Maybe she forgot to feed her cat.

The church was exactly like my dream. A green slab of marble supported a cream-colored larger slab as an altar. Behind the altar, a crimson curtain dangled from the ceiling. A beautifully carved wooden crucifix, gently touched by the candlelight, hung at the center of the curtain. To my left, the confessionals. Beige wood-grained doors held open.

I took in a deep breath and smiled as the warm air filled my lungs. Surveying the walls, I noticed that the stained glass windows represented the apostles. Soft moonlight filtered through the stained glass; patterns of red, yellow, and green danced upon the pews as the clouds moved past outside. Doubting Thomas seemed to smile at me, as if he recognized me as well as I recognized him. I had been here of course. In the depths of slumber, my mind traveled to this place and acted as witness. Cotton acted as witness. And as the old preacher man said, we had another witch to burn at the stake.

Behind you Robert... Cotton whispered in my mind.

I heard the sound of rushing footsteps.

A man said, "Excuse me, sir, may I help you?"

As I turned, the man's face went from a smile to a scared, panicked frown. Short and overweight, his face resembled a shiny apple, the way his skin glistened in the candlelight. It was almost as if he was wearing makeup, the way his cheeks seemed to shine like a piece of fruit. He wore the ceremonial robes of an altar boy. He had a crew cut haircut, little blonde follicles, but, if one did not look closely, you could mistake him for being bald.

He did not know what to think of me, that much was for sure. I could see his mind frantically searching for something to say. His eyes conveyed his thoughts; they darted back and forth, making him look like a confused owl. "Sorry, sir, but may I help you?" He had a high-pitched voice, almost like a squeal. The longer I looked at him the more I pictured a pig roast. This was not Father McKay.

As I cleared my throat, I could taste the remnants of chili and onions, my hobo stew prior to my oh so fun ride down to Quincy. "I'm here for a confession. I have many sins to confess."

The man's eyes narrowed as if he was trying to focus on a pinhead from a mile away. He took his fat thumb to his lip and played with it, kneading it like Play-Doh. I grimaced as I noticed his multiple cold sores.

Finally, shaking his head, he said, "I'm sorry, sir, but you'll have to come back tomorrow during reconciliation hours. I'm afraid that we're not hearing confessions at this hour." He did not look me in the eye. He stared at my tattoo, obsessed, not blinking.

I reached out and grasped his fat, sausage-like hand in mine. Clasping both of my hands around his right hand, I squeezed hard. His eyes bugged out of his head. Lowering my voice to almost a whisper, I said, "I don't think you understand. I have sinned. And I don't have much time. I don't think I'll survive the night. I need to confess my sins before it is too late."

The man's face grew redder; his skin flushed, making him look even more like an apple head. A bead of sweat ran down his bald head onto his chubby cheeks. His lips, overly moist, stammered; he almost drooled as he spoke. "Sir, if you're in some kind of trouble, I can call the authorities if you'd like."

I furrowed my brow and squeezed harder. I could sense the thick lines of skin form in my forehead. I could nearly feel his bones break as I pressed down.

"No cops. Now get me a priest before it is too late. Get me Father McKay. He has heard my sins before. Get me Father McKay."

"Okay, okay..." the man nodded, wincing under the pressure I applied. I released his hands and he almost doubled over. He held his hands together, trying to rub away the pain.

I pointed to one of the confessional doors. "I'll be in that one over there. Now make sure you bring Father McKay. And no cops. Do we have an understanding? This is a house of God. A safe haven. A place for holy men and sinners alike. You wouldn't turn away a man in need, would you?"

He shook his head. "No...no...no sir..."

"Good, now go get Father McKay."

He nodded a last time and waddled down the center aisle, past the altar, back through one of the double doors that sat to the left of the crimson curtain.

The old woman stood up and made direct eye contact with me. Her green eyes were bloodshot. She clutched her bag and nervously waddled towards the entrance.

I opened the confessional door and sat down. It was a box. A four-walled world of wood. I noticed that someone had carved a message in the wall underneath the lattice confessional screen. It read, "If sodomy is a sin then I'm sure fucked." I marveled at the individual who must have sat here, carving that message. Was it in the middle of a fake confessional? Or did someone sneak in here, as a joke? Moreover, why didn't the church staff take the time to remove it? Didn't they ever come over here, at least to clean this side? Even peepshow booths have someone come spray some Lysol from time to time.

I took a deep breath and rested my head on the back wall. Reaching into my coat pocket, I yanked out my gun. I clicked off the safety and sat the gun on the bench next to me. I then reached into my other pocket and produced a potato. I took out my blade and started to peel. I threw the potato skins on the floor. The potato smelled fresh, starchy and raw, ready for deep-frying. The inside felt a bit soft. Perfect.

The door on the other side squeaked open, and then closed. I heard a man's labored breathing accompanied with a shuffling sound. The man across cleared his throat.

"Is something troubling you, my son? The deacon indicated that you were in dire need of a confessional. He said that it couldn't wait until tomorrow's hours."

I smiled. Here's my boy.

"Yes, Father. I have sinned. I have sinned a great many times. Except that God has decreed that they are not sins." I peeled another piece of skin from the potato and tossed it to the floor.

"I don't understand," the screen said back. His voice seemed to have raised an octave.

I grinned as I peeled down around the base of the potato. "You see, father, I have killed a great many people. I have killed men. I have killed women. I even killed a teenager once. But, you see, I had no choice, because God asked me to."

The screen was silent. I heard the sound of shuffling outside the confessional door. I imagined that the deacon was eavesdropping. I stood up and kicked the confessional door. A loud smack echoed through the church, followed by the sound of fast footsteps scampering away.

The screen said, "Please. Go, please leave us alone."

I peeled the last part of the potato and tossed the final piece of skin upon the pile below. I placed my knife in its sheath and put it back into my inner coat pocket. I tossed the potato from hand to hand; it felt cold on my palms.

"You would turn me away, father?"

"You said yourself that these were not sins... that God asked you to. If that is true, then you have already been given absolution, and you have no purpose here."

I laughed a hearty laugh. I could taste tar mixed with onions and beef upon my lips. Nasty habit, that smoking. "Oh, father, I never said I wasn't free from sin. I have sinned."

I waited for the screen to respond but heard nothing. I decided to continue. "You see, father, I've sinned because I've started to enjoy it a bit. Sometimes I can't help it. Culling you demons. You witches. You filth from the earth. Sending you all to the pit. Sometimes it brings me such great satisfaction that I cannot wait to kill again. You see father, I have a gun over here. I hear that door knob rattle, you try to run before hearing my confession, and I promise you, I will gun you down."

I heard what sounded like a dog whimpering, a sobbing sound emanate from the screen. Through sniffles, the voice said softly, "What do you mean 'you people'? What are you saying?"

I picked up my gun and pushed the potato down hard. It clung to the top of the muzzle, engulfing the barrel's tip. A poor man's silencer. "Let me tell you a little story, father. It is the story of a man named Lamech. You see Lamech lived in the ancient city of Ur, in the heart of Mesopotamia some time just after the great deluge. Lamech's buddies had just started writing down the events of the day on clay tablets, in one of the earliest known languages, cuneiform. But Lamech was not as fortunate as his friends were. He was no scribe, and he couldn't even read. All Lamech was good at was tilling the fields, which he did each and every season to provide grain to his city, to his friends, to his god. Lamech was a good man. He loved his wife, and he loved his six sons. Each of his sons had his color eyes and her color of hair. They were the crowning achievement in his life and he thanked his god each and every day for them. Do you know what happened next?

The voice said, stuttering, "N…n… no…?"

I heard the doorknob rattle. I tightly clutched my gun. "Don't you touch that handle, I warned you!"

Sobs emanated through the lattice. "I'm sorry, please. I'm so sorry."

"Let me finish or you're a dead man. I swear to God as my witness, I will shoot you."

"I'm so sorry. Please. Please forgive me. Continue."

"Thought you'd never ask." I loosed my grip; the gun's handle felt heavy in my hand. "Well, that next season, there was a drought. The heavens did not open. Lamech's crops did not grow. He did not have grain to provide to the temple treasury. No matter how hard he worked, no matter how hard he cried, no matter how hard he prayed to his god, he did not have the grain. Do you know what happened next?"

The screen said nothing. All I heard was the whimpering sound of a coward. I tightened the potato, twisting it around the muzzle as hard as I could. I felt blood pump through my veins as anger filled my heart. "The priests came, that's what fucking happened next, father! They took his six sons and sacrificed them, in front of Lamech, his wife, the entire community. He watched as the priests shoved the sword through the beloved flesh of his young, while his wife stood by his side, screaming, begging her god to swoop down and save them. He watched as the priests murdered his family. DO YOU KNOW WHY I'M TELLING YOU THIS STORY FATHER?"

"No, no, why!"

"BECAUSE I KNOW WHAT YOU DID, YOU FUCKING PIG. I KNOW YOUR SINS! LIKE LAMECH, THOSE PARENTS TRUSTED YOU WITH THEIR CHILDREN!"

"What? I don't understand? How? Who? What did you hear? Who told you?"

I stood up and shouted at the screen, holding the potato gun up to the lattice, "SAY YOUR NAME!"

"What?"

"SAY YOUR FUCKING NAME! SAY IT!"

The voice stuttered, stammering behind sobs, "J...J...John. John McKay."

I shook my head as my head fumed with anger. "Goodbye, John." I pulled the trigger and the potato exploded all over the screen. I heard a wet, splatter-like sound as his head exploded all over the inside of the confessional across from me.

I opened the confessional door and peeked my head out. The church was empty. The old woman and deacon were gone. I gently shut my door and pulled my overcoat on tight over my shoulders. I noticed a crimson pool starting to leak from the other confessional door. I did not open the door.

I took a deep breath, exited the church, and caught the Redline back to Boston. Destination: Bukowski's. I needed another drink. Killing can weigh a lot to a man.

Especially when you start to enjoy it. I'm not supposed to enjoy it. Even if it leads to a good performance review and a ticket off this rock, I am still not supposed to enjoy it.

But dammit, I enjoyed that.

Chapter Thirteen

It is January, 1968. Two weeks have passed since I awoke in my room, covered in sweat, terrified out of my skull, the first time a demon had owned my night, owned my dreams. The carnage I witnessed up at Ohio State was now six weeks gone in reality, two weeks from my dream. I have reached the conclusion that my dream was nothing more than the manifestation of my own fragile, cracking mind. You have to understand, when your timeline flows from high school, to the army, to death upon the Normandy shore, to twenty years later in the blink of an eye, you tend to question whether you are sane.

Sanity, in and of itself, is a concept that can be debated. After all, when you meet a regent of the Lord, who drafts you into his holy war on the underworld, things do tend to change. But I deny this at all costs. It is the only way. The only way to function. Any time the image of Omaha beach comes to mind, I block it out. At least I try. Every time I close my eyes, I see Charlie Wilson's eyes roll back in his head. I watch the blood pour from his mouth like a tipped paint can every time I blink. I hear the artillery shells and the sound of flesh burning anytime I am not distracted. I always need the television on, or the radio. Background noise, static, something to dull my senses. Going for a walk to clear my mind is not an option. Clearing my mind is not a realistic possibility. There is no serenity for me. I can never be at peace, never rest, as I hear the cannons on the night air and smell the sulfur of spent gunpowder invade my nostrils. I am haunted. Day and night, the ghosts of Normandy haunt me. The image of the Gateman, laughing, taunting me from his post behind the bar, always there. The strange taste of the beer, always at the tip of my tongue. But I'm not fucking listening! FUCK ALL THAT! It's not real.

I have a job at Pinstar Lanes, a bowling alley in Lancaster, Ohio, a town in the middle of nowhere just south of Columbus. I am a pin monkey, but unfortunately, that is a fun exaggeration. I am basically the janitor. I clean the toilets, scrub the bathroom floors, polish the bowling balls, peel the gum off the underside of the tables, and mop up puke and urine. That is essentially my job, to clean up after the oversized apes that stuff themselves into bowling shirts two sizes too small. Big fat fucks with mustaches, bald heads, and guts that are so large it looks like they managed to swallow entire deer carcasses in a single gulp.

To say I am career-oriented would be an understatement. To say I have advancement potential would be a horrendous, misleading lie. To say that I have given up on a normal life altogether, well, that is pretty much accurate. It is here at the alley that I met Katherine, three years before. She was waitressing in the alley bar that sat just off to the right of the main desk. It has been so long now, I can't remember the name of the bar, something like Al's Alley or some shit like that. After we met and started dating, she managed to quit and get a job working as a paralegal up in Columbus. She has aspirations; if not in her man, well, at least in herself. Luckily, for me, her expectations are low. Many jilted lovers will do that to a woman. And I mean many. Men by the boatload paraded into her life and into her... well, you know. She is no saint.

But certainly neither am I. Not with my thoughts. Not by a longshot.

I am standing behind the main desk, squirting sanitizer spray into the stinky carcasses of alley shoes when I see the ugliest, most awful son of a bitch ever. I see the Ohio State Beast poke his ugly mug out from behind the office door. The office, which sits behind a door to the left end of lane one, is one place I have seldom been, other than the one time to fix the wheel on the owner's swivel desk chair. About all I remember is the room smells like cheap cigars and even cheaper gin. The walls, I recall, were probably once white, but stained yellow from decades of smoke.

My heart falls into my stomach the minute I make eye contact with him. He stands about six-foot-six. He is wearing a black, leather jacket, ripped along the front, no doubt from a knife fight. The inner stuffing of the jacket belches forth from the tear, reducing the coat to more of a skin than a buffer to the elements. Beneath his left eye, I see the scar that haunts me in my dreams. His hair, a sandy brown, falls across his forehead, getting in the way of his vision. He moves the strands out of his eyes with his enormous, swollen right hand, repeatedly as he walks, his gigantic shoulders parallel to the ground while his torso bobs up and down. He makes a clumping noise with his feet as he walks, like the sound a circus elephant makes when walking on concrete.

It is him. I am sure of it. Last time I saw him I was rocking back and forth in my seat like a lunatic, arms across my chest, while I sat legs crossed, a voyeur to his carnage. I saw him rape and murder that poor cheerleader, ripping her stomach open like she was the Thanksgiving Day turkey. It is him.

My mouth suddenly goes dry, like I swallowed chalk. My fingers begin to tingle with energy. I take a few deep breaths. I feel faint; blood rushes to my head, and I see a sparkle of red stars.

"Hey, Bobby, what the hell is wrong with you? You all right? You look like you've seen a ghost."

I turn to see the front deskman, Trevor, standing behind me, smoking a cigarette, left hand upon his hip. He has coffee-colored, long, hippie hair. He is wearing an old, tattered, sky blue bowling shirt with the word "AutoMart" across the chest embroidered in red thread. A wall of rotting alley shoes hangs behind his head.

He holds the cigarette in his lips while he speaks. His thin mustache looks like a dead caterpillar the way it barely moves while he mumbles. "You sick or something?" he says through several missing teeth. Trevor is much like me. Few aspirations. Bowling alley or carny, those are pretty much his only two options in life.

I rest my hands on the flesh-colored counter and bend over, staring down the Beast's back as he makes his way towards the exit. The sound of bowling balls crashing into pins echoes throughout the alley.

I turn to Trevor and ask, "Hey, man. You seen that guy before? He was in the office with Chuck."

Trevor takes a drag and spews the smoke into the air. "Yeah, I've seen him before. Some contractor Chuck hired. Chuck's planning to do some remodeling work on the bar I guess. Why you ask?"

I shake my head as I watch the Beast stop at the last lane, before the exit. He stands there, hands in his pockets, swaying in his stance, shoulders parallel to the ground. He watches a group of overweight housewives with bad hair bowling. "I think I know him. Can't place him, but I think I know him."

"Ah, you've probably seen him up at Ray's Place. He's always at the end of the bar up there, pounding shots. Badass motherfucker. Gets in fights a lot. I'd steer clear of him if I were you. Real mean son of a bitch I've heard. Even for a guy your size. Stay the fuck away from him."

I grasp a towel sitting next to the register and wipe the sanitizer from my hand. "Yeah, you're probably right. Must have seen him at Ray's." The Beast turns and leaves the alley through the double glass doors, out into the cold, dark night.

"You look a lot better man."

"Huh?"

Trevor points his cigarette at me. "The color has returned to your face. You looked like you were going to pass out or something there for a minute. You all right man? Low blood sugar or something?"

I nod in agreement. I notice the clock above the shoe wall. "Yeah, I'm good. Thank God, my shift is over. I'm outta here. I need to go lie down. I am exhausted. Need to take my medicine."

Trevor takes a drag and laughs a smoker's gravely laugh. "They still making you take that shit? No, you are not going to lie down. Nah, you're going to go home and plow Kate, right? I know I would, man." He smiles at me. A yellow toothless smile.

I smile back—so far, all my pearly whites intact. "I should kick your ass, you know that?"

"Yeah, whatever, man." He mashes down the butt into a wine-colored glass ashtray on the adjoining counter. "Take off, man. I'll see you tomorrow night."

I nod goodbye, seize my coat down off the rack next to the shoe wall, and head out into the night.

The bowling alley is only four blocks from my apartment. Katherine has our only car, a broken-down Dodge Dart that guzzles gas and is probably poisoning us from carbon monoxide. Walking is my only option, regardless of the elements.

I loathe these walks. It is on these walks that the memories and sounds come crashing back into my mind like a runaway freight train. It is here I am most vulnerable. I keep telling myself it is just my insane mind trying to make a coup on the last few remaining, normal synapses I have left. I have been denying reality, living in this Midwestern poverty fantasy world. The night air is cold, one of those colds that gets you immediately down at your core, down in your bones, where you feel not an ounce of your own warmth. It is one of those colds that pulls your skin so tight that a mere scratch can open you up like a rotten tomato, spilling your hot entrails all over the pavement, only to watch them crystalize into some deranged ice sculpture.

The street is dark, other than the town center lights that offer little in the black. Busted bulbs hang dark in the night; others buzz and snap, not connecting well. Snow falls softly, spinning in the wind. No sign of the

Beast. I pass by a butcher shop, a bookstore, and the town's general store. No sign of the Beast.

It is then that I hear it for the first time.

You must fulfill your destiny, a voice says in my head. *You cannot run from your calling.*

I spin on my heels and stare down the street towards the alley.

The street is empty. The sidewalks are all shoveled; the snow, piled up high on both sides, creates a corridor-like feel. The wind howls, whizzing over the snow, collecting miniscule ice particles, tossing them into the air. I stand, shivering, as the snow attacks my face, melting instantly. My eyes dart around, searching, probing the dark, looking for the voice.

God has named that man. You must find him. You must cull him from the earth. Eradicate the demon. Slay him and return him to the pit.

I scream down the empty street. "WHERE ARE YOU?" My voice echoes off the buildings. "SHOW YOURSELF!" Wind howls through the streets. A wooden sign, hanging in front of the butcher shop, creaks back and forth.

I am here, Robert. I am here with you. I am in you. It's time you stop playing games.

Suddenly there is a dull roar like sound. The street trembles with a crackling, electric buzzing; I watch in amazement as two streetlights pop and shatter. The glass sprays towards my eyes.

I jump in my stance; I feel a sharp pain scream up my spine. My God, what is happening? Please tell me what is happening. I am so confused. I decide to run as fast as I can towards my apartment. The wind bites at my face, freezing the melting snow that cascades down my skin. After less than fifty feet, I slip on the ice. I fall, arms flailing, into the snowbank at the side of the road. I feel the ice seep through my pant threads, coating my legs in a stinging, frigid slush. I shiver as I stand. I brush the snow from my legs, hear a powerful engine roar, and see yellow lights flash from the corner of my eye.

I turn and see a plow rumbling towards me. The city workers are still out cleaning the streets, while the locals, most let out of work early, are out drinking or bowling.

I scream to the stars, "What is happening to me! Please stop!"

You cannot run, Bobby! You cannot hide. You must fulfill your duty. We have chosen you... YOU ARE AN ANGEL OF DEATH.

The plow practically runs me over as it slams into a car buried beneath the drift. I hear the car horn squeal and the wheels pop from the blast, followed by the sound of metal crunching. The plow driver either doesn't hear or doesn't care. He pushes down hard on the gas as the monster truck gnashes its way through the street, snarling through the snow banks. Through the truck's frozen window, all I can make out is the orange glow from the driver's lit cigar.

I bend down upon my knees and clasp my head in my hands. I can feel the slush seep through the threads in my jeans. My skin burns from the cold. My teeth chatter as I shiver in place.

Robert, it is time.

I say, "No, no, this is not happening. This is not happening." I rock in place, squeezing my head so hard, I am lucky I don't crack my skull. "This is not happening."

You cannot deny your calling. You must obey the Gateman.

It is then that the foul taste of the Gateman's beer, mead, or whatever the hell that awful drink was engulfs my taste buds and cascades down my throat as if I am shot-gunning a tall one. I feel my insides churn, a sharp, grating, ripping feeling that collapses me in two. It is as if something is tearing me apart from the inside out. Tiny claws, teeth or knives, gashing and slashing.

I throw up upon the ice. The hot steam from my processed pizza and beer shoots towards the heavens. Winter stars shine down, peeking out behind dark gray clouds, sparkling in all their glory as the wind howls, sending the snow twirling and swirling. I feel a heavy pressure form in my inner ears. I can hear nothing now, no sound of the wind, no cars or plows, only the thundering of my own heart. My head stings like a migraine.

You belong to us now, Bobby. We have a job to do, you and me. It is time we begin.

Chapter Fourteen

I woke up with a chill. It is cold down here in the ground. My head hurt as usual. Memories of freckles; the taste of strawberry lipstick.

Cotton wheezed. "You dreamt about her again last night. I've told you, that is a waste of our time. You let her cloud your vision."

I held my head in my hands; the tomb was dark. Cotton's casket buzzed like a hive. "Stay out of my head."

The box shook as he spoke. "You need to get past those memories. You need to let her go."

I shook my head. "I can't."

"But you must. Each night she enters your mind we lose another opportunity. You're letting your past dictate your future. This ghost that haunts you, she doesn't even love you as you love her. You're wasting your life. You must forget."

"I don't want to forget. I am proud that it still hurts. I'm proud that she still haunts me. I'm proud that she is still there. It happened. It means what I felt was real, was pure. I may have lost her, but those moments were real. My love for her was real. And no one, not even you—you old bat—can take that away from me."

I stood up and lit the lantern above my bed. Shadows of spiders danced along the tomb's walls.

Cotton said, "God is the answer. In God, you will find your path. All that matters is the mission. You must fulfill it."

I rummaged through my footlocker, looking for tea bags. I was out of coffee. "It was God who took her from me."

The box buzzed. "Perhaps with good reason. Have you ever considered that? Perhaps you were never meant to be with her."

Shit. No tea. I'll have to get some more. "I tell you what, one day, when I get the chance, you better believe I'll ask that asshole why."

"Fulfill your quota. Complete your mission. Then you can."

I pulled a dirty sweatshirt on and started up the ladder. Cotton said, "Where are you going?"

I spat down towards his casket. "Out. Need some tea. Coffee, anything. You need something? Want me to get you anything?"

"You jest."

"Yeah, that's right, you're fucking dead and I'm not. I'm going out and don't fucking follow. She's my memory and you cannot take her from me."

"Robert..."

The ladder rungs felt cold on my skin. "Bye, asshole. Don't follow."

Chapter Fifteen

Slight sidebar, if you will indulge my rant but for a moment. This is my rant towards hypocrites, for over the decades, I have seen more than my share. When you don't age like I do, human beings become somewhat of an anthropological study: creatures at the zoo, endless, slobbering zombies mulling about the city streets and shopping malls. It is hard not to study them. Or be offended by them. I suppose I could marvel at them. But for some reason I tend to be negative. Can't imagine why.

Hypocrisy seems to be rampant in the world. This should come as no shock to you, as I am sure that you have seen it. We are all hypocrites to some degree, mere monkeys pretending to play dress up and act as if we are civilized creatures. In the end, we are no more civilized than the ancients who enjoyed slaughtering bulls to their angry gods. Only difference is we have killed God, destroyed God, rendered Him as a concept to be a trivial pursuit of the uneducated, underdeveloped, easily mislead psychotic mind. For what use is God if we can explain the world? We have stripped Him of his throne.

Our own advancement has warped our minds so much that we have fallen into a malaise of insanity. The examples for our psychotic behavior are many, even in today's educated world. There are grand examples, such as our dictator friend in North Korea, or our crazy, daffy duck like terrorist and former enemy Osama Bin Laden. Then there is evidence on a much smaller scale, minute examples that one could over look if one was not paying attention. For instance, take a visit to the Public Garden in Boston.

The Public Garden sits nestled next to the Boston Common, on the edge of the Back Bay neighborhood. The Back Bay itself is not a bay at all; in fact, it is giant landfill that is slowly sinking into the earth. It is here that some of Boston's most notable landmarks, namely the glimmering razorblade, aka the John Hancock Tower, and Newbury Street, the famous street of collagen, trophy wives, fake lips, hips, and overpriced boutiques, reside.

In the Public Garden, you will find imported trees from all over the world, shading a smooth, asphalt path that winds along the side of two man-made shimmering ponds filled with duck shit. Swan boats, essentially large paddleboats, take silly tourists on two mile an hour rides through the duck shit.

As you walk through the garden, you will find several signs aimed to keep you following the rules.

Stay off the grass.

Do not feed the swans.

Pick up after your dog, $200 fine.

The latter particularly boils my blood. Pick up after your dog. Do not let your dog shit all over the walk. We would not want a tourist to step in it. The hysterical factor is this: the enforcement of the pick up after your dog law is a police officer on horseback. A horse that continuously misses its shit bag. A horse that craps all over the walk. So, while they have gone to every precaution to keep the walkway free from dog turds, still watch where you step, as you might wind up knee deep in a pile of horse crap.

Chapter Sixteen

I woke up to find Cotton in a particularly foul mood. I kicked the sleeping bag off me, pulled a few worms from my face, and tossed them into the corner. Despite how warm it was outside, the hot July morning sun beating down, it was cold down here in the earth. My tomb was dark and damp; it smelled of mildew and rot. I shivered as I awoke; all I could think of was a cigarette. Cotton was spouting at the mouth as I sat up.

"This world is decaying faster than I ever imagined. These poor, suffering souls. The glare of the world has become too powerful. This is our problem now. For long, I felt we were lost amidst a sea of sin. Forever drifting further and further away from the core that is God. However, it is not so much that we have changed, at least not so much as the distractions have. I could not pretend for a moment that I could comprehend the technologies of the age. But our minds are too engrained here, in the moment, with little learned from the past, ignorant of the path ahead of us."

I said, "Oh, shut the hell up, old man," and fired up a cigarette. The heat of the ash felt good on the back of my throat. I blew the smoke into my meager earth-walled crypt, immediately regretting my decision. The smoke hung in the middle of the room like a ghost, suspended, not moving. Since I knew there was no shot I could die from smoke inhalation I bore it no mind as I sat trapped down there in the dark, the only light from the candle I lit beside my bed. The smoke grew dense and sent me into a coughing fit.

Cotton's coffin spoke to me, "Sit up, and put out that foul thing. Or at least use your pipe."

"It is morning; someone might see the smoke out the top."

"Then put it out and listen. I have much to talk to you about."

Next to my cot, down upon the floor sat an old rusted Maxwell coffee can. Muddy water filled the can about half way up. A sea of cigarette butts mulled amongst the sludge. I tossed the cigarette into the brine, whereby it joined its many brothers and sisters, recently deceased from many nights before. Slaughtered peasants from my nightly indulgence in bad habits.

I ignored the old bones and turned on my radio. Many years back I jimmied a wire up to the surface— it protrudes at the base of the tomb, no soul the wiser. As long as I don't play the radio to loud, I'm safe to tune in. The morning sports talk hosts crackled on, debating last night's pitching decisions; another blown save. Bullpen, yet again shit this year.

"I don't understand why you listen to that drivel. You should mind your books. Engaging in these affairs is a waste of your time. More importantly, it is a waste of my time. I don't understand your zest for such trivial matters."

I sat down on the edge of my cot and rubbed my knees. Pain shot through them as if I had been out playing basketball all night. Shadows flickered from the candlelight. Earth stains covered my gray sweatpants. It has always been hard to keep my clothes clean, living here, down in the pit as I do. "Look, Cotton, I enjoy it. I don't want to get cut off."

"Cut off from what? You should be more concerned about your soul than some meaningless baseball game. In addition, that music you listen to, if you can call it music, rots your mind."

"I need to stay connected."

"To what, these sinners? Stay connected to these poor, damned fools? For whatever reason why?"

I shook my head; a heavy smoker's cough belched forth. I held my fist to my lips and winced. My chest burned. "I don't want to end up like one of those lost Appalachian mountain jackoffs, cut off from society, deluded and delusional. I hear some of them don't even know who the president is. Some think Eisenhower is still in office."

"It's a waste of our time."

I stood up and spit in the corner. Too much tar, ash, and nicotine. "Well, lucky for you, time is one thing we seem to have plenty of."

I fired up one of my cooking cylinders and plopped my pot down on top of it. Emptying some bottled water, I tossed in a tea bag. More than ever, my eyes felt heavy this morning. Something did not feel quite right.

Cotton said, "We need to discuss last night's dream."

I stared down at the brown bag; it floated amongst a sea of rust-filled water. My pot was getting old—time to fish for a new one. "Nothing to discuss. No dream."

"Oh, but yes, there was. You see what I mean? Too many distractions, you are beginning to forget."

The water started to bubble under the heat. "I didn't have a vision; I think I'd know if I did."

"I beg to differ... you had a very vivid vision. Instead of possessing the recall you should have, your mind is clouded. You are losing touch. You act sometimes as if I am not here. As if I do not know where you go. I know where you were last night. I always know."

I raised my arms up as if to protest Christ on the cross. "So I went down to Lansdowne, big deal. I wanted to be near the park. I didn't actually go in though. Not like I can get in, at least not during a game anyway."

Cotton's coffin rattled; I could hear the wood squeak and moan. "You were out too late. You drank two bottles of bourbon. You stayed up till four in the morning listening to that drivel, that puke rock you listen to."

"It's called punk rock. And look, I just wanted to try to catch a ball; if Big Papi could've just blasted one, I could've snagged it as it bounced off the parking deck. I wasn't the only one there. There were at least three other guys hoping for the same thing."

"We are on an eternal quest to slay the demons of this world and you're out trying to catch baseballs?"

The pot filled with mud-colored tea. I took my collapsible, army issued tin cup and poured myself my morning caffeine. "It's important. It is important to me. You would not understand, you old Puritan bastard. You lived when the world sucked. You never saw a home run. You never witnessed a touchdown or slam-dunk. You've never seen the greats of the games. You are just some old, washed-up bag of bones from a dead era. Fuck you. If I'm stuck on this rock with you then I'm at least going to try and enjoy myself from time to time."

His box stopped rattling. It seemed to gasp as the wood settled. "Do not let the glare of this world blind your eyes. You will lose your vision."

I took a sip of my tea and winced—awful. "Don't give me that glare bullshit. You can bitch all you want but I catch you listening. I heard you sing along to one of my songs one time. Don't tell me it hasn't had an influence on you too. You may be dead, but you're still listening."

"I do not. I care not for such things."

I took another sip and then tossed some tea towards his casket. The scalding hot liquid splattered across the wood. "Spare me, old man. When I first met you, you were all 'hither me this' and 'thoust me that' like some Shakespearean douchebag. You hardly talk like that anymore. Don't give me that shit. You're changing, along with the world. Even you cannot help it."

"Stop wasting my time, Bobby. It is not worth discussion. What is worth discussing is your dream."

I sat down at my table; my only chair creaked under my weight. I clicked on the lantern overhead; it swayed back and forth. Cotton's coffin came more clearly into focus. Shadows danced like a child's kaleidoscope across the walls. "I told you, I did not have a dream."

"Oh, but you did. I'm surprised you don't remember, given who it was."

"Who what was?"

"The next member to make our list. You remember him. The robust, apple-faced imposter. Our sweaty little deacon friend."

Memory flashed before my eyes, I recalled the deacon's fat, confused, yet terrified face. "The one from the church, Father McKay's boy. That guy?"

"Yes, him."

"What makes him a demon? I was already there, wouldn't I have known then?"

A warm mist started to fill my tomb; it appeared as if it seeped from underneath Cotton's casket. I could feel my hairs stand to attention as the air became electric. The copper pipe, my smoking pipe that lead up to the surface, buzzed and crackled. I watched in amazement as miniscule blue sparks flowed across its surface in a wave like pattern. My overhead lantern flickered, and then died. The candle beside my bed blew out. The only light the ghostly embers of blue flame that trickled across the pipe like water.

Cotton said, his voice a whisper, "Sometimes they are where we least expect, hiding in plain sight. The greatest trick the devil ever played was convincing the world that he did not exist. This is where we now reside, in his world, yet no one is the wiser. The world has forgotten him. Forgotten his minions. They are multiplying, in plain sight. The deacon has emerged. You must eradicate him."

I stood up and took a deep breath. I shook my head in disagreement. I felt my way through the dark and sat down hard on my cot. I saw the faint shadow of a spider crawl down the wall to my left. With a slam of my fist, I quickly ended the poor beast's life. "Why didn't I dream of him?" I wiped the spider carcass upon my sweatpants; to my surprise, he expelled a large quantity of blood.

"You did. You just do not remember. I have remembered for you."

I rubbed my forehead; my skin felt dry, dehydrated. Another migraine attacked behind my eyes. The pain seemed to claw behind my sockets. "Shit."

"What is the matter?"

"I have to go back to Quincy."

"So?"

"I hate riding the Redline. Cesspool."

The blue wave of electricity sparkled and then faded into oblivion. The charge in the air snapped and the mist disappeared. The hairs upon my arm gently rested.

The tomb grew quiet. I sat motionless in the dark. The walls hummed like a wasp's nest.

Cotton said, "You must strike, tonight, before the demon takes an innocent soul. This is an early manifestation; there is still time to save an innocent!"

Shit. Well, I guess that was it. Redline.

Chapter Seventeen

The Beast has a name. His name is Wilhelm Archer. It sounds almost distinguished, seemingly misplaced given the look of his mug. The permanent tattooed tear under his left eye. His red, wind-burned, dehydrated face. Ripped leather jacket. Fists the size of cinder blocks. That, plus it is 1968 and pretty much everyone I know is a Mike, or a Frank, or a Fred. Wilhelm? No wonder he is a tough son of a bitch. Probably got picked on as a kid.

I have been tailing him for weeks. The voice in my head will not stop. Every night I awake in a cold sweat. I clutch the sheets, my hands shaking, my heart thundering. I relive the vision, repeatedly, the Beast standing above that poor girl. Gutting her every night. Forever. Trapped in a time loop, I'm forced to relive the memory every single damn night.

It is getting out of control. One night I scratched Kate so bad she woke up screaming, blood soaking the sheets. It looked like a deranged animal had clawed her back, a wolverine in search of food or perhaps some vicious animalistic sex. I have to put an end to this. Every night is the same; it has gotten to the point where I have started to sleep on the couch. I don't trust myself.

Each night, the voice says, *Follow... Find him.*

Every night I awake, covered in my own sweat and piss. For some reason—as my subconscious mind dives into the deep—I will, at the same time, tend to lose total bladder control.

The Beast has not come into the bowling alley again since that night. He did his odd job, fixed the chair, got his pay, and went about his merry way. I have asked around, however, and I found he works in shipping and receiving at a department store, the night shift.

Kate continuously begs me to enter therapy. The bump on her stomach has grown; a reminder of what is coming, but these thoughts I have will not stop. As much as I try to make them go away, they return. I hear the voice. It reminds me, every night, of my past, of the dog tags hidden away in my dresser drawer. My tags are my telltale heart; I try to hide them, I try to pretend they do not exist. I have taken every attempt to bury them beneath the floorboards of my new life. However, they still beat, still haunt me. I cannot run from them or my memories. The constant reminder, the image of the Gateman, assaults me each night as the sun sets upon the horizon.

The voice says, *You know what you must do. You must avenge that girl. Send the demon back to the pit.*

About two weeks ago, Kate started to go to bed early. She never makes it past eight o'clock before she passes out on the couch. The creature in her stomach saps all the energy and life from her. She can barely keep her eyes open. They scaled my job back to only a few days a week. I am home more than I should be. The thought of looking for work does not interest me. I have trouble simply getting through the day.

When you start to hear voices in your head, you start to question whether you can actually function as a human being. When the voices talk to you constantly, throughout the night, early in the morning, sometimes unexpectedly, like when you are on the toilet, it starts to hamper your ability to cope. It distorts your ability to get up each morning, to shower, shave, and put on some decent clothes and go find work. And what skills do I have anyway? I am useless; I offer nothing to Kate, or to society. The only reason she is with me, at this point anyway, is the ticking time bomb in her womb. Wild, crazy sex and booze brought us together. It also brought us more than we ever bargained for.

These thoughts enter my head as I sit, shirtless, chest exposed, in my beat up, ripped leather recliner. The air conditioner wails, barely keeping up with the steam of the night. The sun sets late in Columbus; it is nine as the sun finally clears the horizon. Kate lays horizontal upon the couch, balled up in the fetal position. Despite the damning heat, she is curled up in a wool blanket. She always has to have something on her; she cannot sleep without the feeling of pressure, the fabric upon her skin. Me, after all I have been through, I can sleep in the backyard with all the grubs and bugs without a care in the world.

I watch as her chest rises softly, and then returns. She is fast asleep. The television spews nonsense. I am not even paying attention. I rarely do. I sit here and drink, trying hard to drown out the voice that will just not shut up. Over and over, it is a relentless onslaught.

Follow… find…

152

I can hear it again as I sit here. I take a swig of my malt liquor and watch Kate sigh. The air conditioner makes a metallic, almost slicing sound as it starts to sputter and kick. It is only a matter of time before it will go, and we don't have the money to replace it. Kate has been working her ass off for those bloodsucking lawyers. And here all I do is drink myself to sleep each and every night. Some catch I am.

The bottle feels cool in my hand; the glass sweats with condensation. Cool rivers flow across my skin. The humidity is brutal.

Our living room isn't much at all; nasty coffee and booze stained flower print wallpaper surrounds me. Off to the side, a small kitchenette. The room smells of spilt beer and stale cigarettes. I know I shouldn't smoke in front of Kate and, believe me, she lets me have it; I just wait until she goes to sleep.

Our apartment is only a two bedroom. The second bedroom has, over time, transformed into a nursery instead of the dumbbell weight room I previously set up. Kate painted the walls a soft yellow, ready to anticipate either sex. I don't know what the stork might bring, and I am not sure if I care. The entire concept seems so foreign to me. Like it isn't real at all. How could a man like me be a father? How could I raise a child when I can't even take care of myself? I am a deadbeat. A deranged, broken lunatic with memories of a war fought decades before. A war that I try so hard to bury beneath the floorboards within my heart and mind. A war I'm not sure I was ever at. Yet the dog tags. The Goddamn dog tags.

A crib sits half assembled; I will get to it soon enough.

I hear a rattling sound come from our bedroom. Kate grimaces, then turns away, face towards the back of the pink, flower-print couch; her wool covers bunch as she turns, exposing her back and her yellow T-shirt. I stand up, fix her dragonfly printed blanket, and then head down the hallway towards the noise.

I stand, wearing only my boxers, at the bedroom door and take a swig. The beer tastes cool upon my throat, calming the constant burn caused by too many cigarettes. The room is a mess. Stained laundry covers the scuffed hardwood floor. The bed is a disaster; the covers form a heap by the scratched wooden headboard.

I hear the rattle sound again. There in the corner, I see my tall wicker dresser, six drawers top to bottom, shaking back and forth as if a giant rat is trying to escape.

I feel dense pressure on my inner ears. The voice booms, "Follow. Find him!" I wince and take another swig of beer. The top dresser drawer shakes as if something is trying to get out.

My heart sinks as I realize what it is. My telltale heart. Driving me to madness.

I place the bottle down upon the floor and tip toe into the room as if someone is watching me. It feels like someone is watching me, even though it is, at the same time, impossible. Yet… there is something. A presence; I am not alone.

The rattling turns violent; the drawer slams upwards but not out. The dresser leaps a few inches from the floor, then crashes back down. The crash echoes off the walls. I hear Kate moan from the other room.

I touch the handle and it burns my skin; I recoil in pain, clasping my right hand with my left. I kneel down, pick up a used pair of my own briefs and grasp the handle, pulling the drawer open. The shaking and rattling stops. Inside, nothing; I see nothing but mismatched brown and off-white socks. I dig through the socks and there I see them. My dog tags. Burning a deep red.

The voice thunders in my head, *Follow... and find him! You cannot deny your destiny any longer!* I clasp the tags tightly and feel the inscription burn into my skin. The pain brings me to my knees amidst a sea of dirty underwear. I hold the tags tightly in my fist as my skin bubbles and pops. Damn it hurts.

"If I do as you say, will you leave me alone?!" I stare towards the ceiling and slam my fist to the floor. Tears streak from my eyes. I feel them career down my cheeks.

Follow... Find him. We are tired of your attempt to ignore us. You cannot ignore Him.

The dresser topples over and falls towards me; the drawers do not fall open, over-stuffed as they are. I punch the dresser and watch in amazement as it blows apart like balsa wood. The broken pieces career towards the four corners of the room. I drop the tags to the hardwood and marvel at my hand.

The voice says, *You have been called. Time to do your duty...*

I stand up and stretch a wife beater undershirt on over my exposed chest; my arms feel powerful, as if I have just lifted a triple set. There on the back of the door, a mirror. I have not worked out in weeks but my muscles pulse as if I had just banged out twenty pull-ups. My veins throb upon my biceps. I look enormous. I flex and smile. I had always wanted guns like these. I feel the sudden urge to let go. To give in. Maybe it's the booze. But look at these guns.

The time is now, Bobby.

I rummage through a sea of smelly, sweat-soaked socks and dirty undershirts. Beneath a pile of stained clothes, I find my black steel-tipped combat boots. I tug them on, pull up some ripped jeans and tip toe down the hallway the best I can, trying my best not to wake Kate. I feel wide awake. I'm not tired at all. I'm not tired for the first time in a long time. As long as I can remember.

I stand there for a moment watching her sleep. I take a sip of warm beer from a half-empty bottle that rests upon the television set. It tastes awful. Flat. Her chest moves so slowly; she is lost in a dream, lost in a world I can only imagine. I take her car keys from the hook by the door and tip toe out into the twilight wearing only by my wife beater t-shirt, ripped jeans, and dry, mud-stained black boots.

The night is hot; sticky hot, the kind of heat that makes you loathe your own humanness, your own scent, smells, and excretions. Nights like these, it is disgusting to be a human.

The Beast works only about ten miles away. I had previously convinced Kate a year back to trade in her boring old Dodge Dart for a hard top 1965 Ford Thunderbird. I love this car; black paint and gorgeous rims. This is one of those nights where the top has to be off.

The wind rushes past as I drive, hot and burning as if I am inside a stove. There is something sinister about the early night; there upon the horizon the moon looms a blood red. The dense smog gives it a ghostly quality as it stalks behind a smoky veil.

Despite the fact it feels as if I am driving through an exhaust pipe, I can't help but light up a cigarette. I pull up to a red light, reach for old reliable, and fire one up. The suburban streets are teeming with children out catching fireflies, last chance to stay up late and enjoy the summer while it lasts. In another month the first hint of the destroyer will come, the leaves will start to turn and our little world will begin its descent into death as winter's icy grip starts to squeeze.

I drive to the department store and park near the back entrance. The store sits in the middle of a parking lot, each side with an identical glass walled entrance. It is a tall, looming store with twenty or thirty-foot ceilings. Behind me is a strip mall that shares the same parking lot. Half the storefronts are empty. There I sit, I smoke, I wait, and I contemplate. The voice will not relent. Happy now, asshole?

Good, Bobby, good. Very good...

I wait until the sun falls behind the hills, as the blood-red moon turns to a bright white, and begins to raise high in the sky; the stars start to poke through the black lace of the night. I wait until just before ten, when all the cars have left the parking lot, when I know that the Beast will be making his rounds to lock up.

He will start at the far east door and then make his way around. I have watched him do it before; there is a process to it. The doors are solid glass, two at each entrance. Each door has a latch at the bottom and the top to help brace it. He will close one door, latch the bottom, then the top, and then repeat with the other. The last step is to lock them together in the middle with his keys. This means I have some time.

I look around to see if anyone is watching. The parking lot is empty; empty beer bottles and discarded newspapers mull about the concrete, the only car Kate's T Bird. The strip mall storefronts are dormant, save one off to the right. Through the storefront glass, I can make out the silhouette of a lonely janitor sweeping the floor.

I open the car door slowly, and then do not shut it. I do not want to make any noise, in case I have mistimed the Beast's schedule. He always goes in order. Careful not to kick a bottle, I tip toe through the parking lot. I make my way to the door, look back over my shoulder to the empty lot once more, and then duck inside.

The store is dark. He has already turned off the overhead fluorescents; they buzz softly along the ceiling, powering down. Miniscule light comes from the tiny bulbs under the awning that sits in circumference around the outer wall. A sea of clothing racks stands silent in the dark. To my right, a jewelry case glows blue, but I am not here for that. I have much larger aspirations. I sneak through the racks of clothing, keeping low. They smell of dust; times are hard, the store has not been doing well. Foot traffic has been down, not just here, but pretty much everywhere. I feel my heart leap into my chest as I suddenly see something large standing before me. A mannequin dressed in a polo shirt.

I look down at my watch; he is probably at the last door now, behind me.

Staying low to the ground, I wade through the racks of dusty clothes until I come out by the door to shipping and receiving. It has one of those rubber "flapper" doors that you can pull a dolly through without damaging anything as it closes upon you and behind you. I pull the rubber door aside and sneak in; the door squeaks as it slaps shut, rubber upon rubber. I find a place to hide down an alley of shelves. Light bulbs, dustpans, and dusty boxes surround me on all sides. The smell of cardboard dominates the air.

I crouch down and wait, fists to the floor. The concrete feels cool against my knuckles.

Suddenly the door creaks open and flaps shut. I peek around the corner to watch the Beast saunter by me towards the back. His shoulders bob to the ground and move as if in unison.

To my right, upon the shelf, I notice a screwdriver.

The voice says, *Bobby, it is time.*

I clutch the screwdriver tightly. It feels cold against my hand. I rush him from behind. He hears my footsteps and turns at the last minute.

He yells, "What the hell?!"

I leap towards him and shove the screwdriver into his abdomen. To my surprise, it slides in like a knife into cake. He screams and punches me on the back of the head with his concrete-like fists.

I can't believe it, I feel very little. As if a six-year-old has tried to take me out. Like some gnats batting about my ears. I am invincible. He can do nothing.

I grin and shove him against the concrete block wall.

He shouts, "Who the hell are you?" He holds the screwdriver with both hands, eyes in utter disbelief at the shiv sticking out of his stomach. "Why, why, why?!" He struggles to stand; his legs give out underneath him.

I shove him back against the wall; his head hits the concrete brick. Blood trickles down the side of his face. He slowly slumps to the floor. He holds the screwdriver tight with both hands.

"Oh, I think you know why. I know all about you, Wilhelm. I know what you are."

He wheezes heavily; blood trickles from the screwdriver down his wrists to the floor. Little red pools form beneath the drips. They mix with the dirt of the floor giving it a motor oil like appearance.

"I don't understand." He holds the screwdriver unsure of what to do. I know he's trying to decide whether or not to pull it back out. Bad move. He'll bleed out. I wonder how dumb he is or isn't.

I smack him aside his mouth; his eyes tighten with anger. He snarls a broken grin; several teeth are missing. I say, "I know what you did to that girl. I know of the demon that exists within your flesh." My words seem to come from somewhere else, as if scripted by someone else.

He looks up at me in disbelief. A thick line forms in his forehead. His face flushes red, and the scar on his left cheek seems to tear apart as it starts to pulse. "What? What did you say?"

The voice in my head says, *End it, Bobby.*

I feel no longer in control, my motor functions robotic. I reach forward with my bare hands and wrap them around his throat. I push with my thumbs upon his Adam's apple. His eyes grow wide. I push and push until I hear a crack, a gasp, and then a wheeze. I do not let go until his neck collapses inward.

His legs rattle their last rattle. He shits one last time. He dies holding the screwdriver with both hands. Probably should have pulled it out. Could have defended himself. Or at least tried. Coward.

I stand up, my heart racing. I feel that same rush of fear mixed with adrenaline that I have not felt since Normandy. My hands shake; blood stains my fingers. Blood that is not my own.

To my right I see a bailing machine, a giant blue metal contraption of hydraulics and force. This machine crushes empty cardboard boxes into cubes.

The cubes return to the warehouse to be recycled. An endless cycle of cardboard birth and death. This gives me an idea.

I grab the Beast by his workboats and pull him across the stained concrete floor. His body makes a scraping sound as his rings scratch upon the concrete. They scratch two lines as I pull. A trail of blood follows behind him. The bailer is only about an eighth full. I pull the iron rod from its clasp and tug the door open. In goes the Beast upon a pile of crushed cardboard. I shut the door, pull down the metal rod, hit the red button, and down come the hydraulics.

Last sound I hear is a crunch. The world eradicated of this terror. A demon sent to the pit. Crushed beneath my boot.

Chapter Eighteen

I have never gone back before. I was a one hit wonder. Never have I returned to the scene. It was an odd premise that Cotton put before me, two demons, colluding amongst each other, preying on the weak together. It was odd to me that the visions came separately. I didn't even remember the second one. I took Cotton's word for it. I had to. He had never steered me wrong before. I was here to do my job, to do my duty. I best follow his guidance if I ever wanted to fill my quota. My unknown quota. My seemingly never-ending quota. It was important to have direction. I needed someone to point me, to aim me, to pull the trigger of vengeance and rage that was I. Without that, I'd be nothing more than a swinging cock full of bullets, aimlessly marauding through life, probably knocking off liquor stores and stealing women's purses on the subway. I was a degenerate. I am a degenerate. For me to exist without my purpose I'd be a lost soul of havoc let loose upon the city. And we could not have that. This is why my job means everything. Without it, imagine the monster I would become. And monsters have no place in this world.

The sky was buckshot with endless stars. It was one of those warm summer nights where the air felt like pea soup, thick, difficult to breathe, like God stuffed the world inside a Cuban cigar. I labored through each step. I could feel the sweat form a small lake above my ass crack, a little Lake Superior of disgusting animal excretion puddling amongst the fibers of my sweatpants. I was happy to be off the subway. Air conditioner busted. One awful ride through a swamp down to Quincy. Trapped inside a subway car, when the humidity is this bad, is one of the worst feelings in life. Feels like a Nazi death train; next stop the gas chambers.

The streets were teeming with the insane. The heat drives them out of the woodwork like rats. As I walked from the MBTA stop, I passed by a drunk passed out in a ditch, amongst a sea of cardboard, fast food wrappers, and cigarette butts. Two male teens, tattooed from head to toe, with nose rings and pink hair, sat on the curb, smoking cigarettes while drinking cheap beer in tallboy cans. Not a care in the world. They had no concern for the absent police; yet I could hear sirens screaming in the distance.

A man in a long white bathrobe strutted about, staring at his feet as he stumbled along. As I followed him through the intersection, I watched in amazement as he walked right out in front of traffic as if he were Moses. The cars parted like the Red Sea; he made it to the other side safely, amidst a barrage of profanity.

The air was heavy, thick, weighing me down. It made me want to crawl next to the drunken hobo and hamburger wrappers and call it a night. Yet, the air reminded me of long ago, of summer nights lost in memory, back then when I had not a care in the world. Back before I shipped out, back when I was with her.

The very thought made me sick to my stomach.

It was best not to think of her. To not dwell on the past. I could not fall down that tunnel. A tunnel to which I could never return. Those days were behind me and had to stay there. To think of that past was akin to drowning in a well. Those memories trap you, take you down beneath the surface, below the water, choking, sinking, and killing the mind. The past can be a mind killer if you let it. There is only one method for survival. Full speed ahead, hard and fast.

Burn right past them all.

The smell of exhaust was thick upon the night air, the smog dense, pushing down, punishing the ground with all its angst. The night stunk of ash and soot, as if hell had unleashed itself upon the world. I turned the corner and there stood the church, dark in the night. Behind the stained glass windows, I could make out a single, solitary light. It moved amongst the glass, a ghostly lantern prowling in the dark. Someone was inside.

I pushed past the yellow police tape and stalked around to the back of the church. The parking lot was mostly empty; the only cars were an old station wagon, a Toyota Prius, and an old model, late nineties, rusted up Camaro. There I found the back door beneath a burned-out bulb. I grasped the black iron railing and pulled my living carcass up upon the brick steps.

I pulled upon the rusted handle but it would not give. I put my weight into it and kicked the wooden door. The loud smack was inaudible upon the night air; it mixed in amongst Quincy's howls, police sirens, and traffic. I looked around to see if anyone saw or heard. Emptiness; not a soul in the parking lot. Above, a few clouds passed quickly; the moonlight danced upon the windshields. I leaned over the railing—there, a bulkhead.

I hopped over the rail and landed on the bulkhead with a thud. My steel tipped boots clunked against the door. I stood up, hands tightly wrapped around the rusty handles. I pulled and pulled until I felt it give way. I practically fell on my ass as I flailed backward, arms flapping in the wind like some deranged seagull.

The steps before me were wooden, worn, the second one cracked. It lead down into the darkness, into the crypt.

I looked around to see if anyone saw me. The moonlight shone down upon my face like a police helicopter looking for an escaped convict. Too exposed.

I ducked inside and pulled down the bulkhead doors behind me. I took out old reliable and flicked it on. My lighter caught as usual, its soft glow shooting shadows across the walls. Shapes mulled about in the dark.

The basement was relatively empty. A single light bulb, unlit, swung overhead. I saw various card tables and old wooden chairs collecting cobwebs. The room smelled of dust, mildew, and rot. There in the corner I saw an old grandfather clock, glass busted about its face, some of the numbers missing. Next to it was a door to a toilet. I went in and flicked the light on. I pulled down my sweatpants and took a dehydrated, hangover-fueled, deep yellow piss. I jiggled the handle to flush, then realized that no pipes connected to the toilet. It was just sitting there, a castaway porcelain bowl. *Shit*, I thought, *my DNA available to the entire world.* I opened up the back of the toilet; it was empty. No water.

Fuck.

I found the stairs and pulled myself up with the help of the handrail. I felt weak for some reason. I never feel weak. My knees burned; my bulky felt heavy in my boots.

I came to the top of the stairs and then gently creaked open the door. It opened into the rectory; the room was dark save the moonlight creeping through an open window. *Crap*, I thought. That would have been easier than the bulkhead. Too eager, I hadn't surveyed enough.

Common sense told me that there'd be no shot I would find the deacon here. However, Cotton insisted he would be here.

"Cotton?" I whispered. "Where is he?"

No response. The only sound I heard the sound of traffic from the window.

"Cotton?"

Still nothing.

Why wasn't he answering? Was the son of a bitch taking a nap? Now? Of all times? When he knew I might need him?

The lights turned on as I felt cold steel upon my neck.

"Freeze!" a voice said. "We got you, you son of a bitch!"

I felt a sharp pain at the back of the head.

The last thing I saw was the ceiling as I spiraled towards the ground.

I remember very little. Other than a lingering sense of being very pissed off.

Cotton?

Where are you?

Chapter Nineteen

I close my eyes and take a long gulp. The bourbon tingles my lips. It has been six weeks since I crushed the Beast. Six weeks since I heard the sound of his bones crushing to dust underneath powerful hydraulic-driven steel. Four weeks since the news stopped talking about it. At first, I was big time news. They droned on and on, each night, looking for answers, looking for the killer that, for some reason, showed up blurry—just enough—on all the security cameras while the background still came in crystal clear. The police are baffled. The media is baffled. Yet time moves on, people get bored, and they move on to the next flavor of the week. I'm old news now. I got off scot-free. I should feel remorse. But I don't. I did what had to be done. I did what the voice told me to do.

Kate can't stop though; she keeps talking about it. She has been really into the story. Every night she keeps bringing it up. My only option is to get out, to come here, to the alley bar, amongst all these obese beer-swilling, chain-smoking dipshits.

I know that I'm changing. I can feel it in my limbs, down in my core. I don't feel as tired as I used to. My knees don't burn as they did. My bulk, once so heavy in the Earth's malicious gravity, no longer weighs me down. I can't sleep, yet the circles under my eyes are gone. I don't understand what is happening and that scares the shit out of me. I don't get hung over. My days seem longer. The world is slowing down. My muscles are huge. And yet I haven't lifted a weight in I can't tell you how long.

I drink to numb it out. With drink comes numbness. I can't numb away the memory of what I've done, but with enough excess, I can stop the world from crashing down all over me, even if just for a moment. It requires a lot of booze. I was always a heavy drinker, but now it takes ten times as much. Very expensive to say the least.

I sat there with Kate earlier tonight at the dinner table, lost. She served this awful skinless chicken meal and green beans. She's trying to be healthy. Wants me to be healthy. Wants that thing in her stomach to be healthy. But I just stared at my food. That's all I could do. She droned on and on. But I wasn't listening. I saw her mouth move but didn't hear a word. I can tell by the look in her eyes that I'm starting to lose her. But that is probably well enough. She's slipping away. I'm not surprised.

It's not that I don't love her, or don't care. I know what she's going through. I know what is coming. But I killed a man. I killed him with my own two hands. I crushed his windpipe until I heard it crack. I watched as his eyes rolled back in his head while he shit his last meal into his torn underwear. I can't be a father. I've become a monster. And this world has no place for monsters.

This bar is my refuge. It smells of cigarettes, booze, and sweat. In the corner, a gang of overweight truckers are playing pool. To my left, a couple of cheap hookers are talking by the jukebox. I take another sip of my bourbon. I love the way the warm feeling greets my lips, the way my chest feels as it crawls down my throat. Bourbon straight over ice is a powerful elixir that brings me closer to the numbness I seek. Every night I come here to watch whatever is on the bar television that hangs to the upper right. It was here I watched the reports come in on what I had done. It made for good entertainment, if only for a while.

I take yet another sip and rub my eyes. Need to keep pounding. Suddenly my head feels very heavy. Odd; I haven't been able to get fully drunk. The sound of the porcelain billiard balls smacking behind me sounds as if it's coming from down a long corridor. The bartender, a middle-aged man with acne scars, begins to fade into a haze of red and black. The music, background noise I am not paying attention to, begins to swirl out of step, the RPMs off, played on the wrong speed. I feel the barstool beneath me begin to sway.

Suddenly I'm falling. Like before. I'm falling fast in the black. The sounds of the bar are distant, muffled static. I no longer feel the glass in my hand. I no longer smell cigarettes mixed with puke. I do still taste the bourbon on my lips. I hear what sounds like rushing wind as I fall.

I smack into something hard and feel a sharp pain careen up my spine. I see stars mixed in a shade of hazy red. I rub my eyes and shake my head. I open them to find myself standing at the entrance to a kitchen. I'm in someone's house?

A dark red stain covers the lemon-colored linoleum. Dry blood smears the floor. Behind me, a living room; rust-colored shag carpeting, a lime-colored couch with matching love seat. Tube television on a wooden table. Rabbit ears bent to the side. The smell of pine sol mixed with something earthy... weed.

I hear the sound of muffled cries from around the corner. As I peek into the kitchen, I see a young woman and two children. The woman has long brown hair that falls down across exposed shoulders. She is wearing a long brown hippie dress with a sunflower patch about her belly. Tears streak her freckled cheeks. She huddles in the corner, back against the wall; the two young children huddle against her. There is a boy. He can't be more than seven; he has short brown hair and wears a red baseball uniform with a matching Cincinnati Reds cap. His eyes are a steel grey. Frightened, his eyes well with tears. A little girl, no more than five, also with long brown hair, clutches her mother's leg. The girl is wearing a pink dress with a ladybug pattern. I have the sudden feeling that I know them. I don't know how or why but I feel like I know them.

My heart thunders in my chest. What is going on? Why am I here? Am I dreaming again? Did I pass out on the bar? Was the smack I felt from my head hitting the brass rail while I fell? But why does this feel so real?

A pea-colored refrigerator stands between them and the range. I see a bloody handprint across the front of the refrigerator door. A trail of blood leads from the door, to the floor, across to the eat-in kitchen. As my eyes follow the trail, my heart sees him before they do. It pounds in my chest as he comes into focus. There, upon the floor, sits a man.

He has blonde hair that hangs in long, messy strands down across his forehead, landing gently against ruby red cheeks. His hair is short in the back, long only in the front. His nose is pointy and sharp, too long like a witch, with a big bony bump in the middle. Veins pop from his skin. Blue colored lines fill his face like a spider web. He wears a white coat that resembles something that a doctor would wear, like a lab coat. Blood stains the white garment. Dark beads of crimson fall from his fingertips towards the floor. He studies his hand and smiles; pointy teeth glisten from the recessed lighting overhead.

I want to scream but I can't. My tongue feels heavy as my heart thunders in my head. Fear claws at my mind as I've only known once before. That one time, when I heard the bullets ping against the metal door, waiting for it to drop. I freeze, unable to move. I feel like I'm frozen to the ground, a helpless statue. Useless. Helpless. Vulnerable.

Something fleshy and bloated sits before the man on the floor. Flesh, hair, and blood. Is it a pig? There's no head. What the hell? What is going on? Oh, God, what did he do? It is body. A naked body. All except for the underwear. There are holes in the body, deep puncture wounds, gushing with blood so dark it might as well be molasses. Or motor oil. Oh, God, what did he do?

I see at the man's feet two types of saws. One saw is a regular handsaw, tiny blade between two yellow handles. The other is bigger with jagged crocodile teeth. Both saws are dripping with fresh blood. The man sits here, grinning, smiling at me, staring right through me at the trembling family behind me. He doesn't see me.

Blood flows from his teeth. Realization hits me like a ball bat. I know now what he has done. He is out to dinner. He is at the buffet. He is enjoying a gourmet meal of pure carnage.

I realize now that this is another vision. This is Ohio State again. This is the cheerleader torn up, yet again. I feel so much guilt as I know I can do nothing. If this is like then, then this has passed. This is a waking moment of horror that has already occurred. My heart sinks as I listen to the sobbing that emanates from the corner. The poor woman. The poor kids. Forced to watch, wondering if they would be next. This bastard. This fucking horrible human being. No wait—that's it, isn't it? He isn't a human being. He's one of them. A DEMON.

The man smacks his lips as blood flows down his chin, dripping like chicken gravy. Out of the corner of my eye, I see the severed head, resting amongst the dining room table chairs. You son of a bitch.

With a sudden smack of light, I feel myself rip back to reality. I almost drop my glass as my body shudders in a convulsing spasm of disgust. God dammit. Not again. Not again. God, not again. Shit.

I pull back the rest of the bourbon in a single gulp and smack the glass down too hard on the bar. The bartender frowns at me.

I say, "Another."

"I think you've had enough," he frowns as he takes the glass from me. His mustache wrinkles up under his nose like a baby rat.

I sigh a sigh of defeat. "Please, rough day. I'm sorry."

He says, "Very well, then," and clinks in two ice cubes. I watch in dire need as he pours the brown gold over the ice. "But you're done after this. Cut off."

I take the glass to my mouth. The minute that warm bourbon touches my lips, I see him. The man. The blonde fucking freak cannibal. Directly across from me, sitting at the bar, sucking on a dry martini. He wears rouge about his cheeks and appears to have a thin layer of red lipstick. A tint of blue eye shadow tickles the skin beneath his sunken eyes. Two tired bowlers sit to his right, mocking him between their sips. He doesn't seem to mind. He stares straight ahead, boring holes into my head with his eyes. He wears a blue, silk scarf. He certainly isn't trying to fit in. This is a bowling alley after all.

I say under my breath, "What the hell is he doing here?"

I feel my nerve endings sting with nervous anticipation. A lightning wave of pain cascades up my left arm, burning. A voice says, *Kill him.*

I close my eyes. *Not again, I cannot. Not again.*

The voice says back, *You saw. You saw what he did. You know what you must do.*

I don't think I can. I can't do it again.

Nevertheless, Bobby, I know you want to. I know you need to. I know you better than you know yourself.

I take a sip and close my eyes. *Who are you? What are you? Why are you in my head?*

I am your guide, Robert. Trust in me, and all your sins will be forgiven. Do not be afraid of the evil that exists in this world, or the feelings of your heart. Man was born inherently evil. It takes every ounce of his being to resist that evil. To not succumb. There are things that exist on this plane. Entities that have broken loose. Creatures that have free reign, free to walk amongst us. Free to corrupt us. Free to dominate us. Free to take us. He is lost. A demon clings to his heart, and it has changed him. Has turned him into hell on earth. You must send him back to where he belongs. You must send him home. He has no place here amongst the living. No right to this freedom.

I grit my teeth and hold my head in my hands. With my thumbs, I squeeze my temples as if to block out the voice. *What I saw, you say he has done this? This is real. He killed that man? Just like before…*

The voice seems to come from farther away this time, as if it is shouting across an empty field. It sounds hoarse, almost sickly. *I wish I could tell you that you have precognition. That what you saw has yet to pass. That you can prevent it. However, I cannot. There is blood, much blood on his hands. Lives ruined, destinies destroyed, worlds collapsed—all at the hands of this creature before you. If you do not stop him now, he will kill again.*

I'm going crazy, I think. *This cannot be.*

Robert, I have been with you since the beginning. I have been here, hoping you would listen, hoping that you would open up that hardened heart and hear my voice. I have been with you since Normandy, my son. You are not crazy, and you are certainly not alone.

The man across stares at me, his eyes a cold steel wax. He looks like a mannequin more than a man. His skin glistens like hard plastic in the bar light. He holds the martini in his left hand; a lit cigarette dangles from his right. There are only two men sitting at the bar now: him and I—it is getting late, almost closing time.

The voice says, *In twenty seconds, he is going to stand up and go to the bathroom. Follow him there. Take him there.*

I shake my head and stare into my glass. *How do you know this? I don't understand. Who are you, who am I talking to? How could you know what he is about to do? I don't understand!*

The voice whispers, *I have a different vantage point. I am not omnipotent. Nevertheless, I see the world from a different angle. Time slants at different angles. Trust in me, Robert, and you will know I speak the truth in five seconds when he stands.*

Bullshit.

One.

No fucking way.

Two...

Three...

I'm crazy, I know it...

Four. You are not crazy.

I won't do it.

Five. Yes, you will.

The man stands up; my heart falls in my chest. He places the martini upon the coaster and walks out the bar towards the alley.

FOLLOW HIM.

I stand up. My legs obey the voice. It's not like I'm fighting. I'm not a robot, with no control. No, that isn't it. I want to follow him. I need to follow him.

That poor family.

I find the alley mostly empty, only a couple of teenagers smoking cigarettes, rolling away in the last lane. The pins crash and spray against the lane's backdrop. My co-worker Trevor stands behind the counter, spraying down an army of shoes set out before him. A lit cigarette dangles from his wormy lip.

I see the door to the bathroom swing shut, and I know that the voice in my head told the truth. It was right. He was right. Whatever he is.

My shoes feel heavy as I walk to the bathroom. Never has it seemed so far. I pass the game room to my left; one sad, lonely fat kid with bad acne-coated skin plays pinball. To my right, I pass a young greaser; he's wearing a white T-Shirt with a pack of cigarettes rolled up in the arm sleeve. He stares at the floor as I pass.

175

When I enter the bathroom, I see the man alone at the urinal. I scan the room quickly—we are alone. I stand there for a minute, breathing heavily, not saying a word. The room smells as any bowling alley restroom would.

The man says in a German accent, "Did you get a good look?" He stands pissing against the porcelain, swaying in his stance, barely able to hold himself up. He steadies himself by leaning his left arm on the urinal porcelain. "Did you come for a close up?"

Hatred wells up in my heart. All I can think of are those kids. That poor woman, the poor man, his life reduced to nothing more than a meal for a mad man.

The German sways in stance; two hands now upon his cock. He grins and sprays his piss all over the wall to the right of the urinal. He laughs like a toddler at play, finally out of diapers for the first time. I walk up slowly and run my fingers through his hair, digging into his scalp with my nails. I clench his long blonde bangs in my mitts and rip down.

"What the hell are you doing?!" He screams. He falls to the floor with a smack. I hold his hair in my grasp and tug. I pull as hard as I can and drag him toward the stall. Dick still in his hand, he pisses on his slacks as I rip him across the floor. His black leather shoes leave scuff marks on the tile as his legs flail underneath him. "What are you doing? Stop! Stop!"

I kick open the stall door, and then clutch his head with both my hands. Before us, the toilet sits, full to the brim with piss, toilet paper, and a couple a rounds of beer shits. I squeeze his temples with my thumbs and with both of my hands push down as hard as I can, shoving his face into the cauldron of filth.

He kicks, he claws, his body convulses and shakes. He screams beneath the surface of the water that bubbles a grotesque stew of excrement and puke. But I hold fast, I hold firm, and I hold down. His muffled screams grow dormant. I hold him down so hard that the toilet shatters beneath us. Urine, diarrhea, paper, and toilet water cascade across the bathroom floor. I drop his lifeless body amongst the exploded excrement. It lands with a wet smack, contorted and broken. He wheezes and gasps his last breath of air. His dead, purple tongue hangs from the side of his mouth.

I stand there for a moment, saying nothing, feeling nothing. It is the fact that I feel nothing that, in a sense, is shocking. I do not feel hate, nor fear. I feel nothing at all. There is something very business-like about what I've done. I am punching the clock. Processing the payroll. Unloading the truck. Laying the brick. I am doing MY JOB.

Good, Robert, good. You have done well. It is now time for you to stop fighting who you are. What you are. You are an Angel of Death, Robert. Moreover, it is time you come home.

Later tonight, I'll leave Ohio. I won't look back. I'll never see the buckeye state again. I'll never see Kate again. I'll never see my child. I won't know his name. I won't see his freckled face.

Until that one day.

Chapter Twenty

"Robert Turner, do you know why you are here?"

Hearing my name took me a moment. I hadn't heard someone living say it in so long. Been what, thirty years? I had always used a fake name when I tried my odd jobs, the small jobs, the scratch jobs, the beer money jobs. The jobs that paid just enough to keep up a measly gym membership so I could shower occasionally. 'Course, I had let that lapse a while back now. Hadn't had a shower in about a month. And you could tell, too.

To hear it now, after so long, took me by surprise. They say you really die the last time anyone says your name. Perhaps only now was I coming back to life.

There are those moments when you know that the person across from you, sitting there in his perfectly tailored suit, taking a sip from his hot cup of Joe, thinks that you do not have any sense at all. That your brain is full of marbles, full of gravel, completely and utterly void of reason or purpose. It is at these moments that you realize the conversation that you are about to have with this individual is going to go absolutely nowhere because your ability to explain your thoughts, or your actions, or why you are sitting there to begin with is not possible. This person will not believe a thing you have to say; he has already concluded that you are insane, and that is the only conclusion that he could possibly arrive at. It is the only definition of your situation that could possibly fit his paradigm of how the world should be, because it is the only way to explain the many things that you have done. It puts it nicely into a tiny little box. A tiny little box of clinically diagnosed insanity.

The room itself resembled a box, a cold steel box. Behind the suit was a mirror; all I could see was the bald spot developing on the back of his head reflected back at me. Not being ignorant of course, I knew someone was monitoring us; it was not as if we truly were alone. While encouraged to speak freely, I knew that was total bullshit.

He was in his late forties, a slight man, thin upon the wind, as if a slight gust or breeze could send him hurtling down an alleyway. It wasn't just the glasses he wore, or the lack of muscle, or the mountain of acne scarring that still remained, but I could tell right away that years of schoolyard bullying had created, in its own right, a different kind of monster, the kind that preys upon those with less stature in the game of life. This was the kind of guy I used to pick on in high school, something that we both knew. He had seen my type before, over the years, amongst the hallways and locker rooms of his youth. I was the kind of guy that would have de-pantsed him, spit shaving cream in his face, then most likely shoved him into a locker for good measure. There he would wait for hours, hoping that the janitor would take a break from his daily drudgery to go smoke a joint amongst the empty shower stalls.

In hindsight, while I was not his particular bully, I suppose I still deserved the amount of animosity that spewed forth from his mouth. For I was a bully, that was for sure.

His face was dry, red from too much sun. Little blotches of burnt skin mingled amongst the paleness of his flesh. The summer had not been kind to him. Certainly, he had a farmer's tan, no shot in hell this guy took his shirt off at the beach club, or pool club, or whatever club he and his privileged family sauntered off to on weekends.

"You do understand why you are here, do you not?"

I grinned, didn't say a word, but nodded. The chair felt like a rock beneath me; clothed in an orange jumpsuit, I felt at home, probably where I always should have been. The stench of bleach and disinfectant hung in the air.

He gave me a menacing look, a look of disgust, of distaste, as if sitting in the same room with me made his skin crawl. I'm sure the way that I sat there grinning like an imbecile did not please him much. He was certainly not at ease.

"You understand why I'm here then?"

I grinned but didn't say anything. I could tell I made him quite uncomfortable; this brought me much joy.

"I'm your court-appointed attorney. It is my job to defend you in court. Do you understand what that means?"

I broke my silence. "Yeah, that means you'll phone it in and then I'll find myself sitting in the chair. Fried meat. A fatted calf, lead to the slaughter. Air gun to the temple."

He sat back, seemingly defeated.

"You do realize that they no longer use the electric chair, don't you?"

I said nothing; I stared him down, seeing if he would blink. Instead, I couldn't even get him to look me in the eye.

In front of him lay a manila file folder. He opened the file and threw some photos in front of me.

"Do you see what they say you have done? Look at them."

I leaned forward; the cuffs held my arms behind my back, around the back of the chair, making the task difficult. I strained my neck in the process. I studied the photos. Two glossies, from different angles, of Father McKay's bullet-ridden corpse. The angle of the shots was from outside the confessional door; upon the back of the wooden boxed confessional, pieces of brain and pockmarks of blood cascaded into a devilish waterfall.

"Yeah, I see them."

He took the photos back and put them away. He shuffled the file folder under his notebook, leaned forward and then clasped his hands. "Did you do it?"

I grinned at him. "Of course I did."

His eyes grew wide. "So, you'll confess? Is there anything to say in your defense? Why did you go back to the church? Why the deacon, why did you not stop at one?"

"I couldn't stop at one. Cotton wouldn't let me."

A vein started to throb in his forehead, as if only now was he suddenly attentive.

"Cotton?"

"Yeah, Cotton, my handler."

He took a sip of his coffee; his hands shook. "What do you mean *handler*?"

I grinned. I leaned in and spoke through clenched teeth, "You wouldn't believe me if I told you."

He pointed at the folder again. "It says here that you told the clerk you were born in 1924."

"Yeah, so? What of it?"

"How about the fact that that would make you ninety years old and you're half that—at most. Why do you feel the need to lie to us? We'll find out who you are soon enough."

"It's not a lie. It's the stone-cold truth, my man. I don't age right. It's sort of slower. That's all I know. Too fucking slow to be honest. That's my problem. I haven't filled my quota yet, so they keep me here. Aging like a slug." I snorted; I felt a little dizzy, something seemed a bit off. I felt strange, almost like a cold was coming on. Something I hadn't felt in seventy years.

"Look, how can I defend you when you don't trust me?"

I sat back and slumped in my chair. My cuffs clanged upon the metal legs. I said, "Can I have a cigarette?"

He looked back at the glass behind him. It was obvious to him that their clichéd ruse did not fool me. He nodded. Seconds later, the door opened and a young, pale-faced police officer tossed some reds along with a book of matches on the table.

I leaned forward and grinned. "Well?"

His eyes squinted. "Well, what?"

I felt like shouting but held my tongue. In a soft voice, I said, "Well, I can't bloody light it with my hands behind my back, now can I?"

He pulled a cigarette from the pack and offered it to me. The butt shook in his hand. I bit at it like a shark attacking a harbor seal. I bit down on the tip. "Well, do you have a light?"

His fingers shook like a convulsing mental patient. He lit a match and leaned in close. I think he half expected me to head-butt him; he leaned in first, and then recoiled without lighting it.

"Come on, don't be a pussy," I said while holding the butt in my mouth. "Just light it."

He closed his eyes for a moment and sighed. After a deep breath, he struck a match and finally lit the tip. He sat back down and shook the match into submission. "You have your cigarette now. Speak the truth." The smell of sulfur now masked the bleach; it overpowered the tiny room.

I took a puff off the cigarette and blew it out of the corner of my mouth while holding it in the other corner. "You want the truth?"

"Yes."

"The truth is, I slay demons. Horrendous, malevolent souls that wreak havoc upon this world. I cull them from this earth. I maim, I crush, I eradicate. I burn witches at the stake. You see, I'm on a witch hunt."

"A witch hunt? So that is what you believe you have done here with this Father McKay? You've burned a witch?"

I nodded while puffing on the cigarette. "Well, warlock really. I guess he is a warlock, he is a dude anyway. Look man, all I know is I have my dreams, Cotton tells me what they mean, and then I execute. Simple as that. My only ticket off this rock. You pussies wouldn't be so bent out of shape about this Father McKay if you knew what I knew about him."

He sat back and crossed his arms across his chest. Despite his tiny frame, a little belly protruded upward, providing an ample enough flesh table to rest his forearms. He was the epitome of couch potato. A lazy, naturally lithe, thin little dude who let himself go. Too much pizza, boredom, and depression made him fat around the midsection. "Tell me more about this Cotton. Does Cotton have a last name?"

"Yeah, sure, Mather."

We sat in silence for a minute, the only sound the buzzing and snapping of the overhead fluorescents.

"Cotton Mather. As in THE Cotton Mather, famous Boston preacher, fire and brimstone, that guy?"

"Yeah," I said, taking another puff; I sat back in my chair and blew smoke at the ceiling. "That guy."

He pointed at the manila folder again. "It also says here that you listed your residence as "Copp's Hill Burying Ground?"

"That's right."

"A cemetery. You live in a cemetery?"

"That I do."

"So, you're homeless?"

I shook my head back and forth; I felt my face flush. I have to admit, I was a bit embarrassed. "Oh, I... well... I wouldn't say I was homeless. I have a home. You see..." I paused, trying to find the best way to explain it to him. "I live with Cotton."

"You live with Cotton Mather," he said, his voice silent, yet quietly mocking me through a proud grin. "You live with a dead preacher, in a burial ground from the 1800s..."

"1600s," I said, cutting him off. I wanted to punch him in the face. "Don't you know your fucking history? You grew up around here, didn't you? Shouldn't you know this? It's local history. I can tell by how you're trying to hide that accent. Did you leave your car in Harvard Yard, boss?"

I blew smoke in his face.

With his thumb and index finger, he clenched the bridge of his nose. He squinted, digging his twig-like fingers into his watering eyes.

He stood up and walked around the back of his chair, his back now to me. He faced the mirror and took a deep breath. "So, let me get this straight. You say you are ninety years old. You live in a burial ground in the middle of the city. You hang out with a dead, famous, Boston historical figure. You have dreams that tell you which witches to... what did you say? Cull from the earth? Cotton Mather, this famous, yet very dead, Boston preacher, interprets your dreams and tells you whom to kill. You kill them then crawl back into your hole in the ground. And you've been doing this for how long? Seventy years? You claim this, despite how ridiculously impossible it is?"

"Well, more like forty years. Hasn't always been this way."

"And you believe this?"

"Wouldn't believe it if it weren't the truth."

"And you'd take a lie detector test to the fact?"

"Course."

"And you'd be willing to meet with any doctor that I bring in here?"

"Course. What the fuck, why not?"

He sighed; he pulled the glasses from his nose and wiped them on his tie. "Well, I think we know our plea then." He pointed his bifocals at me. "You're crazier than shit."

I grinned, took another drag, and blew the smoke towards his face. "You said it, boss, not I."

Chapter Twenty-One

I think about sand quite a bit. Perhaps because, for me, it meant rebirth. I was born again in sand, ripped back from the black to begin anew. It was in sand that I rose, that I stood and defiantly continued my life. In a sense, the beach was my womb, the warm grains caressing my body, keeping me safe, as water lapped at my feet.

Sand is a popular metaphor for time. The hourglass has long represented the cycle of life, the tiny grains that fall, each representing a moment in our lives, minutes, seconds, or hours. Time is something that I have given much thought to. When I think of sand, I tend to think of the shore. I find the shoreline the perfect metaphor for life. We each begin our life at low tide, the ocean receded, endless kernels of time across the beach. We build castles and fortresses with our time, but the tide comes. It always comes. We can try to hold on, to hold it back, but cannot. The harder you squeeze sand the quicker it slips through your fingers. You cannot run, you cannot hide; the tide will always come in. Time will always slip away. No castle can survive the tide. The tide engulfs everything in its path. The tide always wins.

Sometimes, despite our attempts to cling to the sand that is our life, unwanted sand clings to us. It embeds itself between our toes, cakes itself upon the backs of our legs, an annoying itch that will not go away. These are our unwanted memories. Those moments of time that we cannot forget, that we need to brush away.

Yet... this does not quite apply to me, not in its traditional sense. It wasn't until I went to Cape Cod in the early eighties that I felt an affinity for this metaphor. I tracked a demon down to a small motel in Brewster, a tiny little borough that sits nestled along Cape Cod Bay. There, after I slit the demon's throat with piano wire, I took a trip down to the shore to wash my hands. But I found no water to cleanse the deed.

It was low tide. Here, at the interior of Cape Cod Bay, the water recedes for a mile, sometimes a bit more. It appears as if God himself came down with a giant straw and sucked the ocean dry. Gone. Only a desert remains. An endless sea of unlucky flopping fish, trapped crabs, and small tidal pools that dot the landscape. This is my life. The tides, the ocean that descends on us all, has left me alone. I am alone out there on the Brewster flats, endless grains of time in all direction. If the tide is coming, I cannot see it.

Chapter Twenty-Two

The snow falls fast past my eyes. Not quite white out conditions, but I cannot see much more than a few feet in front of my face. The wind howls in my ears. It is dark out. I cannot tell the drifts from the road itself. It is so hard to see out here in the night, with this deluge assaulting my face. I shiver as ice slides down my neck. I'm going to die, I know it; I never should have hitchhiked during this weather. I'm going to die out here on I-90, a frozen popsicle of stupidity. A dead snowman in upstate New York.

A voice says in my head, *The elements will not harm you. They cannot harm you more than the day harms the night. The night falls, but the day will always rise. You cannot die, you of eternal life.*

The words repeat in my head, over and over. He talks more and more each day. I've started to get used to it, as much as it frightens the hell out of me. I'm never alone.

I feel my feet going numb. Frostbite can't be far away.

I see headlights penetrate the darkness, a ghostly, wraithlike light that fights through the snow with ferocity. I hear a roar then a squeal as a black pickup truck pulls up. The snow falls fast past the beaming headlights. The engine coughs, then sighs as it shifts into park. I can barely see as the door opens. The snow flies horizontal by my face and melts upon my lips. I can taste the salt of the road, mixed with sand; I smell gasoline and oil, as the engine sputters and pops, angry that it had to stop.

A deep, raspy voice says to me, "Get in."

My heart flutters for a second, unsure. But what choice do I have? I haven't seen a car for over an hour. The last guy kicked me out at the last rest stop. I suppose I have no choice.

I slide in next to a man, shut the door, and rest my backpack upon my knees. It and I are soaked through. My eyes sting with snow and ice. My vision is blurry; it is hard to see inside the cab. My hands, too frozen to clean the ice from my eyes. The smell of bologna sandwiches and beer hits me. I stare ahead and warm my hands upon the heater. Outside the wind roars. No cars. No trucks, just us, sitting there along the side of an empty highway.

The man asks me, "What are you doing out alone like this?" My arms and lips tremble; I huddle in my coat but cannot speak. My teeth chatter too quickly. I'm a goddamn mute.

The voice in my head says, *Answer him*. I close my eyes and shake my head in a vain attempt to drown it out. Please go away. Not now!

"Son, why are you here?"

I lean back and stretch my neck towards the ceiling, muscles cracking; I feel an icy river cascade down my skin, wetting my shirt. I wipe my eyes on my wool coat and the man finally comes into focus.

He is short, much shorter than I am. His feet barely touch the pedals. He wears a thick white coat. Animal fur, white and ash colored wolf fur, spews from the neckline, nestling against his skin. He is bald with deep, black circles under his eyes. I feel a lump form in my throat.

I recognize him. "I… know… you."

The man grins and puts the pickup into gear.

He pushes down hard on the gas. The truck leaps through the snow, sliding, skidding left and right, almost spinning out, but we recover, swerving back in line. No cars lay before us, none behind. I can't see the road, only heavy, thick white snow that falls faster and faster. It looks like we're flying through space, hurtling through the stars the way the snow flies across the headlights.

I stare at him in utter disbelief. "You… you were in France. I don't believe it! You're the Gateman!"

He grins and clutches the wheel.

I squeeze the side of my backpack; the skin upon my knuckles cracks open like ripened fruit. I cringe as I say, "I don't believe any of this. I'm dead, aren't I? I'm back there, on the side of the road, face down in the ditch, aren't I? I know it. I'm dead, aren't I?"

The voice in my head says, *Far from it.* The Gateman says. "You should listen to him. He's here to help you."

My heart thunders in my chest. "Wait… What do you mean… you hear it to?"

He smiles. All gums and little dagger teeth. "Of course I hear him. He is your guide. Your guide that you ignored for too long. I told you to seek him. You've been ignoring my wishes."

I reach for the handle. Suddenly the doors lock automatically, as if a ghost inside the machine is anticipating my thoughts.

Oh, you're not going anywhere…

This can't be real. It cannot. I have always wondered if my reality is actually reality. I'm losing my grip. Is the world as I perceive it to be? Or is there a thin veil that hangs over the world, just enough to keep me from the truth? And what is that truth? Am I dead on the beach after all? Is this nothing more than a purgatory for my soul? If it is, I am failing miserably. That day in France is years long by. But fewer than how they feel, for I have vaulted across decades in the blink of eye. Just who is this man? What are his intentions? And by the look of the shit eating grin he has on his face, why does he seem to be enjoying it so much?

He laughs and then snorts as these thoughts reverberate around my thick skull. "You should hear yourself, Bobby, so self-absorbed, so important you think you are. Unfortunately, my need for you is much less than that. As I told you in France, your task will be simple. It is now that we finally assign it to you. You tried to hide for so long. You buried those dog tags, the ones you now keep hidden in that backpack, within your dresser drawer for so long. You cleaned toilets, scrubbed floors, and drank plenty. But you cannot drown us out; no liquor on Earth can accomplish that. You cannot run, nor can you hide, from your calling. It is now time you must heed that calling. So that you can fulfill why I brought you back in the first place."

I feel a tingling in my bones, one I have felt before. The last time I felt it, I was sitting at the bar in that French ghost town, sipping down that putrid, disgusting, yet somehow incredibly inviting liquid.

God's mead as it was. So it is true. I didn't dream that up. He is right. I have always kept those dog tags. I know—I've always known. As much as I tried to hide it from myself. It is true.

He says, "Open the glove compartment." The truck lurches forward. Outside, the snow pelts the glass, melting and streaking instantly in a hydro spider web.

I pop it open; inside there is a bottle of Bourbon and two glasses.

"Poor us some. You could use a drink."

Wait. This can't be real. I close my eyes and with my thumbs, I push down hard. Red stars explode in the dark. Something is off.

He says, "Take a pull on that bottle to see if this is real!"

I sigh as I screw off the cap and oblige him. The bourbon feels smooth, with just enough bite and heat as it slithers down my throat. He points at the bottle. "That's good shit. Pour me some."

I take a highball glass and pour the glass half way up, then hand it to him. He balances the steering wheel with his knees as he fiddles around with his pockets. After a few seconds, out pops a little bottle of what looks like maple syrup. "Want some?" He tops off the bourbon. "This mixture is truly heavenly."

I shake my head; God knows what's really in that bottle. Besides, I like my whiskey straight. I pour myself a glass and stare out the windshield. My heart starts to calm; the thunder turns into a flutter.

He snorts again as he puts the syrup bottle back in his pocket. He daintily holds the glass of bourbon with his left hand as he makes hand gestures with his right, as if he's offering sign language of what he's about to say next. His knees hold the wheel as we bounce along. "Bobby, you my friend, are nothing more than a mustard seed shot into a mountain. But once you take root, you will start to blossom, you will grow, and with time, you can accomplish what you've been sent here to do."

"And just what is that?" I take a sip. The bourbon tastes sweet upon my lips. Sweet enough on its own. Doesn't need any syrup.

"To erupt a volcano, to unleash an avalanche! Your sponsor will tell you your tasks, one by one. All you must do is listen to him. You obey him, you do as he asks of you, and you can gain passage."

The fluttering of my heart returns to its thunder. I feel it pounding in my chest; an emptiness forms in my core. I imagine I am sinking, deep down into the brine, within the cauldron of Normandy, witches brew for the damned. "Gain passage where?"

He takes a sip and smiles as the truck slides slightly to the left, then back to the right. The wind howls. Suddenly, we careen upwards, then down hard with a smack; the back tail fins and slides across the snow. He uses his knees to get us back on course. He laughs as the truck again swerves left and right. Not an ounce of fear. He does not seem to give a shit at all. I can't even see the road, it is nothing but white noise, snow upon a television screen, channels gone, antenna busted.

"Do you mind if I smoke?" He takes his last sip of the bourbon and tosses the glass between us upon the console. He takes out a pack of cigarettes. "You want one?"

I say, "No," and sip my whiskey.

Fucking liar, the voice in my head says.

"You see, Bobby, he knows you better than you know yourself". He lights the butt and hands it to me. I cringe at the thought of how it had touched his gray, corpse-like lips.

Do not be such a child.

"Fine." I rip the butt from his hand and take a drag. The ash feels wonderful upon my throat; the mixture of ash and bourbon is intoxicating. "You need to answer my question. Passage where?"

He takes a pull, then blows a perfectly formed smoke ring at the windshield. "Why, off this rock, of course."

"But to where, where to? Heaven? Hell? SPEAK, DAMMIT, STOP BEING SO FUCKIN' COY!"

Settle down, Bobby.

"Yes, please do settle down, you get so worked up all the time. You have already done so well. You eradicated that demonic soul from this world when you stomped down upon his throat. That triumphant crunch that you heard was but one of many trumpets awaiting you. Then that dainty German boy! Bravo! You do that again, and again, and again, serving our purpose. And you go up, not down. That is really all you need to know. You are a soldier, Bobby, a soldier of God."

"You want me to murder people? What God would want that? I don't understand. I can't believe what I've done. I had to leave. I had to get out. Get away."

He holds the cigarette in his mouth as he clenches the wheel with both hands. He squeezes hard; blue veins pop along his knuckles.

He chews on the cigarette while he speaks. "The earth is the devil's playground. Read your scripture. Lucifer is the prince of this world. This is his domain. And he is corrupting, lying, cheating, stealing, fucking, and clawing his way to the top. He is eating this world, piece by piece. Town by town. Movie producer by movie producer, politician by politician, hooker by hooker, broker by broker, lawyer by lawyer. This is his world. God needs our help. This is our role here. Our purpose. Moreover, if you do your duty, you follow the will of your sponsor, you will succeed, and fulfill your destiny. The Beast, as you called him, was but the first. Your German friend, an appetizer. There are many more like them, their souls corrupted, their minds damned to lives of sin. The darkness is creeping in, eating away at the light. Faith is dying out. Year by year, more falls away."

He takes a long drag and blows the smoke out of the corner of his mouth. I don't know what to say. I close my eyes and listen to the silence. The silence takes me fierce and blindly. I lean back and stare at the smoke-stained ceiling. The shadows upon the beige-colored felt dance from the wavering headlights. Suddenly they become one and I realize I am staring into darkness.

That darkness will take us all.

"It will take us all, Bobby. There are those of us, assigned by God, who work on this plane, fighting back against the Prince of Darkness. We are few, but we are persistent. Soul by soul, we will win back the world. We will win by the eradication, the purification, of the demons from this world."

I take another drag and feel the ash coat my tongue. "No, I can't. I can't do this. If it is right, then why do I feel so much guilt? They deserved to die. I know they did. But if I was doing God's wishes, then why do I feel so hollow? I can't do this... I wish I never made it off that beach."

The Gateman's eyes grow darker. The black circles under his sockets start to expand, encircling; he looks like a crazy raccoon. The darkness surrounds his eyes.

Two pools of ink. "You ignore this calling, and the beach is exactly where I will put you. And you will die. You will feel the searing pain of death as you pass from this realm, as you fall down the tunnel. But you will not like where the tunnel leads. It leads to the Prince. He will be waiting for you. You can sit at his feet and suffer, in darkness, for eternity. On the other hand, you can fight him here. Here on this Earth, you can fight him, you can slay his demons, do what you were bred to do. Let us face it, Bobby, you were never anything more than cannon fodder. With that ten-cent head, and those massive guns you call arms, all you were ever good for was a fight. You are a soldier, Bobby. Now it's time to go to war."

He clutches the wheel tight and swings his body low to reach the pedals. He slams the breaks down with ferocity; his cheeks flush red. We come to a screeching halt. The snow falls gently outside the window. Out in the darkness, I can make out the shiny ribbon of a moonlit river. A hillside, slowly sloping, stretches out in front of us, coated with a soft white blanket left-over from the storm. The flakes fall softly now, glittering in the moonlight as the clouds part and the stars peek through. "GET OUT," he says.

I do not hesitate. I cannot bear to spend a second longer with this man. I open the door and step out into the cold bite of the night. The wind laps at my neck and my ears, stinging them with the reality that, despite the storm's end, the world is still frozen. To my right, the pointed tower of a steeple looms against the sky. Up high, along the spire, two windows glow like eyes, looking down upon me. I see headstones littered upon the hilltop. A black, wrought iron gate stands before me. Red bricks cover the recently plowed and salted streets. Behind me, the roar of a city.

My driver rolls down his window and then pulls himself up and out. He sits upon the doorframe and smokes his cigarette. He blows another smoke ring that disappears into the night sky. He points towards the stones. "There. There upon the hill. You must go there. That is where you will find him."

I look back at him, confused; I can feel the skin upon my forehead wrinkle, giving away my ignorance. Find what?

He spits at the ground and frowns. "There, you damn fool. That is where you go. That is where you will find him."

"Find who?"

"Your sponsor. He is there."

I gaze back upon the hill and see nothing. Gravestones, snow, coldness, and nothingness. "I don't understand."

"Walk amongst the stones. Listen well. You will find him. You must listen to him. Your soul depends upon it."

Chapter Twenty-Three

The interrogation room door squeaked; in walked my rat-faced lawyer. He appeared less sweaty than our last encounter, perhaps he was now more at ease, having met me once before. Or perhaps now he was less concerned about the prospect of me leaning across the table and gnawing his pointy nose off. With him sauntered in a crab-like creature, a slightly balding stout little man with legs a little bit too short. His overall appearance took me for a second, as his build and movements resembled the Gateman's, but he lacked the pointy teeth and snarled impression. He looked like a worn-out insurance claims adjuster.

I sat with my hands cuffed behind the chair again. I had grown accustomed to the feeling of metal against my skin. My lawyer, in an attempt to kiss my ass, dropped a green-colored glass ashtray on the metal table before us, then delivered a pack of reds from his suit coat and lit me up a butt. Rather than obliging— the last thing I wanted to do was to become friendly with this jackoff—I shook my head and leaned back in the chair. He crushed the butt against the bottom of the ashtray in dismay.

"Robert, I'd like you to meet Dr. Poland. He's gone through the results of your MMPI test and would like to speak with you."

The doctor sat down across from me. He carried with him a leather-bound notebook; it overflowed with papers. He seemed a bit disorganized; as he opened the notebook several papers spilt out and flipped to the floor.

My lawyer said, "I'll get that." The doctor shuffled in his seat, struggling to get comfortable. The smell of nervous sweat oozed from his glistening skin.

"So, what's the verdict? Am I crazier than a retarded monkey? What's the deal, doc?"

The shuffling subsided; he folded his hands on top of his mound of papers. He spoke in a high-pitched, nervous voice. Obviously, he was well abreast of my reputation. "Before we begin it, I would like to administer another test."

"Come on... out with it. I'm dying to know."

He shook his head; a bead of sweat rolled down across the wrinkles of his forehead. "It is necessary that I collect as much information as possible before I can make an informed diagnosis. The MMPI test is but one method that I use. Are you familiar with the Rorschach test? I think you might find it enjoyable."

"I've heard of it. That the one where I gotta look at a bunch of pictures and tell you what nonsense I see?"

"It seems you are familiar to some extent. Yes, I am going to show you a series of items, but not pictures. Rather, inkblots, images—they call them plates. You're to look at the inkblots and tell me what they represent to you."

"Sounds silly to me."

"The test was created in 1921 by Hermann Rorschach and has been widely accepted in the field of psychology for over seventy years. We use this test to analyze personality and emotional functioning. It is quite a compliment to the MMPI. I prefer not to rely on one method, but by imploring more than one, I can make a full diagnosis, without test bias. Shall we begin?"

I sat up in my chair and hunched my shoulders forward. I looked up at the lawyer who stood in the corner, arms folded about his chest. "I think I'll take that cigarette now," I said, nodding towards the ashtray. He picked up the pack, carefully placed the cigarette in my mouth, and lit up the butt. The match flame felt warm, scorching my lips.

Dr. Poland said, "Let us begin." Amongst his mountain of papers, he produced a manila folder; inside, I could see the corners of photographic quality paper. "It is important not to get nervous. Tell us honestly what you see in the pictures. It is in your best interest to understand fully your mental health. You can turn the card, look at it from different angles, take your time and provide us with your best possible answer."

I puffed on the cigarette and exhaled from the corner of my mouth. "Gonna be hard to turn the picture with my hands tied behind my back..."

The Doc's red, bloodshot eyes grew large like sand dollars; I could sense what he was thinking.

My lawyer spoke up, "Just tell us which way you want Dr. Poland to move the picture for you and he will."

"Fair enough," I said. I shifted in my chair; one of my cheeks felt numb, all pins and needles. My shoulders were tired; it was hard to sit like this.

Dr. Poland produced the first image from his packet. His sweaty sausage-like fingers shook as he pushed the picture across the table. "Tell us what you see here. This is the first plate; I will show you ten in total."

I chewed on the cigarette; the smoke burned my eyes. I squinted; my tear ducts felt raw, dehydrated. I saw before me the image of a bat. "It looks like a bat, or a moth or something. Or if I'm looking straight down on it, it kind of looks like it could be the top of some sci-fi type spaceship or something. Depends upon which angle I take. Can I consider angles?"

"You can consider anything you like when interpreting the cards. It is how you see the image; we cannot tell you the right or wrong way. There is no right or wrong way, only how you interpret the image before you."

"Well, I guess I'd say it mostly looks like a bat. So, am I crazy then or what?"

He pulled the image back and stuffed it in his folder. The paper caught the edge; he stuffed it in, bending the photo. "I cannot share with you any interpretations of your answers until we get to the end of the test. I wouldn't want to influence your responses in any manner." He produced the second image and placed it upside down in front of me. "Are you ready for the second plate?"

I nodded, "Sock it to me, boss."

He flipped it over; it was not in black and white. Blotches of red filled the top and bottom of the image. "What do you see here?"

"Can you turn this one sideways?"

He nodded and turned the image. I squinted; the red oozed off the page. I had seen it before. Blood.

"Turn it back."

He obliged. I stared at the image, not sure what to say. Did I want to seem normal? Was that my goal? Of course, I knew in my mind that the more normal I seemed, the more likely it was I'd wind up in general population. I sat there for a minute contemplating, chewing the cigarette end as the smoke wafted up my nostrils.

What did I want? How did I want this to go, to shake down, to play out? Prison would be hell, yet I'd lived hell for so long perhaps it would be a welcomed change. I had animal-like tendencies, this I knew. To them I was a monster. But they didn't understand my story. I was only doing my duty. What God intended. Where was I better off? Amongst the poor, slobbering fools of a loony bin? Or right there in the pit? In the cage with the demons... I had it then. I knew where I needed to go. I needed to go to county. I needed to find my way into lockup. Those poor bastards locked in there with me... just think of the opportunity... I could complete my mission. But was I still on my mission? Cotton, that son of a bitch, had left me, abandoned me. I was an orphan now, alone, confused, and lost.

At least in prison I could crush some skulls. So, I decided to tell the truth. Obviously, I was not insane. I couldn't have made the whole thing up. I met the Gateman. I saw him with my own eyes. Tasted that awful beer. No use in pretending I was crazy. Might as well tell the truth.

"I see blood. A tunnel. A gateway of some sort. I don't know, this one isn't as clear as the last one."

He snorted and then spoke. "Do your best. The images that are coming, some will seem more easily known than others; the purpose of the test is to mix it up a bit so that there is control."

"Well, I see the blood more clearly than the tunnel. Like something is bleeding. It looks almost as if the blood is moving, but I can't tell what exactly is bleeding. Almost looks like the sides of a mouth, when you turn it sideways. Like someone punched in the mouth." I chuckled through clench teeth, and then puffed on the cigarette.

"I see," he said. He delicately pinched his index fingers together, then, clasping the center bridge, he pushed his glasses back up his sweaty nose. I took another puff of the cigarette and blew the smoke across at him.

"You judging me, boss?"

He shook his head. "No, no, no. I'm merely assessing your response." He took a few notes on his yellow legal pad with his shiny, executive-style blue pen. The value of that pen could have fed me for a week.

As he sat there writing, I started to think about prison. I saw an orange sea of menacing, foul creatures, clad in their standard prison issued jumpsuits. I pictured myself amongst them, the only bright light, a bastion of good amongst all the evil. I would be a soldier, a crusader; I would take back the holy land, beating them to a pulp over and over. Of course, I could not fully eradicate them. While Massachusetts didn't have the death penalty, I'd wind up in solitary confinement for sure if I were too violent. That would do me no good whatsoever. Alone, there in the dark. I could picture nothing worse than sitting in the dark, alone with my thoughts. Truly then I'd be a prisoner... a prisoner of my own mind. So, while I suppose I couldn't kill them, it sure would be fun to kick their ass repeatedly. If eternity was my damnation, eternity upon this rock, then at least I could stomp on some demons while I was here and have a little fun.

He produced the third card.

"Easy. I see a squashed frog. Someone stepped on him, crushed his little bones. He's bleeding on the ground."

He pulled back the card, took a second to write a few more notes that I couldn't make out. The smoke from the cigarette started to burn my nostrils. It became difficult to hold it in my mouth. He placed the fourth card before me. I took a puff as I leaned over.

I felt a sudden sense of fear at the image. I must have broadcast it all over my face as the doctor sat back quickly in his chair. He nervously twirled his pen amongst his fingers. His eyes darted back and forth; no eye contact.

I saw Satan, or what looked like Satan, to me anyway. He stood towering over me, his feet aiming to crush and destroy my utter insignificance. It was terrifying. Certainly, I could not tell him that.

"I see a soldier, a samurai maybe? He is standing above me, looking down at me. I'm at his feet, perhaps I'm lying on the ground and he's staring down at me, hovering above me, ready to strike."

That felt like a safe answer. No way was I going to tell this guy what I truly saw.

He placed the next image in front of me. For some reason this one was difficult to look at. It certainly looked like a bat again, although different, more like a bat man or a moth man of some sort. I was having trouble concentrating though; it was as if the image was moving before me. I could almost make out the shapes of little, miniscule people mulling about. No, more like writhing about.

"This one of those eye trick pictures?"

He looked at me curiously. His glasses slid down his nose. He caught them before they crashed to the table. "Please elaborate."

I said, "You know… hold on," and took another puff. The cigarette had burned down too low; it was about to singe my lips. I looked up at the lawyer. "Hey, you suit. Can you take this? Either that I'm going to spit it at this doctor fellow." He left his corner position, cautiously took the cigarette from my lips, and smashed it in the ashtray. Ash tinged his fingertips; he wiped them off quickly on the inside of his jacket.

Dr. Poland asked, "What were you saying? Please continue." He twirled the pen at lightning speed.

"You know, one of those eye trick images where it looks like things are moving. I've seen one of 'em before on a billboard downtown. Makes your eyes think things are moving."

"You see moving images in the picture?"

"Yes."

"Tell me what else you see."

I hunched my shoulders forward and shook my arms. Lactic acid nightmare. Hard to hold yourself in one position this long. "At first I thought it was a bat. Looks like a bat, or a bat man. Kind of looks like he's got two crocodile arms. Then it started to swirl a bit. Must be one of those eye trick pictures."

"Very interesting, thank you." He smiled at me. Yellow stained teeth.

I wanted to reach across the table and rip those teeth out. "Tell me what you see then, Doc. What am I supposed to see?" I tried to stand; I lost my balance and the chair crashed back down.

"Now, now, no need for hostility. It is important that we administer the entire test."

"Fine."

He put another card down on the table.

This looks like the gateway to hell I thought. "It's a gateway."

"Hmm," he said. He placed yet another image before me.

"How many of these do I have to go through?"

"Ten in total. Three left, after this one. Take your time. What do you see?"

I squinted at the image. Looked like another tunnel to me. I was starting to see a pattern. I wondered if I was imagining the tunnel I fell through. The one that brought me from France to that cornfield in seconds flat. As I focused, I saw the image come into light. "It's a lamp. One of those reverse image thingies. The lamp is hidden amongst the ink. Tried to trick me with that one, but I saw it."

He then placed a very colorful card on the table. Blues, pinks, grays, and oranges exploded from the image. In the middle, I saw the image of a creature with giant, bat like wings. This was not like a bat man though. More like a dragon man. A demon man. Lucifer himself, standing above the fire, above the pit of hell. No way could I say that though. He would definitely think I was crazy.

"I see a vagina. A big, sweaty vagina. You happy?"

"You need to take this seriously."

"I am. It does kind of, sort of, look like a vagina. Been a while I admit, since I've seen one, but that's what it looks like to me. Course, perhaps my ex-wife had a weird looking gulley hole!"

"Do you see anything else in the image?"

"No."

"You don't see the four-legged animals?" He sat back, seemingly satisfied. He put the expensive pen in his mouth and clamped his teeth upon the end.

There he was again, with that mocking grin. I could feel my blood boil. My cheeks felt hot, flush with rage and fury. "Give me a reason to come across this table, keep smiling like that."

The lawyer finally spoke up. "Calm down, Robert, Dr. Poland is here to help you. He is here to provide his professional diagnosis so we can discuss your plea."

"Fine." I could feel the blood rush from my cheeks. A headache formed instead, drilling from the inside, behind my eyes.

Dr. Poland said, "Only a few more to go. Tell me about this next one."

"I see an explosion. An atom bomb. Mushroom cloud billowing up from the ground. Cloud kind of looks like a cow's face though. That is a weird one. I don't like that one."

The doctor sighed deeply. He stacked the picture with the rest. "This one now is the last card." He placed it on the table. Very bright in color, this one didn't bother me as much as the last one.

"Sort of looks like how I'd imagine a coral reef. Sea life. I see some sea horses floating around in there."

He returned the card to the stack, and then began to stuff them into his briefcase. "Very good, Mr. Turner. That completes our test."

I slumped down in my chair, attempting, with no success to relax my shoulders. "Well, how did I do?"

He stood up and backed away from the desk. "I will type up my diagnosis and provide it back through Mr. Lorenzo here."

Rick Maydak

I shook my head and gritted my teeth. Through clenched teeth, I said, "No, no, no. That is not what you said. You said you'd tell me the results of that MMBBI or whatever the hell you called it test. Then you made me look at these pictures. You tell me what you think." I clenched my fists and felt a searing sensation scream down my arms to my mitts.

The doctor glanced over at the lawyer; he clutched his leather-padded notebook as he backpedaled towards the door.

Anger welled up inside me. "Do you think for one moment I'm going to let your stumpy little ass out of here without telling me the result of the test?" I pulled forward with my cuffs as hard as I could. I felt my shoulder pop and my arm go limp. Twisting like a contortionist, I freed myself from the chair and stood up. I kicked the chair behind me; it fell to the floor with a bang. "You owe me an answer." My left arm hung at my side like a dead limb.

My lawyer stood between us, arms outstretched. His eyes darted frantically towards the mirrored glass. "Now, Mr. Turner, there is no need to get upset. Dr. Poland will provide the results as soon as he can type up his diagnosis."

"Bullshit. He told me at the beginning he would give me his diagnosis today. Now. While we are here." I flipped my dead arm up over my head; the cuffs passed before my eyes. With my working arm, my right arm, I grabbed the glass ashtray and smashed it against the table. It broke in two; I smiled at the sharp edges.

My lawyer yelled, "Mr. Turner! Stop!" Before he could say anything else, I grabbed a glass shard, brought it to his neck, and then threw his body back

208

against the door with a thump. I leaned in hard against him with my body, using my hips to hold him in place. My left arm dangled like a dead tree branch while my forearm pressed against his neck. The broken glass dagger pressed gently against his jugular. I squeezed it so hard I cut my palm; blood trickled down my wrist.

The doctor scuttled into the opposite corner and cowered to his knees. He clutched his briefcase against his chest. I could hear shouting outside the door and the shuffling of feet.

"Now listen up, you fucking pigs! I have this rat's back firmly against this door. You push it open and you'll shove this guy's birdlike neck right into this piece of glass—do you understand?" The shuffling ceased. I heard murmurs and clicks. No doubt, they were getting their guns ready. "You stay out there or this man dies; and the blood will be on your hands, not mine. I warned you!"

The lawyer's lips trembled like two oversized maggots. I could smell his stress sweat waft through his clothes.

"Please," he stuttered as sweat squeezed its way through the pours of his face. "Please don't do this. No good can come from this. Please release me. I have kids."

I pushed my knuckles against his Adam's apple. The sharp edge of the glass pierced his skin slightly; a trickle of blood rolled down his throat and stained his collar.

"You," I said, through clenched teeth. "You shut up." I looked towards the doctor huddling in the corner, a frightened dog amidst a sea of loose papers that he clutched against his breast. The briefcase lay upon the floor, busted open. "And you talk. Now, or I push forward."

"What do you want me to say?" His fingers lost their grip; some of the papers wisped to the floor.

"Well, am I crazy or not? Or am I just a very pissed off man? Out with it! I want the results." I could smell the lawyer's breath, egg salad, his face mere inches from mine. My ear was almost against his lips as I cocked my head sideways, staring down the doctor. I could feel his lips trembling softly against my skin.

The doctor looked up at me like a cowering child who had disappointed his alcoholic father. His glasses dangled precariously on the tip of his nose.

"What can I say that will stop you from doing this? From hurting him..." He paused for a moment, "Or me?"

"Tell me the truth and I won't hurt anyone. Lie to me and I'll know. I can smell a liar a mile away. I want the absolute truth. I'm tough, I can take it. Am I crazy, Doc? Do I have a screw loose? What about those inkblots? What was all that nonsense about? Tell me what you wrote down. Tell me what you think."

"The results aren't good. If you want me to tell you the truth, they're not good."

"Explain. What do you mean; did I see the wrong things? Explain yourself. I don't mind cutting this pig's throat. You know I've killed. What's one more? I'm already looking at life!"

He dumped his papers to the floor and picked up his leather-bound notebook. Opening to his notes inside, he began to read to me.

"The first image, you said it was a bat. Many folks see this common answer. Also acceptable is a moth, any winged creature. The second image..." He paused for a second, "The second image, you said you saw blood, lots of blood about a bloody mouth. This is concerning. The most common answer is two people looking at one another. Instead, you focused on the colors, seeing the red, interpreting it as blood. If you can't see the people it is believed that the subject has trouble relating to people."

"No shit. Continue."

"The third image, you said looked like a squashed frog. Again, you mentioned you saw lots of blood. I honestly do not know what to make of this response. This card is typically used to determine whether the subject has any homosexual tendencies. People see either two women with large breasts or two men with protruded erections. You saw neither. Rather, you saw a dead animal, and again with the blood reference. I feel there is much hatred in you."

"So, you're saying I'm not gay then…"

"This is a controversial card. I for one feel that it is useless. I don't think an inkblot can determine whether or not one is a homosexual."

The lawyer's shirt was wet and clammy; he was starting to soak through. I could feel his sweat meander its way through the hairs upon my arm, leaking like motor oil.

I asked, "Then why the hell did you waste my time?"

"It is important; it's part of a series. You have to take the test as one. For the sake of completeness."

The lawyer whimpered.

"You be quiet," I said. Outside the door, I could hear the shuffling of many feet. They were amassing. "You sons of bitches, in case you can't see from the fucking mirror, I've got this piece of glass right on this milquetoast's jugular. You make one move to open this door and he's going to spray like a broken hose, you got it?!" The taste of nicotine and tar backed up in my throat. I spit in the opposite corner, then stared back at the doctor. "Continue!"

With his hand, he wiped the sweat from his neck, then ran his fingers through what strands of hair he had left upon his head. Due to the sweat, his hair slicked back, giving him the look of an Italian mobster. "Fine, fine.

The next card is the father figure card. You saw a menacing samurai staring down at you. Anything conceived as threatening indicates that you don't handle authority very well."

"Again, no shit. Go on."

"Do I have to go card by card?"

"I want to know your diagnosis. What about the next one, the second bat."

"Had you stopped at bat, I would not be concerned. However, you saw crocodile-headed arms. This indicates hostility. That is not as bad as what you indicated next. You saw moving people. To use your words, you said that they were writhing amongst the ink. This is a concern to psychologists."

"Why? What does it mean?"

He stood up and began to pace the room. "And then the other cards, you said you saw a lamp in card seven. You could not see the animals, the four-legged creatures in the next card. In card nine, you saw a mushroom cloud, an explosion. This indicates severe paranoia. These results along with the result in card five tells me all I need to know. But I would never diagnose without also considering the MMPI."

I pushed my fist against the lawyer's throat; he let out a muffle, and then swallowed hard, gulping at the air.

I went on, "So tell me about that test then. I deserve to know. You fuckers made me sit in front of that computer screen answering those sadistic questions as if it was some sort of satanic exam. I deserve to know."

Dr. Poland stopped his pacing and stared at his feet. "The MMPI has ten scales in total. The scales measure different potentials of psychological disorders. I don't like to view them in isolation, which is why I gave you the Rorschach, to see if the results coincided. I am very concerned. You scored terribly in scale 6, indicating a high degree of paranoia. You also scored terribly on the social introversion scale, and poorly on scale 4, which shows a lack of acceptance of authority and amorality. This coincides with your Rorschach. But I won't tell you what I'm really concerned about unless you drop that piece of glass."

"I won't. Tell me."

"Drop it or you can forget it."

"I'll gut this pig, I told you."

He took his glasses off and wiped the condensation off on his cufflinks. "No, you won't."

"Why do you say that?"

"Because I realized something as we've been talking. I read your file. I know you won't kill him because *he's not on your list.*"

I felt the pain behind my eyes get worse. A jackhammer went off in my head. A sudden, powerful migraine hit me like an aluminum baseball bat. I could hear the ping as it hit my skull; stars formed in my eyes and I dropped the shard.

The door pushed open as an army of police officers barreled into the room. The lawyer went flying to the ground. I fell hard on my back; the piece of glass stabbed into the underside of my left leg, puncturing the skin.

A red-headed, overweight, ginger-faced cop yelled, "Don't move!" He dug his knee into my sternum. "You move and I'll shoot you! Don't think I won't!"

It felt as if his knee would crush my abdomen, like cracking open a lobster tail. He breathed heavily above me, gut billowing from his slacks.

The doctor stood up and walked over to me. I turned my head to the side and stared at his shoes. Loafers tinged with dried mud. I could barely talk, the cop's knee pressed down so hard. He held the barrel of his gun against the side of my cheek. Two fat, white, donut-eating cops sat on my legs. Out of the corner of my eye, I saw the lawyer struggle to stand... deep pit stains ruining his suit coat.

I whispered, "Doc. Please... you got to tell me."

The doctor stood next to me, hands in his pockets. He looked down at me like a disappointed father, disciplining his son. "You did very poorly in scale eight. You have bizarre thought processes, strange perceptions. You have no family and are socially alienated from the world. You saw the lamp in card seven of the Rorschach. You saw people moving amongst the ink of plate five."

He leaned in. I grimaced as the cop pushed the gun into my cheekbone. The doctor continued, "You live in a hole in the ground that you dug in a cemetery. You claim to speak to a dead preacher. You claim to have seen ghosts. You also claim to have been born ninety years ago. You claim to have visions that only the dead preacher can interpret for you. You told the police you are on a mission from God. You believe you are killing demons and culling the earth of their filth."

He paused, and then stood back up. "You failed the tests I administered that coincide with these delusions. I am sorry, Mr. Turner. You are not crazy. I'd never use that term."

"What... what would you use?" I asked, stuttering, the headache shattering my synapses. Bolts of red-colored lightning dominated my vision. "Please..."

The doctor cleared his throat. He took a moment to pick up some of his papers. Stuffing them into his notebook, he said, "Schizophrenia. You have Schizophrenia, Mr. Turner. One of the worst cases I've ever seen."

Chapter Twenty-Four

I'm sinking in the black. Water surrounds me, cold like ice. I fear for my life. The only sound my heart thundering in my head. I see nothing. Black emptiness; the void.

I sense something swim past my legs. A soft siren song fills my ears. I feel the gentle kiss of a mermaid's lips caress my feet.

Thank God, I am saved. My rescuer. My heroine, my love. Her lips tickle my toes. I hear laughter.

Then I feel a sharp pain as her fingernails dig into my skin. My nerve endings scream. She tears at my flesh. Blood fills the water around me. The whore.

She pulls me down.

Chapter Twenty-Five

It seems like such an odd proposition, to wander through a graveyard at night, hoping that the dead will somehow come alive and talk to you. I must be crazy. This is madness. Certainly, I feel a level of madness descending on me, or perhaps the feeling that I am somehow the victim of a practical joke cooked up by the divine. The big dog upstairs must really be getting a kick out of this, assuming He is there at all. I have no real reason to believe in the big dog other than recent events pointing to His existence. Certainly, I have tried, over the years, and despite the fact that I have been told directly by one of His agents of His existence, I have to say, I still spend my nights in flat out denial.

It is much easier to live in denial of the divine than to embrace it fully. It is the consequences that matter. If you fear that you will spend the rest of your eternal life burning in the unholy flames of Hell, chances are, you will approach each day with a desire to do good. To be good. To not be such a sonuvabitch to everyone.

They say proof is in the pudding, after all. And here before me, in the cold Boston night, amongst broken tombstones jutting out from mounds of snow, I have my proof. I feel more vulnerable at this moment than I ever have in my entire life. For before me, amongst the stones and swirling snowflakes, stands my evidence. Rather, floats my evidence.

He is not substantial, he is not wearing clothes, nor is he naked. Nor is it a he or a she, actually, at least not visually. I only know it is a he because of the way his voice penetrates my ears and soul as he speaks.

He says, *Welcome,* in a voice that seems to come from miles away, a voice deep, haunting, and yet tired. He sounds exhausted. This poor bastard needs a nap; his first one, his dirt nap, obviously didn't take.

I glance around to see if I am alone. The wind howls as the snow spirals through the air. Moonlight penetrates through a crack in the clouds, lighting up the Charles River that looms behind the stones. Off in the distance, coming deep from within the bowels of the city, I hear the roar of a plow and the sound of metal scraping against concrete and brick. A few flashing lights reflect off windows that ping pong the light through the city streets. But there are only two souls out tonight. One is mine, the other floats in front me. Everyone else is safe behind closed doors, fires burning, radiators blasting. Boston freezes like the North Pole.

He has no legs, none that I can see anyway. This being of light, a dense sort of glow without a glow, starts to form shape around the torso. His midsection is blurry, almost like static on a television, his face is flat and smooth, with dense, sunken sockets where eyes should be. No nose or lips that I can see. The spirit holds his arms out to his side; in each hand, (although I can scarcely make out any fingers) he holds what appear to be lanterns. Behind him, to the right, above the trees and gravestones, looms a colonial church. I recognize the church, I've seen it before, in textbooks, but I cannot place it. Something significant. Something relevant to our collective past.

I know I should be afraid, but I'm not. I just spent one hour in a taxicab from hell that somehow crossed all of upstate New York in one-tenth the time it should have taken. But instead, I'm curious. I am here for a reason. I am supposed to be here.

Welcome, he says again, sounding exhausted. He makes a grunting sound, coughing yet not coughing.

My mind races, searching for something to say—anything to break the confusion. I say, "I thought the dead couldn't get sick."

He says nothing, just hovers there, lanterns held out at the side, shoulders sagging under the weight. The longing look in the empty eye sockets gives me the impression that he is not a happy soul. He seems lost, longing for something or someone else.

I say, "Why don't you put the lanterns down?" I huddle in my coat. The wind picks up and tosses a swirl of snow down my neck, stinging the exposed skin beneath my chin.

He hovers but does nothing more than cock his head from side to side, as if studying me. The lanterns drop lower but do not leave his grip; he slumps a bit forward as if the weight is unbearable. Grunting again, he only says, *Welcome.*

Tree branches creak as the wind picks up. Behind me, a sign flaps against a shop door. He holds up a lantern, and points into the graveyard, as if suggesting I should enter.

I stumble up the steps towards the spirit; he does not appear to get closer as I ascend, rather the opposite, he seems further away with each step I take, as if he is slowly back-pedaling down a hallway that I cannot see. Smaller now, he is but a faint whisper of light that is slowly fading. He speaks one last word, only the word *Welcome*, one last time before he pops from existence. And just like that, he's gone.

It is cold here in the dark amongst the stones.

If you have ever been in a graveyard at night then you know it can be quite a spooky place, to say the least. I never viewed myself as being afraid of much, but when you stand in a graveyard in the dark of night, many hours past the witching hour, then get a nice welcome from a tired ghost, well, things can be spookier than normal.

I have often marveled at those who would say that they would be terrified of a ghost. I have heard people say that witnessing a ghost would be the most awful thing that they could imagine. I offer a different viewpoint. If you see a ghost, celebrate. Even if the ghost is an asshole and not a nice fella like my welcoming party here. Even if the ghost rearranges all your dishes at night or pours blood in your toilet or hangs diapers upside down from the ceiling. Even if your ghost is the biggest prick you've ever met, dead or alive, I still stand to reason that you should celebrate.

Here is why: now you know. You FUCKING KNOW that there is something after death. And that knowledge is quite powerful to your life. Do not be so self-important as to think you now have a pest you need to eradicate like a common city rat. Don't hire a ghost buster; try to make friends with the dude. Don't bring in a priest, do not do an exorcism. Play chess, watch television. Shit, he may end up being the best friend of your undead life. However, chances are, he will in fact be a prick, which is why I believe these fuckers are here in the first place. They must have done something. They are lost. They are stuck in between. I wonder what my friend here did. He did something.

This is what I tell myself as I stand here in the dark, the hairs on the back of neck standing at salute. My world is crumbling, my psyche taking a major hit, my sanity, certainly always questionable, now, teetering on the brink of disaster. However, I feel good to be alive. It is better than the alternative. Imagine being stuck here forever like that poor bastard. Time slowing to a crawl. Living forever. Sounds awful. Oddly, I do feel haunted. Perhaps that comes with the territory, whether they mean to or not, they leave you haunted. Why did he carry those lanterns? They seemed so heavy in his hands, and yet, it didn't seem like he could put them down if he wanted to. I wondered what he did. And just who super-glued those lanterns to his poor dead fingertips?

Maybe one day I'll find out the answer to that question.

Amongst the snowdrifts, I see a path, shoveled perhaps six or seven hours before; now snow covers it, but it is not nearly as deep as the banks that loom on both sides. The wind creates drifts amongst the stones; some are almost completely buried, others only on one side, the wind daring to discriminate.

I walk down the winding path, amongst the bare trees as the wind howls and the city roars in an eerie silence behind me. No cars upon the city streets in this Nor'easter.

I stop for a moment and look backwards down the path, towards the gate, but do not see the spirit. I see townhouses that run perpendicular to the graveyard. I wonder what it must be like to live across from the dead. I imagine a little kid up there now, up late at night, way past his bedtime, staring out his bedroom window, seeing me standing there at the gate, talking to that tired ghost. Would he have seen anything? Would he have seen what I saw? Or would he have seen nothing but a tired wino standing there out in the elements, a walking mental patient, talking to the brick wall as if it were his best friend?

I hear a crack as a branch loses its war with the snow and careens towards the earth. It lands about twenty feet down the path, which turns my gaze back. It is then that I see it. The only stone that stands completely free from the snow, as if God himself commanded that not a single flake should taint its sacred head. The snow beneath my feet crunches as I walk closer. As it comes into focus, I realize it is not a headstone I am looking at, it is more of a box. An old brick box, jutting upwards from the earth. Only one word adorns the side. "Mather" it says in big letters across the brick facade.

Despite all I have witnessed, despite my bumpy car ride time warp through the snow with my bourbon swilling ageless wonder from France, despite seeing a ghost for the first time in my life, despite the realization that perhaps I really did die and get reborn on that beach—despite all that, I finally feel sheer terror.

The box seems to sense this, as it seems to shake, ever so slightly, vibrating in the night. It gives off a tinny like hum, buzzing, bee or wasp-like. I can't tell you why, but I want to place my hand upon the tomb.

Slowly, I approach, apprehension building in my chest, my heart heavy, thumping, as I reach outward with my hand. What will happen? Why do I sense I'll be shocked with some sort of electricity? I'm nervous like I'm about to touch an electric fence. I lay my hands upon the stone. It is not as I expect. It is warm. Not hot, not burning like a cauldron, but warm, warm and inviting like mom's cookies.

A voice says, *Welcome.* It is different from my welcoming lantern-holding friend. This is a powerful voice. An orator's voice. This is a voice that could carry, that could command a room, captivate a population, start a war, or mesmerize a congregation.

I hold my hands firmly against the warm stone, enjoying the warmth that it offers my cold, shivering fingers. The voice booms again.

Welcome home, Mr. Turner.

I recognize this voice. It is the one in my head.

Chapter Twenty-Six

There was a lot of media at my trial. The killing of a priest was big news, good for headlines, great for ratings. I was a television sensation, a public menace, a deranged lunatic, a monster straight out of a Hollywood movie. Sweaty little men with various kinds of badly groomed facial hair packed the courtroom full to capacity. They feverishly typed away on their tablet computers. I would make the morning copy or blog or whatever it was that people read these days. The room smelled of stress sweat and feet.

I would be on the channel five news; they would talk about how the cops captured me, and they would sensationalize my living conditions. A reporter would be coming to you live from the North End. There would be footage of Cotton's tomb, video of my cot, empty soup cans, and dirty ashtrays. They would drone on for hours about how I lived there deep in the ground, a walking zombie, a killer, a stalker, a midnight wraith. Tabloids would suggest I was a rapist, a sodomite, a pedophile, jacking off every night amongst the gravestones of dead colonial heroes.

I would get my twenty minutes of fame, they'd be sure of it, and then I'd fade away from their memory.

The priest killer, put away forever, another lunatic, another confused paranoid schizophrenic.

Just what drives a man to these conditions they would ask? They'd wonder how my delusions started, how I formed my beliefs, how I could possibly claim the things I claimed. They would never know that the priest I killed molested those boys and that I had rid a demon from the world. They would never know the truth.

Question was… did I know the truth? Paranoid schizophrenic. That is what they called me. Hearing it now, sitting here next to my rat-faced lawyer, coming from their mouths, it certainly did sound like I was insane. Dr. Poland's tests all but confirmed it. Cotton's voice had left me. I had no more visions. I felt normal for the first time in a long time. Yet, here they would crucify me for insanity.

The jury was composed mostly of soccer moms and business clad sad sacks. This one woman in particular would not look at me. The others would glance over from time to time but not her. She wore a blue scarf about her neck that matched the caked-on blue eye shadow that looked like twin lakes beneath her bright blue eyes. Her hair was out of style, a perm that matched the eighties more than today. She would not look at me at all. I took this as a game of course, and stared her down, seeing if she could catch me looking at her out of the corner of her eye. After a few moments, I could tell that she did; her eyes darted everywhere but at me, conveying her nervousness.

I almost laughed when Dr. Poland took the stand. He appeared comical to me, he looked like an egg with legs. He was dressed up for the occasion, light blue suit complete with bow tie. Of course he wore a bow tie, of course he did. Only a guy like him would.

My lawyer stood up and approached the bench. The Judge, a middle-aged black man with a frosty mustache said, "You may begin."

It was strange listening to what they said now. Now that Cotton's voice did not cloud my mind, now that I had been able to get several nights of restful sleep, no dreams, no visions, no horrible nightmares, I felt good. And from what Dr. Poland told that murder of crows that constituted the jury, that throng of soccer moms, I too began to realize the truth.

He said I experienced paranoid delusions. That I believed that I was on a crusade gifted to me by an agent of the Lord. That I believed that a dead preacher from Boston's past talked to me on a constant basis. That I cut myself off from society. That I broke into a cemetery and dug a hole into the Mather tomb, desecrating part of the city's history. He talked about how I had failed the MMPI, how I saw creatures and people writhing within the Rorschach inkblots.

He said I killed a man. He described how I stalked into the church, went to confessional, and then stuffed a potato on my gun. He talked about how I pulled the trigger and sent Father McKay's gray matter all over the inside of the confessional. He talked about how I went back, drawn like a pig to the trough, to suffer the deacon the same fate; only this time, my luck ran out and they got me. But that isn't true at all. I was set up. Cotton set me up. And I don't know why.

Dr. Poland took a crimson handkerchief from his breast pocket. He wiped the sweat from his brow and addressed the jury. The sound of nervous, scuffling feet and sniffling sinuses echoed through the room. "This particular subject has me more concerned than any patient I've dealt with in the past. There have been many well-documented cases of schizophrenia that have been highly studied. Captured in school journals and textbooks. For example, there was the famous case of the subway killer. This killer believed, beyond the shadow of a doubt, that he was on a Nazi concentration camp train, bound for the gas chambers. Those poor people that sat there, on their way to work—to him, they were Nazi guards. He slaughtered three people with a steak knife before a throng of men jumped on him, taking him to the floor."

The doctor paused for a moment; with his handkerchief, he wiped his glasses. He looked up at me; his eyebrows looked like fuzzy little caterpillars. "This man here," he went on, pointing his glasses at me, "This man here is beyond that. His level of delusion goes beyond what I have ever encountered. His delusions have taken him so fully that he slept in a tomb, an empty tomb at that."

What did he mean empty? Empty?

"We're not sure what he has done to the skeleton. The only thing we know is that the coffin was empty. The bones no longer there. While it is highly possible that someone vandalized the Mather tomb somewhere in our past, it was well documented that Cotton Mather was in fact buried there, in that tomb, up on Copp's Hill."

What is he saying?

My lawyer asked, "What do you think he did with the bones?" He paced the room, his hands clasped behind his back. I watched as my opposition rolled his eyes. The state's lawyer was a fat man with a fat neck in a big black fat suit. With big fat rolling beach ball eyeballs.

"It is uncertain. He thoroughly believes he is talking to Cotton Mather. This aspect of his delusion confounds me. I cannot find any reason, even within his schizophrenia, part and parcel to his paranoia, as to why he would remove the bones. The only explanation I can think of is that he was not aware. Someone moved the bones years ago, before he dug his way in. Alternatively, perhaps the well-documented burial was a farce. It's highly possible the bones were never there to begin with."

My lawyer continued his examination. "This paranoid delusion, this Cotton Mather, entirely within his head, a second personality?"

The doctor shook his head, "No, no. I do not believe it is a full-blown second personality within him. He does not morph into this second person. Patients with split personalities take on the identity of the other. In this case, he only speaks to Cotton. Cotton is a voice in his head. Part of his delusion, part of his paranoia. The patient has invented this character. His condition has led to seclusion. He cannot relate to society. The Cotton Mather invention is a means to human contact, even if it is not real and only exists within the realm of his mind."

My lawyer stared at the jury as he asked, "Is he a cold-blooded killer? Do you believe he acted with full awareness of his actions? Premeditated murder?"

Dr. Poland shuffled in his seat. The sound of typing dominated the room. "He was one hundred percent aware of his actions. The murder *was* premeditated. The bringing of the potato to the crime is evidence enough. And he did return to the scene, to do it again. If it wasn't for the stakeout, he could have killed another. However, while he was aware of his intentions, he was only aware within the realm of his delusion. Within his sickness, he was fully aware. But it was the sickness that drove him."

My lawyer paused and then walked over next to the jury. He put his hand upon the wooden railing and surveyed the crowd. Looking back at the doctor, he said, "Does he belong in a prison?"

The doctor shook his head in disagreement. He addressed the jury as he spoke, "He belongs in a hospital. This man is mentally ill. We must study his brain. His paranoid delusions are grand. We can learn much from him. His crime was unforgiveable. Rather than throwing him in prison, a place he would probably prefer—he in fact probably would welcome it. Remember, he believes he is hunting demons. What better place to find that quarry than within a maximum-security prison? Rather than feeding that beast within him, a crime he committed could lead to good. If we can learn from this subject, think of all the future patients we could aid. This is an opportunity for science. I implore you, make the right decision."

He looked back at me and smiled. I was stunned. I could not comprehend how the bones were missing. I stared down at the floor. Worn wood, scuffed from the boots of endless criminals. Such misery and insanity these walls had seen. Maybe I deserved to be a lab rat. Maybe that was the best end for me, where I belonged. A scientific experiment, a carved-up frog. But one thing just did not sit well with me. Where were the bones? They were there. They had to be there. It did not add up.

Chapter Twenty-Seven

Hell is quite different than I pictured it. I am not sure exactly how most people picture it. I know that some will not at all, will not entertain it for even a moment, too terrified of their own imagination. Others conveniently do not believe in it at all. It is much easier to live your life clinging to the notion that there are no consequences for your own actions. It is freedom. Freedom to rape, pillage, plunder, and fornicate at will. If there is not a hell, there is no need to be nice to your neighbor. No reason to help out your fellow man—instead, you can take a dump right on their front lawn, I mean who cares, right?

If nothing occurs upon death, what is the point of any integrity? Might as well get shitfaced every night, knock off a few banks, and piss on your neighbor's favorite gardenias. With no repercussions, no judgment, you are free to be the most selfish sonavabitch you can be. Be all that you can be. Claw your way to the top; money is everything, cash is king, faith is pointless. Shoot up a mall, kidnap some puppies, and belittle someone stupider than you.

Make fun of the retarded, beat up a little kid. Take a shit in the community swimming pool. Why stop there? Steal a car, crash it through a McDonald's, run over a jogger. Ten extra points if you knock off the shoes.

But... if you do believe in Hell, I can assure you it is more different than you ever thought. Not that I ever really knew what to expect. I suppose I was like most: I pictured fire, brimstone, a bunch of horny demons running around with pitchforks and their exposed pricks hanging and bobbing about.

To tell you the truth, there is very little mention of Hell in the bible. Most of what we know about Hell came from writings over the centuries, interpretations, dreams, Dante's *Inferno*. That is how we picture Hell, straight from the minds of writers and Hollywood directors.

It is very different from what you might think. I suppose I thought in Hell, a man's life of sin would crash upon him in retribution. I always thought that the rapists would be ganged raped themselves by an army of leathery stinking sweaty horny demons. Over and over and over. The Porn star drowned in a pool of ejaculate, over and over and over. The greedy, money stuffed down their throats until they explode, over and over and over. Point being, over and over and over was what I pictured—your own worst sins done back to you for eternity. Over and over and over.

But that is not what it is like. I'll tell you what it's like. I've been there. It's dark. That's it. It's just dark. No light. Close your eyes as tight as you can on the blackest night and there you are: in Hell.

There is no sound, not a peep, just eternal darkness and nothingness as far as you can see, with not a whisper upon the wind. Shit, there is no wind. No sensations. You are not burned at the stake; you are not tortured over and over and over. Instead, you just are. You just are.

You are eternal, that much I do know, there is something there other than nothingness, but it is nothing more than a form of nothingness. There in the black, for all eternity, nothing more than you with yourself. With your own thoughts. Your own mind. Just you and your past, in your head, played over and over and over... so I guess it really is still over and over and over.

I'm here now in the dark. My eyes do not see. My heart does not pound. I do not feel cold, I do not feel anything. I don't know where my feet are, if I have feet, or if I am physical at all. I don't know how long I've been here.

But I know it's long.

I can't blink my eyes or scratch myself. The darkness is colorless. It's hard to say it's black when it is more that it's nothing. I have not seen or heard a demon. No one has tried to pitchfork my ass. I'm not sure if I have an ass. I'm not hungry. I'm not tired. I'm not amped up. I'm not afraid, but I probably should be. Aren't I waiting to burn? Instead, I feel calm. I am just here. I'm not sure where here is. I'm not on earth, I don't think. I'm not beneath, down in the core. I'm not floating amongst the clouds. I'm not on a distant planet. I'm not anywhere.

But I'm still here.

I can see pictures, if you can call it seeing, but it is not really seeing. They are not in front my eyes, they are not in my head, I'm not sure if I possess a head. They are as if they are pictures in a waking a dream. It is as if I'm in my room, in the middle of the dark, during a blackout, the moonlight sucked from the earth. As if I'm sitting up in my bed, awake yet asleep, dreaming of my past. Of her.

Her I see clearly. I can see her freckles. I may not have a face but I can see hers. I cannot touch her. I cannot talk to her, but she seems to notice me somehow. Perhaps it is nothing more than my memory, but she smiles at me. Her teeth glisten in a moonlight that is not there. I smell the saltwater of the ocean behind her, yet I have no nose. I can taste the lingering hint of her lips from a kiss just passed, but I have no mouth.

She does not speak, she just smiles. Her red hair bounces across her bare shoulders. I try in my mind, if I had a mind, to take my gaze from her face but I cannot. She is the only thing I can see with the eyes that I do not have. Behind her the ocean roars, I hear it with ears long since gone. The world around her is out of focus. The only thing I can clearly make out is that smile. It warms and tingles the heart that I no longer have, stopped beating, buried, worm food so long ago.

How long ago I do not know.

I am in Hell. I cannot touch her. I cannot move limbs that I do not have. But her beautiful face—the lingering senses of a time since passed, tingling the nerves long since buried and decayed—brings me but a moment of peace. But then she frowns. She tells me to leave. She tells me she doesn't want to see me anymore.

And my heart sinks. Once again, I am alone.

It is empty here. I am the only one here.

They must all be up there. Running loose. Wreaking havoc.

I should be up there with them.

Rick Maydak

I should be there, hiding amongst the rafters, instead of down here, drowning in the well.

Chapter Twenty-Eight

They sent me to Seacliff Psychiatric Hospital in Fall River, Massachusetts. I found it ironic that the largest mental facility within the state was located in the same town as one of America's most famous lunatics. Lizzie Borden called Fall River home. To this day, there is much debate about whether or not she committed the famous murders. In fact, the courts acquitted her; she was free to live out the rest of her life with her sister, until pneumonia took her.

The town, these days, is quite proud to exploit this "tradition," murderous as it may be. There are local beers brewed in her name, a Lizzie Borden bed and breakfast, and guided tours that you can go on. In fact, I believe the beer is called "Bury the Hatchet," having had one once before as I sat at a craft brew pub in Boston after a kill. It was one of those better kills; I got the bastard right as he was opening his Chrysler LeBaron's trunk. I stabbed him in the back of the neck and then just dumped him in. Took his wallet before leaving and enjoyed a nice meal that night. Chicken parm' with a side of linguine.

Of course, I wouldn't be going on any tours anytime soon. My new home loomed upon the horizon.

The hospital looked more like a Gothic cathedral than a place of wellness. It was apt, I thought, sitting there as the car drove us up, that only a place straight out of a Batman comic book is where I'd end up. The spires stood tall to the heavens. Lightning tore the sky apart; ash-colored clouds stalked the horizon. Perfect, I thought, it could be no other way. Had to look like this.

My room was not much bigger than a prison cell but I did have the room to myself. The bed was a twin size, the mattress stained with the feces and urine of countless other lost souls, the frame a rickety aluminum. There was a toilet behind a doorless partition. Only one dresser, built into the wall. No television, no mirror, no books, no nothing. The walls, a boring vanilla white. Didn't want to rile up the blood.

The room had that nice hospital smell to it, antiseptic mixed with urine.

They sedated me for the better part of six months. It was my fault, really, I can't blame them. My first night in my room I tried to break the door down with my bare hands. For some reason I decided I'd howl like a wolf to see what they would do. I figured that if I was going to be insane, I should at least act the part. I mean, when in Rome, right?

They put me on several different medications. 'Course, they failed to inform me of the side effects; they were of no concern to me as far as they minded.

I quickly found that abnormal weight gain was one of them. I never had six pack abdominals, but I was always in shape. My ninety-year-old frame could pound some pushups, bang out a shitload of pull-ups, and I was quite fond of planks. I kept my military training. Core strength, above all. My body, a tank, a land rover, with cannon arms and classic barrel chest. I prided myself in this.

Back then, back in the hole, down in the earth, there next to Cotton all those years, I kept my regiment. I did pushups every morning, sit-ups and planks every night. I had hung a bar across the roof of the tomb, perfect for pull-ups and reverse grippers. It was important to stay in shape. I had to sculpt my body—I was a killing machine. But these drugs tired me. I was exhausted all the time. And despite the fact that I barely ate I was gaining weight like a sperm whale.

I was thirsty all the time. My mouth felt and tasted like the inside of a fireplace, yet they did not allow me to smoke. This was just the beginning. I started to get nosebleeds, constantly, something that the doctors could not explain as they said it was not a side effect that they knew of.

They kept me to my room. For months on end, I'd sit there and stare at the wall, all the while feeling my muscles atrophy and watch as my stomach grew ever larger.

They would bring me out from time to time to walk a path of grass just outside my room. They kept me separate from the others. I would see other patients off in the distance, but came no closer than a football field. They were easing me in. There were other killers here. I was not alone. Seacliff had a reputation. We were the craziest crazies on earth. The looniest lunatics, the wackiest whack-jobs, the nuttiest nut-jobs.

I hated being alone. I guess I had always been alone, or so they told me. Cotton was a fabrication of my mind. He was not real. I made him up, or so they said.

I was a sicko, a sick, sick, sicko they told me. I had created this story all in my head. I belonged here.

This was truly my home.

The only thing though—as I sat there upon those too crisp, too dry sheets, sheets so smooth they could rip your skin like sandpaper—I realized there was a problem with their arrogant logic. Something that they did not consider; something that kept me grounded in myself. My dog tags. I still had them. They never took them from me. I still wore them around my neck. This was all the evidence that I required. I did not dream up Normandy. I remembered that beach. I remembered the way the boat bounced in the ocean, the way the air smelled like sulfur, the way my ears burned from the booming cannon fire upon the ridge side.

I remembered stalking through that town, the dead man's shoes, the way the beer had tasted. A taste I would never forget. Honey mixed with earth, a touch of grass, and the biting sweetness of too much fermentation. They could drug me, they could accuse me, and they could shut me off from the world. But they could not take reality away from me.

I don't know why Cotton left. He set me up, that asshole, I knew that. Problem was, I did not know why. He had masked my presence from the authorities for years. One time I even walked out right in front of a cop, but because Cotton was with me, the pig never saw me. Just stared at his shoes while shoving a Pop Tart down his throat. It was one of Cotton's special tricks, to keep me hidden.

Why did Cotton betray me? Was I not a good soldier, a proper mercenary? I had failed in my mission, yet no one told me why or how I failed.

Once in here, I did not attempt to count the days. I never did down in the deep either, down in the earth, down in the hole. Once I cleared the first decade, I stopped. There was no point. Made no sense to start now.

I met with doctor after doctor but they never said much. They asked how I felt; asked about my moods, did I sleep, did I eat, and did I feel any side effects from the medication? These seemed like low-level types, none of them possessed the presence or knowledge of Dr. Poland.

Dr. Poland; for some strange reason I began to miss the crab-like psychologist. I found him amusing, he was comical to me. He carried such a strong opinion of me; he seemed to have a genuine interest in me, which made me interested in him.

It was a cold morning when the door opened and in walked the orderly. I had never seen him before, a stout black man, ballpark mid-forties with a beer gut, ashy skin, and bushy eyebrows. Hair in that sort of nineteen-eighties mid-level afro.

I sat up in my hospital gown pajamas; my balls dangled between the fat of my legs. The aluminum frame of the bed creaked beneath my weight. I had to be pushing two seventy. Disgusted with myself, I covered my gut with the folds of the fabric. I asked, "What is it?"

He said, "My name is Malcom. Please come with me." He stood in the doorway, leaning in, his hand firmly grasping the doorknob. "Get dressed; you've been allowed gen pop. You can come to the living room."

"Living room?"

"That's what we call general population. There you can meet other patients. There are books. There are board games. There is a television. The docs have decided you can handle it. The medication, they said, is taking."

"Taking? Taking? You call it taking? If you say so, boss."

I stood up and lumbered over to the dresser. I dressed myself in gray sweatpants and a navy-blue sweatshirt. They didn't offer us much. No wild colors allowed. Did not want to rile up the blood. As I pulled on the sweatshirt, I felt the coldness of my dog tags against my skin.

The orderly stood at the door, holding it open for me. "Gen pop is a good thing. You want to go to the living room. Do you good. Did I mention there's a television?"

"You did."

"Come, I think you'll like it."

The hallway was a nondescript shade of nothing. Whites mixed with beiges mixed with dirt and stains. The tile beneath my feet was a lime green shade of snot. It smelled of disinfectant.

I passed many doors: doors of mahogany, doors of steel, and doors of white. The hallway was longer than I remembered—the last time I had gone this way was on my second day. I remembered very little. The overhead fluorescents buzzed like a hive as we passed by, the orderly steadfast by my side. The hallway was empty, just him and I.

The end of the hallway opened into a room the size of a bus garage. The stench was overpowering. Sweat mixed with skin, salt, and the endless unclean. Hebephrenic life mulled about before me, the lost, the damned, the confused, the rarely showered, hadn't had a bath in two weeks crowd.

There were about six windows on the far wall. I noticed that wrought iron bars were firmly in place; one would not want one of these crazies escaping out into the night, descending upon the unsuspecting town below like some medieval Frankenstein.

Men in hospital gowns sat at little tables playing checkers. A man with long, gangly hair said, "King me!" Across from him, another man sat; he smiled, with many missing teeth and gums too red. He scratched himself as if fleas were insulting his body.

To the far left, in the upper left corner, a television, a tube television from the early nineties suspended against the wall. It cackled, spit, and buzzed to life. Set on CNN; I saw Wolf Blitzer's ugly mug dawn the stage.

The orderly pointed to the television. "See, I told you there was a television. You are welcome to watch. You are welcome to do anything you like, of course, within parameters. You can play some games, check out that shelf of books, or watch television. You are allowed to talk to other patients, although I am not sure you would want to. But you can if you like. We won't stop you." He pointed to the orderlies that stood like gargoyles, prone upon the wall. "We will be watching you, but don't worry; just to make sure you are safe."

My orderly friend took a space upon the wall, leaned back, and stared at the television.

A dusty shelf sat beneath the barred windows. I watched my slippers as I scuffled across the black and white checkered floor over to the window. I thumbed through the musty novels. Not much to choose from, all nonfiction; they did not want us paranoid freaks to adopt some story as our own. Books on wheat and grain production. Books on sports: Red Sox, Bruins, Larry Bird, Pete Rose. A couple of cookbooks in case any of us wanted to dream about a meal that was never coming.

The room smelled like cat piss, yet there were no cats.

A man stood in the corner looking out the window; he rocked back and forth and clutched a stuffed teddy bear. Behind me, there was a row of metal tables. Two sad souls sat across from one another, working feverishly on a puzzle; upon closer examination I could make out that they had finished half of the British Parliament building. Big Ben loomed.

So, it had come to this. This is where I would end. Here amongst the urine-soaked lunatics, dusty books, and puzzle pieces. Amongst the lost, the forgotten, I would wither away. This was my hell. Two things occurred to me. One, if I was truly crazy, if they were right about me, then I'd be stuck here literally forever, their guinea pig, to stick needles in, to shove experimental drugs down my throat, to have my brain examined like a lab rat for the rest of my natural life, and probably even after. They'd carve me up and send pieces of my brain to various universities so privileged white kids could further their education.

The second thought I had though was this: what if I wasn't crazy? What if they had it all wrong? I could not decide which was worse. If they were wrong, and I was aging at a much slower pace than the world, then I would be here forever. This would be my eternity. This was Hell. I had already found it.

There was a couch set against a white support beam, faced towards the television. A man sat there, a man so frail his skin hung like a wet bag against his bones, bones that seemed to poke and jut through like poultry at the supermarket. He had long, greasy hair that hung down across his eyes; longer in the back, it rested upon his shoulders. He sat hunched forward, as if stuck in the position, arms dangling between his knees, knuckles almost touching the floor. He hung his head forward, neck pointed down, like a sick dog, yet his eyes remained trained upwards, staring at the television.

I decided to take a seat next to him; I could barely stand. *These damn drugs*, I thought. I used to be able to chase a demon six city blocks, now, a simple jaunt down the hallway and I was huffing and puffing like a geriatric.

The television buzzed with excitement. Wolf was braying about the Hadron Collider, whatever the hell that was. I sat back and rested my head against the back of the couch; slouching, I slid my ass down in an attempt to get comfortable. My gut protruded outward, making me sick to look at. Fuck.

The man next to me pointed to the television; he hung his head low, yet craned his neck upwards as he spoke, "Those sickly fools going on and on about that collider. Searching for the God particle. Idiots." His hair dangled like a mop.

I said, "'Excuse me?'" I rested my hands upon my stomach. I noticed out of the corner of my eye how my orderly was watching us. "What are you talking about?"

He pointed again. "That super collider. So they find the particle, big deal. Won't destroy God as they hope. They are going to smash atoms together, that's what they're going to do, but those fools don't even understand what they are doing. What if they create a singularity?"

"They're trying to destroy God?"

He placed his hands upon his knees and sat back. He was so frail he looked like a concentration camp survivor. "They're always trying to destroy God. What they don't realize is the closer they get, the more they see the face of God. They aim to do the opposite, yet they will only find more evidence."

I said, "Whatever you say, pal." I leaned my head back and closed my eyes.

He went on, "You ever hear of the Anthropic Principle? That the entire universe was set into motion just for us? Every single aspect of the universe exists to bring about our creation?"

I didn't answer him. I just wanted him to shut up.

He stood up and pointed at the television, "Oh, they would love to prove we're nothing more than some random accident that occurred in a backwater. Oh, they'd love nothing more than to eliminate accountability from their selfish lives. Those fools!"

Malcom, my orderly, interrupted. He hurried over and put his powerful hand upon the man's shoulder. "Jerry, quiet down or I'll take you back to your room."

My newfound friend, Jerry, chewed his gums; his eyes darted back and forth, surveying the hospital personnel who had started to coalesce near the door. He nodded at the orderly and quietly took his seat. After a few moments of silence, he leaned in close and whispered, "The universe is not random. Did you know that gravity is roughly 10 to the 39th times weaker than electromagnetism? That, if it were any less than that, then stars would burn too fast and be too small?"

He produced a red handkerchief from his pocket and blew his nose; his long hair flung wildly. He went on, whispering, leaning in close to my side while stuffing his snot covered rag into his sweatpants. "The nuclear weak force is 10 to the 28th times the strength of gravity. If it were any weaker, the universe would not possess any hydrogen. No hydrogen, no water. How about that, can you imagine no water? No water, no humans; no humans, no beer. Be a travesty."

"No beer would be a travesty," I said, immediately regretting the response. Now he would think I was interested.

"If the difference in mass between a proton and a neutron were not exactly as they are, we'd have no chemistry, no life. It has to be perfect. If the nuclear strong force increased by just two percent, there would be no protons, no atoms. If it were five percent the other direction, there would be no stars. And water, I mentioned water. Think of water, how amazing it is. In its solid state it floats. If it did not float, the Earth would be frozen all the way through. This is the most unique molecule, water is. We are made mostly of water, of course. And they think they can debunk God…" He leaned in and put his head on my shoulder; I could smell his awful, sour milk breath. He whispered as his cheek rested on me, "Those fools. They cling to string theory because it still gives them a randomness aspect."

I sat up; his head slid off my shoulder. He recoiled and his oily hair brushed against my skin. It felt like spaghetti. "Look, pal, not interested."

He stood back up. I could tell he was getting agitated. His face flushed red with anger; his eyes boiled a cauldron black. "When the universe was 10 to the minus 43rd seconds old it had to know how many neutrino types there would be at a time of one second. It had to know this so that when the universe expanded forth it was at the right rate—it's all math, man, all math! We are an equation, someone wrote the code!"

I stood up and started to walk away; the orderly came over and stood between us. "Jericho! I told you that was enough. Now sit down."

He pointed at me and screamed, "Why don't you care? Tell me why you don't care!"

I didn't say anything as I walked towards the door. There, another orderly met me, a pasty-faced ginger who reminded me of that cop—might as well have been his twin. He could tell I wanted to go back to my room, he didn't stop me; rather, he held the door open.

Jericho stood upon the couch and screamed at me while I left. "I know why! I know why you don't care! I know what's inside you! I know!"

As I passed out into the hallway, I could hear Jericho scream to the other psychos within the room. "They think they can disprove what is known? Those damn fools. They turn that thing on and they have a better chance of starting a black hole and sucking us all straight down to Hell than they do of disproving the Almighty. That is all they want to do, those self-important know-it-alls!"

The hallway was long; I could hear Jericho's shouts echo down the hall as I made my way towards my room. "The universe had to know in advance what it was going to be!"

Chapter Twenty-Nine

They say the Romans executed St. Peter upside down. Some say that it was because the Roman soldiers were having quite a bit of fun. Fucking joke to them. Others suggest it was because St. Peter demanded that he was unfit to die in the same manner as his Lord and savior. Legend states the he would not die, which perplexed the drunken Roman soldiers to no end. They stabbed him, tried to burn him with fire, but he would not succumb. Finally, they chopped off his head. This St. Peter could not withstand. It wasn't like his head rolled around shouting obscenities at them.

The real reason scholars suggest that he did not die as quickly as the soldiers preferred was in fact because he was hung upside down. Death in the ordinary position of crucifixion causes suffocation. However, one cannot suffocate while hanging upside down. I suppose we will never know the truth, at least not from the medical community. But, I decided at the very least, I could test the hypothesis. Collect some data. Propose an experiment as it were; you know, contribute to society. So, this is where I was in 1995 after I broke into the Blue Hills Reservation after dark.

The Blue Hills is a beautiful place. I would imagine most folks outside of New England would never have imagined that one could go skiing and see the Boston Skyline all at the same time. It is the last remaining refuge of colonial forest that remains after all these decades of sprawl and so-called progress. Boston is congested. To say the least. A big, congested, sprawling mess of concrete, asphalt, glass, and wires. All laid down upon cow paths from over two hundred years back. A giant, unorganized mess, not counting snobby Back Bay. But out here in the Blue Hills, especially at night, one can find the peaceful serenity of God's country.

The St. Peter crucifixion had always bothered me. Not that I didn't believe the claims or the legend, but mostly because I found it curious that crucifixion upright caused suffocation but upside down did not. I felt that the only way to figure this out would be to do an experiment. There had been much data about the subject of upright crucifixion, but the upside-down method was mere folklore. It was time I found out. And what better way than to hang a demon upside down.

I had left him there three days before. Rumor had it that it was on the third day when they sliced St. Peter's head off—if he lived up to that point, it would be interesting to see if this guy made it that far, as well.

The air was cool; it was one of those mid-October nights where the moon looked enormous as it lulled above the trees like an alien spacecraft. The air smelled clean, the way that only pine trees can make it smell. As I crested the hill, I saw the crucifix, lost in shadow, facing the city skyline. I figured that if I was going to hang him up there alive, I should at least give him a good view.

The night was quiet; the only sound I heard was my own crunching footsteps, snapping twigs as I approached. I half expected him to holler to me, begging for assistance. Instead, I heard nothing.

The sky was clear that night; Boston glittered upon the horizon as the demon's back came into focus.

"Enjoying the view?" I asked, as I approached. He said nothing, nor did he move.

I had placed him just on the edge of a cliff, only a few feet back, just enough room for me to stand in front of him and tie him off. I clasped the top of the crucifix and leaned around.

Shit.

His face was gone.

Something ate his face.

Now I would never know.

Then again, what the hell ate his face? Just what was in these woods?

I heard a howl upon the wind and decided to get the hell out of there.

Much safer back in the womb. I mean tomb.

Seriously, I meant tomb.

Chapter Thirty

The room was cold, like a meat locker. I'd been in one once before, one of my many odd jobs. I was a butcher for three weeks once; got fired because I was creeping out the patrons. It was there that I really honed my craft with knives. I wasn't partial to knives per se. I used my gun much more, but there were times when my knife skills came in handy. And, it was important to learn how to cut muscle and tendon. I could have used a few more weeks on the job. I never was good at it.

"Tell me, how much do you remember about your parents?"

I did not like this man. He resembled a bifocaled scarecrow; a long, thin, bony man with steel gray eyes and a pointy nose. His hair was a charcoal black; too much gel, slicked left and right with a long, pasty part right down the middle. My newest head doctor, my latest shrink, the next in line to try to examine the inner recesses of my mind.

I felt dried out, how I imagined a heroin addict must feel after going cold turkey. Everything about my existence felt weak, thin on the wind, despite the fact I had ballooned into an orca whale. I stared down at my gray sweatpants; man, my knees hurt. "I don't remember much. Images mostly, more than anything."

He sat there, leaning back in his chair; about his desk many discarded papers, a pendulum rocking back and forth, pictures of perfect, sandy brown-haired children with perfect teeth and perfect smiles. Perfect blonde wife with a gorgeous smile standing in front of a perfect cul-de-sac fucking house. Check. This guy could cross it off the list. Successfully procured the American Dream. He had the American Dream, in all its glory. Now he had to deal with the nightmare that was I.

Behind him, there was a corkboard; pinned to it were various papers that I couldn't make out, too blurry. My eyesight seemed to be failing a bit. Damn drugs. The room smelled of expensive aftershave.

"I want you to try. Tell me about the images. What do you see? How about we start with your mother?"

I shook my head and rubbed my knees. "I don't remember much. I can see her with long brown hair… eyes blue… a sky blue. Green dress. I smell flowers. A book. Children's book. She's reading to me."

"Do you remember her name?"

"No."

"Tell me, do you remember anything else about her? What about the book? Tell me, do you remember anything about the book in particular?"

"No." I looked up at the ceiling; white spotted plaster. "Look, Doc, I really don't remember. What's the point of all this?"

"Tell me about your father then."

"He was an asshole, used to beat me with his tire iron. That what you want to hear? Need some reason why I hear voices, Doc? Looking for some psychotic underpinnings from my past? Some reason for all this…

delusion, as you call it?" I rested my elbows upon my knees and my chin upon my hands. Man, was I tired.

"This works best if you take this seriously."

I took a deep breath and sighed. "I honestly do not remember a thing about them, other than a few images of what they looked like. My father was a big guy; all I can remember is a hard hat and stained clothes. Soot. Construction worker. Maybe a miner. I don't know. Face red, thick lines in his cheeks. Eyes red; bloodshot. I think he was a drinker. That's all I got."

"Tell me about your childhood. What was it like growing up?"

Still holding my chin in my hands, I shook my head back and forth. "I don't remember."

He rested his hands upon his desk and formed a triangle with this index fingers and thumbs. "Please. You must remember being a child. You remembered what your parents looked like, that was a good start. Give me one memory from your childhood."

"I don't remember much since Normandy. Look. I told you people... shit. Look, man, I'll talk to Dr. Poland. Let me talk to him."

"I've been assigned to you now. Robert, you must know that you were never at Normandy. This is something that you have made up. It is not real. It is an illusion. You would be in your nineties."

"I don't age as fast as you."

He pointed to a manila folder on his desk. "I have your medical records right here. We have thoroughly examined you—there is nothing about your physiology that is out of the ordinary. We estimate that you are in your early forties, which would place your birth in the early seventies. I hate to break it to you, but you are not a ninety-year-old man."

I stared him down. All I wanted to do was leap across the table and break that pointy nose.

"Robert, up until this point, we have not been able to identify your origins. You do not come up in any police databanks. We took photographs of your teeth, took your fingerprints. We have no official record of your existence. There are hundreds, thousands of Robert Turners in the United States alone. We need to understand your past, how you came to where you are now. It is essential."

"I told you about my past. You have dismissed it as raving madness. What more do you want from me?"

"How about your wife? Do you remember your wife?"

I did not say a word; I sat there, staring through him.

"Robert, do you remember your wife? Please, I'm only trying to help."

"Which one, I've had two."

He looked puzzled. One eyebrow rose higher than the other did. "In your file it says that you indicated you were married once, but no mention of another. You were married twice?"

"There was my first wife. From before. Before everything. But you just told me I'm not supposed to talk about before."

"Robert, do you remember your wife Katherine Harris? You told Dr. Jennings you were married to a Katherine Harris of Lancaster, Ohio?"

"You mean Kate? Yeah, I remember her. Nice broad. Bit crazy. Course I imagine that sounds weird coming from me."

He smiled and then nodded. "That's good, Robert, really good. It is important that you remember her. I am glad you remember her. When was the last time you saw her?"

"I don't know, man, must be thirty years, maybe more. I left a long time ago."

Silence filled the room. The only noise, the wheezing sound from one of his plugged nostrils. He twirled a paperclip amongst his fingers. It darted up and over his knuckles, moving in motion, as if he practiced often, a nervous twitch. I was making him nervous. I rather enjoyed that.

"Robert, we did some research on Katherine Harris. We were able to locate her. She still lives in Ohio."

"Not surprising, Doc; she was never the adventurous type. Probably still lives in the same shitty apartment. How is she holding up? Haven't thought about her in a long, long time. Did she age well?"

"Robert, Katherine Harris is thirty-five years old."

My head started to feel heavy, foggy, as if coming out of a deep sleep. The wall behind the doctor started to shimmer and shake. I held my head in my hands. Behind my eyes, tiny daggers started to push forward. I could feel a migraine coming on. "No. Can't be. You've got the wrong Katherine Harris."

"Robert, we've been in contact with her. Out of all the things you have claimed to us, it is the only thing that we have been able to confirm. She remembers you, Robert."

"I don't understand…" The world started to spin.

The doctor leaned forward, hands clasped as if praying; he rested them on the desk, settled amongst the papers. "Robert, I sent Ms. Harris a photograph of you. She knows you. She is your wife, Robert. She says that you went missing five years ago."

My mouth felt like volcanic ash. I could feel warmth vibrate up my left arm; my heart started to pound. Pins and needles in my chest. "Not possible. I know who I am. Not possible."

"She misses you, Robert. I asked her if she knew your family, but she did not. It seems you kept her in the dark about a great many things." He pointed at the file, "She says you left one day after work and never came back."

"I suppose that part is true, that I remember." I thought of the Gateman, thought of our ludicrous bumpy car ride through the whiteout snow. I thought of the graveyard, of Father Newman. I thought of Cotton.

"Would you like to see a picture of her?"

My heart started to pound. I did not want to see the picture—yet I needed to. The pins and needles turned into tiny daggers. I could feel my breath shortening, my throat collapsing. Whispering, I said, "Show it to me."

He placed in front of me a picture of a beautiful blonde woman; rosy cheeks with large, flowing hair and too much lipstick. Her face was a little plump, but her eyes were a radiant ocean of blue. I recognized her. Sort of. Somehow, she was different. Different in the sense that I knew that I knew her, but did not feel like I had known her—not in the way he said I had. Yet I remembered Kate. I remembered our apartment. I remembered our fights. Then I remembered what else I had left behind. "I do recognize her."

The doctor smiled as if I had won him a prize. "Very good, Robert! I am so glad. Tell me what else you remember."

I pointed down at the picture. "I remember that is what Kate looked like thirty, forty years ago. But that was then, not now."

The pleased look upon the doctor's pale face disappeared. He took a deep breath and then placed another picture in front of me, photo side down on the table. "I want to show you another photo, Robert." He flipped the picture over. "Do you recognize this person?"

It was a photo of a small boy, no more than five, six years of age. He had sun-bleached blonde hair, eyes the color of silver clay. He was smiling in the picture; dimples pierced both cheeks. Something about him seemed familiar.

"Robert, do you recognize this child?"

I shook my head and bit my lip. My throat tightened further. Stuttering, I said, "Can I have a glass of water?"

The doctor nodded; in the corner of his office, he had a small water cooler. He stood up, took a paper cup, and filled it while saying, "Robert, you do know why I showed this to you, don't you?" He handed me the cup.

The cool water felt like heaven gliding down my throat.

I knew. "I know what you are about to say. But it cannot be. These are old, old photographs. He'd be a grown man by now."

"Robert..." still standing, arms folded about his chest, he nodded towards the image. "This is your son. His name is Robert, after his father. He was born about the time you left. Robert he's five years old."

I started to rock in my seat, I couldn't help it—it was uncontrollable. "No. No. No. Cannot be. No. Cannot be. No."

He sat back down, and then took the photograph away. He stuffed it into a folder, and then placed it within a desk drawer. He leaned forward, elbows upon the desk. "Robert, this is your family. You left them five years ago and have been missing ever since. You are sick, Robert. I'm here to help you."

"No, can't be true, I know it's not true. I know where I have been. I remember Normandy! I have the dog tags!"

"Robert, it's time I told you. I have examined your dog tags. I know you think that they belong to you. I know that you think they are from World War Two. But Robert, I assure you that they are not."

I reached inside the neck of my sweatshirt, clasped the tags and pulled them out from underneath the fabric. I held them in my right hand. "No. You are wrong. I remember the boat. I remember the cannons; I remember my friend's head speared with shrapnel. I watched him die at my feet as I stood in there, waiting, waiting for the door to drop!"

He leaned back in his chair, seemingly defeated. "I know that you think that, Robert. I know that you believe that to be true. But Robert," he pointed at the tags, "those tags are vintage Vietnam War. They say your name but I don't believe that is your real name."

I could feel my blood boil. "You lie." I ripped the tags from my throat; the necklace split in two. I slammed my hand on his desk. He jumped with fright, and then stood up. The door opened and in walked my orderly pal.

Malcom asked, "Is there a problem here?" He placed his hand on my shoulder and squeezed. My shoulder burned in his vice grip. Suddenly I felt very tired; my legs gave out, and I collapsed back into the chair.

"No," I whispered, "No problem".

Malcom slowly backed up to the door and stood, arms folded across his chest. The doctor poured himself a paper cup of water. He took a long gulp, then wiped the sweat from his brow. He sat back down and stared at me. He didn't say a word. We sat there in silence for thirty seconds. Malcom wheezed through his nostrils.

Finally, the doctor cleared his throat. "You know what I think, Robert? I think you found those tags. You found them lying on the ground, perhaps on a hike. Or perhaps worse. Perhaps you stole them. Or maybe even hurt someone. I think you saw the name on the tags and your mind, your condition, fabricated all of these memories. You believed you were in the army; you believed you fought in World War Two. You are a confused man, Mr. Turner. But don't worry, we can help you."

I hung my chin against my chest. The sweatshirt felt dry against my skin; my own drool encrusted the fabric. "I want to see Dr. Poland. Can I please see Dr. Poland?"

My doctor looked up at Malcom as if to ask him permission. Malcom nodded. He looked back at me.

"I don't know how to tell you this, Mr. Turner."

"Tell me what?"

"Dr. Poland is missing, presumed dead. A tragedy."

Chapter Thirty-One

I always wondered what it felt like when you died. I had felt the searing pain of a bullet lance through my abdomen, followed by numbness, coming to amongst the blood-stained shores of France. But I had not felt that moment of death, where I ceased to exist. The Gateman had said he "brought me back," suggesting I had fallen past the threshold, yet I had no memory of it. Over the passing decades, I concerned myself less and less with the prospect as it seemed so distant, being as invincible as I had become.

Does it hurt? This being the question that many have pondered; problem is we cannot ask anyone because they are not here. Death has finality. Anything other than finality is not death. Certainly, my Normandy wounds burned, an excruciating burn that felt like my skin was melting from my body. But would death itself have a feeling, a moment of pain?

Certainly, if you die by violence, there must be pain. I can imagine that those poor souls beheaded by the Al Qaeda jihadists felt searing pain as the executioners' blades sawed at their necks. But again, that single moment where the nerve endings sever and the head falls to the floor, at that split second—what does it feel like? Was there a final jolt of pain? Certainly, the terror experienced in such a death would be beyond description, but how does it *feel*? Is it electric?

Well, now that I have died I can tell you.

For me, when I died, I did not feel pain. It is very hard to describe. The best way I can paint the picture is it felt like slipping away. Kind of like that feeling you get right before you fall from somewhere high, where your heart flutters and you know you are in for some trouble. Like when you slip on the ice and you know you're about to slam your head on the surface; not that moment when you see stars, head bouncing off the ice, but that split second before it occurs when your core feels hollow. That was what death felt like to me. A falling away.

I wonder now, as I sit here in the black, alone in the void, how my victims must have felt. I knew now that I had overdone it, that I had played up the macabre a bit too much. I was dramatic, a showman, a Hollywood actor. I wanted them to feel fear; punishment they earned. My role, as Cotton had told me, was to punish the sinners and eradicate them from the world. It would be too easy for them to die unaware of the reason why. It was important that they knew the reason why.

The reason was everything.

I did not torture, maim, or keep someone alive to feel pain. When it came time to carry out my mission I was quick and deliberate—but only after they had seen me, only after I had a moment to stand on my soapbox and wax poetic about their sinful existence. The life they led. The people they destroyed, the carnage left in their wake. The dominos they toppled.

260

And there I was, a towering presence over my prey, the single domino, standing tall, standing firm—and destined to stand forever.

Or so I thought. I did not stand forever. So many things I thought wrong… so many things I had wrong for so long.

I'm here now in the deep. There is no leviathan to keep me company. No Anti-Christ to have a few beers with. No demons with which to toss around the football. My thoughts are my eternity. It is odd what you can remember.

Down here in the void, the noise that is the world ceases to haunt; it does not distract. There are no televisions that bark advertisements at you. The roar of jet planes and automobiles is a distant memory. There are no computers, no smart phones. There is no internet access, no Wi-Fi, no hi-fi. There are no mp3s, no downloads, no web-based clouds. No touch screens, no wide screens. No high definition, no streaming, no wireless speakers.

There are no sports teams. No championships, no world titles, no gold medals. There are no soft drinks, no microbrews, and no specially formulated, highly priced and packaged Russian vodkas. No gluten free products, no fish oil, no garlic extract, no weight loss formulas, and no cross fit training. There are no ecofriendly roadsters; no, Hell is not green. There are no blades of grass and no autumn leaves.

There are no low-fat Greek yogurts. No whole grain products, no vegan-based solutions. There are no handbags, no shopping malls, no Wal-Marts. There are no hipsters, no hippies, no goths, no punks, no jocks, and no metal-heads. There are no fully configurable accounting systems. There is no regulatory reporting, no quarterly filings, and no annual reports. No stock prices, no options, no put options, and certainly no futures.

There are no New York City steakhouses, no Chicago deep-dish pizzas, no Denver weed, no Philly cheesesteaks, and certainly no fucking horrendous Pittsburgh hoagies with French fries and coleslaw.

There is nothing.

NOTHING.

Hell is nothingness. Friedrich Nietzsche must be so damn proud. He believed in nothingness as a faith; how surprisingly it seems he was right, at least about this aspect.

When you have no distractions, it is amazing how clear your mind can become. To say my memory is sharp is an understatement. To say I have total recall would be apt. I now recall every single aspect of my life. It is all there, at my fingertips but I have no hands.

I can remember in second grade that time I pissed my pants during CCD class. I hated going there, every Sunday, listening to the boring stories the volunteers watered down for us. Never the Old Testament, no fire and brimstone, nothing but loaves and fishes. I remember that day as if it was happening now. I can feel the warm trickle that started down my left leg, followed by the sudden gush as if the Hoover Dam had exploded. I can remember how my face flushed with crimson, my eyes as wide as headlights as I saw the dark pool form amongst the inner thigh threads of my best corduroys.

I can remember my grandfather. After all these years, these memories were previously lost to me, but I can remember him now as clear as if he were sitting here next to me. I remember how he came to live with us after my grandmother died. How he quickly succumbed to senile dementia. He would wear his shoes on his hands and his underwear on his head, frequently. My mother was convinced he was faking it. He would come to dinner every night virtually naked, sometimes fully in the nude. I remember how one night, to see if he would flinch, my mother served him dinner while she too was naked. He did not bat an eye as my mother stood there in the buff serving him a tray of meatloaf. My mother yelled, "Well, Papa, what do you think, is this how we should behave?"

His only response, as he sipped his water, "Well, Kelly, I guess you're just as crazy as I am."

My mom's name was Kelly. She was beautiful but mostly angry and smelled of gin and weed.

I remember all these things. The first time I hit a home run. The first time I sacked the quarterback. How my father used to take a shit with the bathroom door wide open. How he used to wear a robe too short and would have no issues having my neighborhood friends getting a good look at his dangling balls.

I remember all this. And for so long, I remembered nothing at all. It was as if I had been reborn, my past a lost story from some hack writer. But now I remember.

But mostly I remember her.

If I can focus, but for a moment, I am with her.

I walk with her every day. Her hand feels warm in mine. She smells of sunflowers and honey. We walk each day along a river. The water hisses and bursts amongst the rocks. There, along the dirt path, a wooden bench. We sit there every day. My arm around her shoulder, her long cherry-colored hair draped across my neck, the warmth of her cheek against mine. I can feel her body breathe calmly, soft breath upon my skin.

The air is warm; the sun is setting. I can hear birds flutter amongst the trees; off in the distance the soft roar of the closest road. We are alone here upon the path, just the two of us, in our own private Garden of Eden, our own paradise. Reborn here together in my memory, we embrace, we kiss, we make love amongst the flowers. It is here that I go, my own private Eden. If I can concentrate clearly, I can see the sparkle of her green eyes. I can taste the sweet tenderness of her lips; run my fingers through the silk that is her hair.

It is here I go, to run from the black. It creeps in all around me, constantly winning the war, clawing back. Each moment I cling to her, the darkness fights to overcome. She is but a shining light, a shimmering star against the backdrop of space. She is my cosmos, my Venus, my shooting star.

But then she tells me to leave. That she never wants to see me again. And the darkness creeps back in.

I get angry when the darkness wins. It is like a dream you wake from that you wish you could return to. You try to go back to sleep, to find that same moment, that same feeling but it always eludes you. If there is one freeing moment of death, is that, if you concentrate hard enough, you can return to the dream.

However, it is, after all, just a dream.

Chapter Thirty-Two

I fell asleep quickly despite the uncomfortable mattress. My eyes felt heavy; the drugs weighed me down. Falling asleep here despite these awful sheets was easy. It's easy when you're grossly overweight and sedated with animal tranquilizers.

I wasn't out long, barely asleep. My mouth tasted funny. I smelled an earthy smell, felt an awful draft and I opened my eyes. I was no longer in my room, no longer at the asylum. At first all I could feel was the clump of dirt in my hand, the chill of the autumn night. I was outside. The wind howled past my ears. I winced; slowly the world came into focus. A full late September moon crested the horizon; the black blemished with endless stars, more stars than I had ever seen. I was kneeling; dirt stained my sweatpants. I was wearing only a black T-shirt; my arms were freezing, my skin pulled so tight that a scratch would bleed me dry. As I stood, I saw an endless field of corn stalks, seemingly in every direction, a sea of rustling leaves. There was no sound other than the wind and the cackling of the dry stalks rubbing against each other. By the looks of the sky, it was very late, probably past midnight, but a few hours before a hint of dawn.

Where am I?

How did I get here?

My dog tags felt cold against my skin, the chill of the night turning the metal ever colder.

Where is my bed? Where is my room?

I was not in the hospital.

Was I ever? Or have I been here, down in the ditch the whole time?

The air smelled of decay and coming winter. The earth would be raw soon. It would not be long now before the destroyer came, the God of desolation, the hound of winter.

The remnants of the harvest are not long for this world.

The one constant truth that exists on this rock, is that it *is just a rock*. A giant ball of dust coalesced together by the forces of gravity. Turning and moving, hurtling through space and time, an endless cycle of life, death, decay, and birth. All mere dust. Every living thing, sharing in the same DNA structure, spliced by a master architect and molded like clay into all we know.

But is the architect absent? As I stared up at those endless stars, twinkling in all their glory, I had to wonder, is He there at all? The doctors say I imagined my entire mission. They say that I dreamed up the Gateman. Did I dream up my God as well? Is He nothing more than a construct of my feeble mind trying to make sense of what I do not understand? This world, an existence of myself that I cannot possible comprehend. Am I insane, a paranoid schizoid?

They say that Cotton is a voice in my head, which I created.

No, I'm not.

I turned quickly to see a path amongst the stalks. The wind howled from that direction.

"Who's there?" I called out, my voice but a faint whisper in the night. "Show yourself!"

The voice whispered back, *Follow.*

I shook my head and fell to my knees. I clutched my skull in my hands; I could feel the searing pain behind my eyes well up once more. "No, no, you're not real. You're in my head you're not real."

Follow, the voice said once again.

I buried my head into my knees. With my fingernails digging into my skin, I clasped the back of my neck. "I won't. I will not follow. This is not real. I am in my bed, this is not real. I need my medicine. I need my medicine. I need my medicine. I forgot. I forgot. I forgot medicine!"

The sky cracked above my head. Lightning darted across the sky as angry black clouds swept in, blocking out the moon, disintegrating my stars. The path seemed to jump in the flashing light. Darkness followed, the wind stopped, and I found myself in ink black nothingness.

No sound.

Nothing at all.

I had to wonder, am I dead? Is this what it is like to die? Am I alone in my room, dreaming of my own death? Is my last breath gasping from my decaying lungs? Is my mind collapsing like an imploding star? Will I join the billion souls already in the earth, returned to the dust, a mere husk, dead flesh, a meal fit for an earthworm?

Suddenly, lightning popped the sky once more; thunder crashed, booming in my ears. It was then that I saw him standing on the path.

I could not see his face; his clothes were from another time, relics of early colonial times. The sky turned black when I realized whom it is.

"Cotton! Wait!"

I stumbled forward into the emptiness, towards where I believed the path was. The sky opened up and hail shot my back like buckshot. Lightning burst again; I could see the hail bouncing off the crushed stalks that lay before me. Up ahead, a shadow took the corner.

"Cotton, please, wait!"

The hail stung my neck and rain pelted the path. I slipped and fell; the stalks were slick with rain and ice. The sky exploded again as I saw another turn; there, I saw a man just out of reach. Before he took the corner, he turned to look at me.

His eyes glowed red like the hound of hell.

Lightning crashed another time and the world turned black. I slipped and fell again; I cut my arm on the razor-like stalks. I could feel the blood trickle down my forearm to my fingers. I stood back up and stared up at the sky; the rain pelted my face as I screamed to the heavens, "Please, wait, dear God, make him wait!"

My shirt stuck to my body like a second skin, an unwanted rag. I clawed at it, ripping and tearing. I tossed the rag into the stalks and carried on, my exposed chest red, pockmarked from the ice daggers that rained down.

I turned the corner and the storm stopped suddenly, as if someone had turned off a light switch. Gone was the wind, the rain, the pelting hail. The moon returned; the sky opened back to stars. There was a clearing before me, a single solitary wooden shack, a barn that stood alone.

I heard what sounded like a creaking door. Cotton must have gone inside. There were no windows, just a single wooden door.

As I tip toed towards the barn, I heard a howling off in the distance. It did not sound like a dog or a wolf. It did not sound like any animal that I knew. There was a tinny, almost mechanical cry to the howl, like an early nineties dial-up modem crossbred with a lion.

What the fuck?

The door to the barn smacked closed. Someone was watching me.

I needed to see him.

The howl brayed again and I realized that, whatever it was, it was getting closer.

I heard what sounded like stalks crunching. Fear ran up my spine like liquid water. I leapt to the door and ripped it open. Slamming the door behind me, I could hear something breathing outside. Something big.

I turned to see an open room with a vaulted ceiling, a single light bulb swaying from the end of a long line. Across the ceiling was an array of wooden support beams and cross beams.

There in the middle of the room I saw a man.

"Cotton?"

The man did not seem to notice me. His back was to me; in front of him, something hung from a black iron hook. Behind my eyes, I could feel the pain return.

"Cotton?"

He did not turn around. As I stepped closer, I saw a wooden table adorned with many sharp knives next to the man. Two saws. A pickaxe. Red blood stained the axe.

The man was big, bigger than I was. The thing in front of him was not as big. The thing in front of him moaned. A soft moan. A moan of desolation. A moan of loneliness. A moan of realization. A moan of acceptance. Of giving up.

The man clutched one of the knives and slashed the thing in front of him. The moaning ceased; he returned a blood-soaked knife to the table.

I realized now that the man, the slasher, was not wearing colonial garb. This was not Cotton Mather. No, this was something else. I could see more clearly now, he wore the dress of a butcher. I now knew who this was. What this was.

I had found my next quarry. I had found my next mission.

I said, "I see you," but the man did not respond. He mused at his knives for a moment, cocking his head side-to-side, unsure of what to use next. Like an artist deciding what color to paint. This was his artwork, his pleasure. His eyes were sunken, as if no eyeballs existed at all. His skin was translucent; blue veins bled through. He picked up a dicing knife and studied it. Smirking, he decided against it and placed it back upon the table, teetering on the corner edge. It fell to the floor. As he bent over to pick it up, I got a good look at what was hanging before him.

It was not a pig.

It was not a young calf.

For this was not a butcher of farm animals.

This was a butcher of men.

I saw a young man in his early twenties, his throat slashed; blood ran down his neck. The assassin had stripped the young man down to his underwear; the innocent wore boxers dotted with yellow smiley faces. There was a large open wound about his stomach and flesh gutters upon his skin, torn down the underside of each arm. The assassin had bound the victim's hands and affixed then to a rusted iron hook suspended from one of the rafter beams. A long, burnt red, rusted chain lead from the hook to the beam.

The young man's eyes were missing; gouged out, not sure how long ago. His purple tongue protruded outward; it hung to the side.

The butcher picked up the fallen knife and went back to work.

The pain behind my eyes grew even stronger. I fell to my knees. I knew how this worked. I had been here before.

"It's not real," I said, while I clasped my head, "You're not real. I probably saw you somewhere but this is not real. I need my medicine. I need my medicine. I need my…"

The man turned around and smiled at me. His teeth glistened like an angry wolf. Bringing a blood-soaked finger to his lips, he said only, "Shhh," and grinned. Blood stained his white apron.

I cried out, "Cotton, you son of a bitch, I know this is not real! You're not real, you son of a bitch!"

The butcher frowned. His eyes glowed a hellfire red. The smell of rotten eggs filled the room. Holding the knife in his hand he sauntered toward me, his legs cracking, not working, crunching, deconstructing into a crab-like walk. His knees splintered as bone broke. I raised my head to see a flash of steel followed by stars and searing pain.

And I woke up in my bed.

I was soaked in sweat, my hospital issued sheets clinging to my skin.

I was out of breath; my chest felt heavy, full of phlegm.

I sighed a deep a sigh of relief. *Thank God, it was not real.* The ceiling spun before my eyes.

Who said it wasn't real?

My room was pitch black. I saw nothing. But I felt a presence.

"Cotton?"

Yes, my son. It is I.

I clutched the covers up over my head. "You're not real. I made you up. They said I made you up."

No, no, no, my son. It is they who are deluded. Poor misguided fools.

I pulled the covers as tight as I could. "Cotton, they say I'm sick. They say I invented you. That you do not really exist. That you were a fabrication of my mind. They say these dog tags…" I clasped at my neck and I realized my chain was missing, the tags were gone.

We've accomplished so many things, Robert. Our work is not yet done.

"No, you're not real. And even if you were real, you set me up. Either way I'm not listening to you."

Dear Robert, what have they done to you? This abominable medicine they have been pumping into your veins. It is corrupting you, confusing you. I have been your guide your entire life. Come, let us study your vision. There is a demon afoot.

I pulled the covers up over my head. "No, Cotton. Not this time. Not again. Not ever again. You are not real. I am sick. I am really, really sick. I must be sick. I have to be sick. I am sick."

"You're not sick, Robert," another voice said. This voice was not in my head. This voice was near. This voice was at the foot of my bed. I recognized this voice.

I sat up to see an outline in the dark: a tall, skinny man who resembled a scarecrow. Jericho. Clothed in his light blue asylum issued hospital gown. I noticed he was wearing only one sock. A red sock pulled all the way up to his knee.

He pounced on me and pushed me upon my back. Tired and weak, I could not fight back. I fell with a thump backwards onto the mattress. He leaned in close; his breath smelled of sour milk and decay. His long oily hair touched my cheeks on either side; my skin crawled in disgust. His eyes were wild and fully dilated. He held my hands down upon the bed and straddled my sternum with his legs, then dug his left knee into my stomach. I struggled against him, but could not move. He had me pinned.

Whispering through clenched teeth, Jericho said, "Do not listen to him, Robert. He is a liar. A cheater. A thief in the middle of the night. He will misguide you and mislead you."

"What? Who? What are you talking about?"

He grinned; several teeth were missing. His gums were as brown as pottery dirt. "Azazel. Do not listen to him. You must not. He will lead you astray. As he's done before."

"Azazel?"

"Yes. The deceiver. The defiler. The one to whom you call Cotton."

Don't listen to him, Robert, Cotton's voice reverberated throughout my cranium, radiating as if my mind were a steel drum. *It is he who is a liar.*

273

Jericho let go of my left arm and smacked me in the face. It stung, harder than it should. "Shut up, Azazel! Shut your mouth! There will be no more words from you."

I stopped struggling. I craned my neck upward. "Hold on a minute, Jericho. Wait right there…" He stared at me, cocked his head sideways; his bangs covered his eyes. He pulled the strands of hair from his face, squinted at me, and concentrated. His face was so sunken he looked like a living skeleton. "Jericho, you're telling me you can hear him?!"

He said, "Of course I can, you fool." He stood up and hopped off the bed. "You didn't actually think you were crazy, did you?"

At the foot of the bed, he knelt down, his arms disappeared below my feet. As he stood back up, I saw that he was holding two pieces of thick rope, about three inches thick.

"What are you doing, Jericho? Where did you get that?"

He grinned at me as he folded the rope over his forearms in preparation. "It has been a while since I've had to do this. But there were times… oh, the stories I could tell you."

"You didn't answer my questions."

He jumped on the bed again, slamming his fists into my chest. The force of the blow bounced the bed; it crashed upon the tile floor. My ribs felt like they were stabbing me from the inside. He smiled again as he held me down with his knees upon my chest. First, he tied my left, then my right arm to the metal bedposts. He made two tight knots; the fabric of the rope burned into my skin as he pulled.

My arms stung with fatigue. I was helpless.

He leaned in close and, with his middle finger, he tapped his fingernail upon my forehead. "Come out, come out, come out, Azazel! Playtime is over."

That stinging feeling behind my eyes returned, pushing as if something was trying to claw my eyeballs out from the inside.

"What are you doing, Jericho? Tell me!"

As he leaned in over me, he pulled from beneath his hospital gown a silver crucifix. He placed it against my forehead, and then kissed it. It felt like he placed a cinder block on my head. Standing back up, he said, "In my past life, I was a Catholic priest. I spent seven years as a member of the elite North American appointed clan of official Exorcists. They say that such prolonged exposure to such events is why I need my medication."

He bent down and picked up a small, leather-bound book. "You poor soul. All these years and you believed you were doing the Lord's work. Only to find that those whom you seek to eradicate have made a Legion amongst your flesh. Now... these events require a witness but unfortunately, we are fresh out. I thought about asking one of the orderlies, but I assure you they would have laughed in my face. You see, they're all a bunch of unbelievers."

He sat at the foot of the bed and patted my leg beneath the sheets. "Now don't worry. This will be over soon."

The voice inside my head said, *Robert, do not listen to this imbecile.* It sounded different from before. Gone was the New England accent. It sounded almost Eastern European, with a hint of Russian.

Jericho rushed towards me and smacked me with the book across the cheek. Red flashes panged across my eyes. "Quiet you! Enough, Azazel." The crucifix fell upon my chest. It felt like a twenty-five pound weight. Jericho smiled and placed it back upon my forehead.

The pain behind my eyes intensified. It felt hot, as if scalding hot water was about to ooze from my sockets.

Jericho sat back down and started to thumb through his Bible. He paused for a moment, closed the book, and shook it as he said to the ceiling. "You see, this is the problem. All these damn unbelievers. Putting us in here as if we are some deranged bunch of lunatics. If these people had been here back in the day, there would be no prophets. No truth tellers. No messiahs. These assholes would have had them all committed and forced them to play board games until their teeth rotted out."

I tugged, pulling as hard as I could, but could not get my arms free. All those years, all that power, all that strength, and here I was reduced to this: a barely functioning invalid. No stronger than a ninety-year-old grandmother or a two-year-old toddler.

Jericho stood up upon the mattress, his legs straddling my sides; the bed creaked. He pointed down at me. "All great prophets are so-called schizophrenics. All had visions, all heard voices. If Moses stood here before us today and claimed that a burning bush had spoken to him the word of God, do you realize what they would do to him? They would tie him to a bed and feed him creamed corn for an eternity! They would poke, prod, and pump him full of drugs! They would brand him a freak, an outcast, a deluded blabbering fool. They would shut him off, confined, and kept from the masses. We now live in this world. The true lunatics are the ones out there, outside the walls, lost in their ways. Do you realize that in this day and age it is more socially acceptable to watch internet pornography than to go to church on Sundays?"

He's deluded, Robert, the voice in my head said, spinning about my cranium like electricity upon a conductor. *Don't listen to this imbecile.*

Jericho's wild expression turned grim. He clenched his teeth, his skin pulled tight upon his sunken cheekbones. "Time to come out, Azazel." He stood before me, bowed his head, and began to pray. "Lord have mercy. Christ have mercy. Christ hear us. God the Father in heaven. God, the Son, Redeemer of the world. Have mercy on us. God the Holy Spirit, the Holy Trinity, the true one God. Have Mercy on us."

My throat felt constricted. My tongue felt numb. My chest felt heavy. A skyscraper pushed down upon my lungs.

Jericho continued, "Holy Mary, pray for us. St. Michael, St. Gabriel, St. Raphael, all the holy angels, archangels, cherubs, and powers... all holy orders of blessed spirits, St. John the Baptist, St. Peter, Paul, and Andrew... pray for us."

I felt what I can only describe as a wet tube sock slowly move about my throat; it felt deep, from my stomach, my core, all the way up to my tonsils.

Jericho fell to his knees. "Pray for us now, all the holy apostles and disciples of the Lord. All holy martyrs and doctors hear our prayers. St. Anthony, St. Dominic. All holy virgins, widows, and saints of God!"

Shut him up shut him up shut him up shut him up, bounced about my brain. The wet tube sock thrashed about my throat like a viper. I pulled upon the ropes and felt the fabric burn into my skin.

Jericho said, "Deliver us, Lord, from all evil..." He returned to his feet. He made the sign of the cross, leaned in close, and placed the bible upon my chest. It felt heavy like a cinder block, pushing my body down hard into the mattress. "Deliver us, Lord, from the snares of the devil. From anger, hatred, and ill will. From all lewdness and everlasting death. By your coming, by your birth, by your death, burial, and holy resurrection. We beg you to hear us."

The thrashing about my throat stopped. I could hear the sound of footsteps outside the door, the shuffling of feet. The door pounded and someone tried to push it open; Jericho had placed the back of the single wooden chair I had beneath the doorknob. Outside I could hear Malcom shout, "Jericho, open this door this instant!"

Jericho continued, "Do not keep in mind, O Lord, our offenses or those of our parents, nor take vengeance on our sins. To recant the holy prayer that you taught us. Our Father, who art in heaven, hallowed be thy name; thy kingdom come; thy will be done on earth as it is in heaven. Give us this day our daily bread; and forgive us our trespasses as we forgive those who trespass against us; and lead us not into temptation, but deliver us from evil!"

The door creaked; the chair dug into the tile and held. Malcom yelled out, "Jericho, open this damn door!"

Jericho ignored him and continued his rant, "Strike terror, Lord, into the beast now laying waste your vineyard. Fill your servants with courage to fight against the dragon! Let your mighty hand cast him out of your servant, Robert Turner, so he may no longer hold captive this person whom it pleased you to make in your image, and to redeem through your Son; who lives and reigns with you, in the unity of the Holy Spirit, God, forever and ever."

The door crashed open as Malcom, along with two fat orderlies I did not recognize, pounced into the room.

Malcom looked down to see me tied to the bed. His eyes practically popped out of head.

"Jericho, what in God's name are you doing? Again?"

Jericho grinned at him as he backed up against the wall. "Exactly. In God's name. That's exactly what I'm doing."

"Again, Jericho? Again?" Malcom turned to the other two. "Take him back to his room."

He leaned in close to me and untied my left arm, then my right. I could smell cigar smoke and bourbon upon him.

"I'm really sorry about this, Mr. Turner. This is entirely my fault. Unfortunately, this isn't the first time."

I could hear Jericho shouting as he was lead down the hall. "You're free now, Bobby! Azazel is no more! No longer will he haunt you! No longer should you be terrified of your own insides!"

I sat up in the bed and touched my throat. I could breathe easily. Malcom looked at me with a worried expression. "Can I get you anything, Mr. Turner? Glass of water perhaps?"

I shook my head, "No. I'm fine."

"We can talk about this in the morning," he said. "First I need to deal with him. Jericho is… troubled. I wish I could say this was the first time he's done this." He moved the chair back into the corner. "I'm really sorry." He shut the door behind him as he left.

I was alone in the dark.

Cotton, Cotton, are you there? I thought, closing my eyes. *Speak to me, are you there?*

I heard nothing, the only sound the hissing of the radiator beneath the barred window.

I knew he was not there.

Nor would he ever be again.

Chapter Thirty-Three

I am sitting in a church and I am next to my mother. It is not a very ornate church, nor is it grand. The ceiling is not that tall; the mahogany cross beams slope to a point. All I can see is a row of ceiling fans running down a beige support beam, white speckled paint behind it. There are about forty rows of pews; the pews are a sandy color, more beige, beige upon beige, beige everywhere, boring and non-descript like how I view the sermons. I am young, no more than eight years old.

Along the walls are stained glass windows depicting the saints. Between the windows, wooden carvings depict the Stations of the Cross, Christ's journey through Jerusalem to his undeniable fate. Before me the alter, a green marble base with a white and black spotted stone surface. Behind the alter a wooden crucifix suspended high, a spotlight upon the cross and the carving of Christ. To the left and the right of the crucifix I can see two reverse profile shadows of our Lord, hanging there in opposite direction, his head, hung low, the shadows facing left and right.

The priest is at the podium. He is an older man, late sixties, bald chrome dome. He is slender in stature and his robes dangle as if on a coat hanger. He has just finished the gospel. I am sitting by my mother's side; she smells of flowers, musk, and gin.

The priest says, "St. Augustine once said, 'Therefore, do not seek to understand in order to believe, but believe that thou mayest understand'—something I feel that we have lost in this day and age. We quest and thirst for an understanding of God but we do so now in peculiar ways. I think another quote from Augustine puts it well. He once said, 'There is another form of temptation, more complex in its peril... It originates in an appetite for knowledge. From this malady of curiosity are all those strange sights exhibited in the theatre. Hence do we proceed to search out the secret powers of nature, which is beside our end, which to know profits not, and wherein men desire nothing but to know.'"

I stare ahead at the crucifix dangling in the spotlight.

The priest continues, "You see, my fellow brothers and sisters, I feel that we too are falling into this temptation. We seek to understand that which we are not meant to know. We aim to unravel the backdrop of space, to see the origin of the stars. Yet, these things we are not meant to know. It is in the name of science that we seek to disprove the existence of God, and I fear that it is out of the most selfish motivations that these endeavors are empowered."

My back tires, sore against the hard wood of the pew. Before me, an elderly gentlemen nods in agreement with the sermon.

"The Word was not brought to us by men. God made the Word flesh. God and no other. The entire human race is but an infant. We are ignorant of our world. We have grown and will continue to grow into adulthood. And perhaps we will learn more of our existence, of the Creator, if He so chooses to allow this. Make no mistake, my brothers and sisters. With each discovery, with each new fact, the Lord, thy one true God, has allowed this peek into his grand tapestry."

I feel a strange pain behind my eyes.

"I read recently that scientists claimed that they had proved the Bible false. They seek to do this at every turn. Through studies of camel bones, a recent magazine claimed that Abraham could not have had with him camels in Egypt, for domesticated camels did not exist in Egypt at that time. This contradicts our scripture. Therefore, thousands of years of history, tradition, and faith is dismissed in an instant."

I squint; the pain feels like a tearing, a clawing of tiny dagger-like hands behind my retinas.

"So quick they were to publish these findings. Word spread so quickly. How happy they were to dismiss all of our beliefs so quickly, with such little knowledge. Nevertheless, there is an explanation, of course, a contrary. I offer a rebuttal."

Tears leak from my eyes. I clasp and squeeze my mother's hand. She does not pay me any attention.

"Abraham was not from Egypt. He traveled to that land from Mesopotamia. Moreover, science has proven that, at the time of Abraham, domesticated camels existed between the Tigris and the Euphrates. He simply brought the camels with him on his journey." The priest laughs. "And here this is front page news. How eager, how quickly we aim to disprove thousands of years of tradition. Moreover, at what aim? At what goal?" The priest stares down at the silent congregation. "Without a God, to what moral law do we abide? By society? Without a God, sin reigns."

Rick Maydak

Before me, I see the crucifix shimmer. Christ's twin shadows, turn; no longer in profile, they stare at me.

284

Chapter Thirty-Four

The pointy-nosed doctor with the pasty part said, "Mr. Turner... tell me, how have things been progressing?" He leaned forward on the desk. He faked a smile. Thick wrinkles formed across his forehead.

Pictures of his kids stared at me. I had started to hate them. Their perfect teeth. Stupid smiles. Oily, shit eating grins. "Good," I said, avoiding eye contact.

"Tell me, Mr. Turner, do you still hear the voices? Is the medication taking?"

I slumped back in my seat and stared at the ceiling.

"Please, Mr. Turner, these sessions are important."

I cleared my throat, and then, to his horror, I spit in the corner. "Doc, I don't hear a damn thing. We done?"

He sat back in his chair and rested his right ankle upon his left knee. He frowned at me in disgust. He twirled a pencil between his fingers; like poetry, it rolled from finger to finger. "Look, Mr. Turner. I understand why you are upset. I have been informed about what happened two weeks ago. I know about Jericho. He unfortunately... suffers from delusions. You see, he was, at one time, a Catholic priest. Unfortunately, though, his path turned for the worst."

"Sob story. Don't care."

He shook his head. "I don't know what you think you might have seen, or what he might have told you. But I assure you that Jericho is not well. However, he does have a tendency to be a bit persuasive. Suggestive. I just want to make sure that his delusion did not somehow derail the progress that we have made."

"Look, Doc…" I leaned in forward and put my fists upon his desk. "Just keep that freak out of my room, okay?"

"Jericho will no longer be an issue. We have denied him gen pop. We will keep him in his room for the foreseeable future. Now tell me, Robert, I am curious. Tell me in your own words if you feel the medication is working. It would seem to us that it has, but I would like to hear you tell your own perspective."

I leaned back in my chair and stared up at the ceiling. Someone had tossed a pencil into the foam tiles above. It dangled above the doctor's desk. "These meds are turning me into a whale, Doc. I can't stop gaining weight. Pretty soon you'll have to get me one of those rascal scooters so I can make it down the hallway."

"Yes, you've complained about this before. This side effect you mention is not a known, clinically proven one. However, exhaustion is unfortunately a side effect. I suspect this exhaustion is the reason for your weight gain. When you came to us, it was obvious that you exercised. You were clearly in shape. Malcom has indicated to me that you spend most of your days staring out the window, inactive." He took a sip of coffee and winced. "Robert, this time spent staring out the window. Tell me, what are you thinking?"

I closed my eyes and took a deep breath. "I'm not thinking much of anything, Doc. It is best not to think. Thinking too much takes me to places that I don't want to go."

He stood up, took his sport coat off the back of his chair, and put it on. He tugged on the cuffs. "Robert, I called you here today because I wanted you to meet someone. I have someone in the other room who would like to talk to you. Would you be willing to come with me?"

"Who is it?"

He opened the door and held out his hand, suggesting I acquiesce. "Come, I'll show you. Nothing to be concerned about."

He led me down the checkered tiled hallway past several doors until we came to our destination. The door was solid, no glass window or partition. I had no clue what awaited inside.

He said, "I think this experience will not only be a welcome one, but it should help us accelerate the progress that we've made."

He opened the door and entered. I followed behind him. As he moved to the side, I saw her. After all these years. Kate. Her blonde hair was even bigger than I remembered. A giant hurricane of hairspray. She wore a crimson-colored one-piece women's business suit. It had big black buttons up the center that ended just beneath two mountains of ample cleavage.

"Hello, Bobby," she said. With a pink handkerchief, she wiped the tears from her eyes. Too much blue eye shadow, as always. "It's good to see you again." She had not aged a day.

My doctor said, "Please take a seat, Robert."

I shook my head in disagreement. "No. I will not take a seat. What the hell is this? What are you doing?"

A tear squeezed out of Kate's eye and cascaded down across her chin. It left a small trail, a tiny river amongst the caked-on concealer. "Please, Bobby; it's been so long, please..."

I backpedaled towards the door. "That's not Kate. It cannot be Kate. Kate would be in her late sixties. I do not understand, but that is not Kate. I don't know what that is, but it is not Kate. It is more tricks. More lies!"

My doctor stood between the door and me. He shut it behind us. For a moment, I thought about rushing him, but my limbs felt too heavy. Like I was weighed down by gangland cement boots. Mere moments from now, they were going to drown me in the harbor. What else could be their aim?

My doctor said, pointing at the chair, "Robert, I want you to hear what she has to say. It is important that you hear what she has to say."

He pulled the chair back from the table. "Now, please, take a seat."

"I can hear just fine from back here." I leaned against the ceramic block wall.

Kate, or whatever that was, nervously crumped the handkerchief in her hands, rubbing her thumbs amongst the fabric in a nervous twitch.

I said, "Well, out with it then. Say what you came to say."

Her lip quivered. Little pools of snot formed at the base of her nostrils. Her eyes welled up with tears. "Bobby, when you left us, you were having a breakdown. You used to have so many horrible dreams, nightmares, all the time."

"This I know. I've had nightmares for decades."

She wiped the snot from her nose. "But, Bobby, every time you would drink, you'd start to talk about your parents. You claimed such awful things."

"Bullshit, Kate. I don't even remember my parents."

She looked at me with longing, sad eyes. "Bobby, you used to say that a lunatic murdered your Mom, Dad, and big sister. You claimed he made you watch as he took them one by one. This haunted you, Bobby, every day of your life. You drank so much to try and not remember. But each time you would get drunk, you would talk about it. Those were the worst nights. You'd always wake up screaming, covered in sweat those nights. I didn't know what to do, I felt so sorry for you."

I stared down the doctor and pointed at Kate. "That's bullshit. I have no memory of that."

Kate stood up and clutched her matching red purse. "Bobby, you used to talk about it all the time. You called him the German. You said that he made you watch. I would beg you to go to the authorities with these memories, but it was only when you were really intoxicated that you'd even consider talking about it. The one time I mentioned it when you were sober you stormed out of the house and didn't come back for two days."

I stormed over to the doctor and grabbed his lapels with my mitts. "Get me outta here! I don't know what game you are playing or what this is but that woman is a liar! She doesn't know me any more than you do! You get me outta here right now. That is NOT KATE!"

The door burst open and Malcom came in. With hands that felt like vice grips, he pulled me through the room. My feet dragged across the tile. I shouted towards the ceiling as he pulled me down the hallway like a rolled-up carpet. "That's not Kate! You Goddamn sons of bitches, that is not Kate!"

Chapter Thirty-Five

I awoke to find my door open. My sheet was missing, my naked body fully exposed. The air was cool, crisp. Glass covered the floor, the window smashed open. The cold night air seeped into the room, through the iron bars like a ghost. I shivered, sweat coating my skin. Outside, the wind howled and I heard thunder off in the distance. The tree outside my window creaked and cracked, struggling against the elements. I perceived the sound of leaves rushing in the wind. Moonlight filled my room, and shadows danced upon the ceiling, swirling leaves, dancing tree limbs.

My first reaction was one of fear. Then confusion. Then emptiness, loneliness, and desolation. Is this even real? Am I destined to go down this path forever? This doubt of reality, something that I cannot escape?

The door to my room creaked, inviting. Was anyone out there? Or was I alone? Jericho, that freak, probably busted out again. Up to his mischievous mayhem once more. God knows what he did in here while I was sleeping. However, this could be my chance to get out of this nuthouse.

With much effort, I struggled into a sitting position. Damn these infernal meds. As each day went by, I felt weaker and weaker. I used to be so strong. Abnormally strong. But here they have reduced me to an infant. I swung my feet over the side of the bed; the checkered tile felt cool upon my toes. My knees screamed as I stood up. I scuttled over to the dresser and put on a pair of gray sweatpants complete with a matching gray sweatshirt. The doorway beckoned.

I tip toed around the glass, careful not to cut my feet. There to the left of the door, I found my blue slippers. I put them on and ventured out into the hallway.

It was empty. Checkered black and white tile in either direction, not a soul in sight. The only thing to my right, an empty water cooler. To my left, up ahead, I saw brown stains upon the floor. Left lead to the living room. Left lead to my freedom. As I stared down the hallway, my mind played tricks with my equilibrium. The hallway almost seemed to bend, slightly shifting sideways. My legs felt so tired. Like a geriatric dinosaur, I lumbered on.

As I made my way down the hallway, I noticed how eerily quiet it was. The only sound was the buzzing and snapping of the overhead lights. Given that it was nighttime, only every third light bank was illuminated; the rest, intentionally dormant. My stomach hurt. I felt sick and the room began to spin. Fucking meds. I stared down at my feet and I saw a stain upon the floor. It was blood, fresh blood, slowly turning brown in the cool October night air that wafted down the hallway from the portal that was my room.

Why is no one here? Where are the orderlies? Where is Malcom?

The trail lead down the hallway to my destination. I passed a bubbler. The living room doors swung ever so slightly in the wind that pushed at my back, careening in from the broken window in my room. I noticed, there upon the white doors—handprints, handprints in blood.

I stopped for a minute and closed my eyes. "Cotton. Are you there?" He did not answer. He truly did feel gone. Not distant, not missing. But gone. As if he had never been there to begin with. Despite my aching, tired body, my mind felt crisp, clear. My eyesight may have been suffering, my limbs may have been burning, but my mind felt as clear as it had ever been. There was only one way out of here, and it was through the living room, through the half fence, half door that lead to the outer hallway, past the offices, where the guard would be. Based upon the blood-stained handprints before me, I had to believe that there was no one there. This place was empty; the heat was either off or had failed. The cool of the night prevailed. This place was a crypt, a tomb. God knew where the lunatics were.

I pushed open the door; the room was dark. Thunder slammed as lightning cascaded across the night sky piercing through the living room windows—there, a shadow up where the television should be.

As I walked into the black, the clouds cleared, moonlight penetrating the barred windows, and I saw something—someone—hanging, arms outstretched, legs dangling, head hanging to the side.

The crucified Christ.

But it was not Christ.

It was Jericho.

Jericho raised his head slightly; blood trickled from his trembling lips. "Help me…" I reached out, my fingers trembled.

"Don't touch him."

I turned to see Dr. Poland standing behind me. He wore a white coat; blood stains streaked like claw marks up and down the jacket.

My insides beamed with electricity. "But… they told me you were presumed dead!"

He grinned; I saw tiny daggers amongst a sea of blood-red gums. "I cannot die. You know that, Robert. You know that I cannot die."

"I don't understand." Outside the thunder clapped again and lightning cracked across the sky as clouds passed by the moon. The room turned dark as the clouds sauntered on. The moonlight peeked through; shadows danced across the walls. As he came into focus, I saw that Dr. Poland was no longer Dr. Poland. It was him. The Gateman.

"Don't look so shocked, Robert."

I pointed at him, my arm and fingers shaking. "Not possible. You are not possible. You are not real. I am getting better. My medication is working, dammit! God dammit, it is working!"

"Is that what you think? Is that what they told you?"

Behind me, Jericho wheezed. Blood trickled from his mouth.

"I don't know what to think anymore. If you are real, then why did you do this? Why did you string him up there like that?"

Dr. Poland—or the Gateman, I should say— stepped towards me and pointed up at Jericho's struggling body. His finger shook as he spoke. "He will be a corpse soon. Sent away. He will become a feast for the pests that truly run this Earth. He is nothing to me, an insect, as they all are. He is a nuisance; he is an annoyance, an insignificant bump along the road."

"If you are the Gateman—that doesn't sound right. The Gateman would not do that. The Gateman speaks for righteousness. He speaks for truth. He speaks for the one and only true God!"

The creature before me began to laugh a deep, chortling laugh. He broke into a cough and spit oozy black phlegm upon the floor. "My dear boy, I don't speak for God! You fucking imbecile. Its time you learned the truth, my little so-called demon slayer. You fucking fraud. You lunatic! You were my unmolded clay and I made you into something so special."

"What? But Cotton… if you're real, he's real. We were doing the Lord's work."

"Is that so? Is that what you think? Do you think the kind, loving, Mr. Puppy dogs and ice cream pushover up there would actually sanction a holy crusade of murder? You humans are so easy. Just a little nudge is all you need, and bam, we have the Spanish Inquisition. Boom and we have the holy Crusades upon Jerusalem."

He grinned; blue veins formed in his cheeks. Moonlight filled the room as if it were mid-day. "These days, with all these distractions, most don't notice me anymore. Those who do can only act on a small scale. This lack of faith in God has a downside, I'm afraid. I should be happier than a pig in shit, but instead, it has resulted in less belief in me, as well."

My heart filled with an icy fear. "What are you saying… are you… you're the Devil?"

He started to laugh so hard he doubled over. He slapped his knee. "Don't I wish? No, you dipshit, I am not the Devil. Maybe someday. He is getting soft. I'm somewhat of a star pupil, so to speak. Maybe I'll audition. Push for a promotion."

A realization fell over me. "You mean all those years, all those times…"

He nodded, grinning so wide it encompassed his entire face, stretching the skin. His teeth glistened in the moonlight. "Yes, yes, yes! You bet. You were not slaying demons! You should only look in the mirror, you fool! It was you, you all along who was possessed!" He nodded towards Jericho's now lifeless body. Blood trickled from Jericho's toes to the floor. "Till that asshole came along. Talk about fate. You and he winding up here together. But he won't cause any more problems now. He has made his way down the tunnel. He's in the black now."

Outside, lightning screeched across the sky. I said, "What is the cost then of all this evil? Why me? To what aim? To what goal?"

He shook his head and laughed. "No goal, you fool. There is no goal, no grand plan, no huge scheme. Don't you understand? This place is nothing but a playground to me. You are just a schoolyard chum I convinced into beating up the retarded kid. That's all you are."

"But why. Why send me here at all? Why did Cotton leave me to get caught? For what purpose?"

He smiled. "You fool. You think you're the only one? Those moments where your Cotton would not respond, would seem to be sleeping, did you really think he was slumbering? No, you moron, he was off playing with others. The casket was never full, always empty. You really did just get caught. He didn't set you up. He wasn't home between your ears at the time. You think you are that important? So deluded." He paused and licked his lips. "You know, most can be pushed to do little things here or there. We've been at this for so long. But you, you are special in one regard. All it took with you was one little nudge and you were off murdering "demons" by the boatload. It was all too easy."

I sunk to my knees. I clenched my fists. Blood slowly trickled across the tile to the left and the right of me. "I'm damned." The tiredness that had crippled me seemed to lift off my shoulders as if a giant weight disappeared. As if I was Atlas shrugging off the world.

He smiled at me, lips crunching up, puckering into a kiss. "Oh yeah, you're fucked. Been fun though. I had a blast. Cotton Mather. Can you believe it? An idiot like you latching on to such an obscure historical figure. Azazel had you so bought in! He is so good. Such a good partner, that Azazel is. We've had so much fun over the years."

I clenched my fists tightly. They felt as they once did. When immortality pulsed through my veins. "So, you are Dr. Poland then, too? You were there, in the interrogation room, fooling me? Confusing me?"

He nodded, humming with excitement. "Well, he was a real man, at one point, but not for some time. I have enjoyed his flesh for a while now. Cannot say it suits me too much. His pecker is really small! Poland, my ass! His last name should be Irish."

"So, what happens if I kill you then?"

His eyes suddenly turned red, then black like oil. The blue veins about his cheeks pulsed. "What?"

I leapt up and grabbed his neck with my mitts, slamming him backward to the floor. As I held him down, his legs convulsed, his bones cracked as his legs jutted out in both directions at a ninety-degree angle, splintering, shattering, tearing bone, taking on a crab-like appearance, something I had seen before. This sonofabitch had played me this whole time.

I pushed and pushed down upon his windpipe; my knees held his small, thrashing frame to the tile floor. He hissed at me and howled like a wolf. I had heard the sound before. In the field, amongst the corn stalks. Here before me, the hellhound, blubbering and spitting blood like all the demons I thought I had killed before.

His eyes turned a hellfire red; the stench of sulfur filled the room. My eyes started to sting. I felt the pain behind my eyelids as before.

Was Azazel fighting to get back in?

I closed my grip as tight as I could as the creature thrashed beneath me. Suddenly, I saw stars, the pain behind my eyes collapsing me to my knees. The power that had returned left as quickly as it had formed. The creature sprawled to his knees; on all fours, he scampered across the floor, slipping and sliding across the blood-stained tile. He careened out into the hallway, smashing into a cart. I heard him laugh as he slid down the hallway and out into the night.

I fell to my knees. I heard the outside door slam shut as a blast of cool air filled the room.

Jericho hung there before me, broken neck, head dangling sideways.

He stared at me with longing eyes.

Chapter Thirty-Six

Cotton once said to me that our greatest threat to humanity was arrogance. Man's need to dethrone God, to take His place amongst the stars as the most significant in history. It was man's aim to bring down the heavens, to claim the stars as his own, to control the tides, determine the weather, and to decide who lives or dies. This is what dominates mankind, the zest, the zeal to determine the basic human right of life. It has started all our wars and delivered all our genocides.

Mankind had now embarked on its last critical step on the evolutionary ladder, the destruction of religion. We did not need it anymore, we had evolved past the need for mystical beings to explain what we could not; science could now do that for us.

Cotton did not believe that science in and of itself was evil, but it did, in his estimation, attract evil men. Men hell-bent on disproving faith in a higher power. Cotton believed there was a movement in the scientific community to disprove a creator. Certainly, Stephen Hawking was one of Cotton's least favorite on the subject. Hawking had long argued against a creator God and instead believed in the concept of the random universe. This was not a new concept. Bertrand Russell wrote in 1935, for instance, that one should think of man as a mistake of randomness, in fact, an unfortunate accident, a sideshow, as he put it, "a curious accident in a backwater." We were not deliberate, nor did someone design us; rather, we were just some random freak show puked forth from primordial ooze that he could offer no real plausible explanation for having been there to begin with.

Cotton found these theories dangerous. It rendered us as nothing more than organic robots, eating, fucking, and shitting our waste across a barren landscape that had no purpose whatsoever. To these men, we were not central to the universe, we were not important in the cosmic sense, we were not special, we were not unique, we were nothing. We were nothing more than drones, falling out of our mothers, born to wear suits, ties, and purchase iPads forever. No purpose. Just consumerism. We were nothing more than our houses, our cars, our televisions, and our clothes.

However, not all in the scientific community would agree. Brandon Carter, a famous astrophysicist from Cambridge—in fact, a buddy of Hawking—argued what became known as the Anthropic Principle. The Anthropic Principle states that all the apparently haphazard and unrelated constants found in physics all have one wacky thing in common: these are exactly the values necessary to have a universe that could create and sustain living beings. Said differently, the universe is a designed construct, just for us. Too much math supported this theory.

This is what I was thinking about as I stared at the cemetery before me. These thoughts and images were in my mind, no doubt, because Jericho reminded me of them. I remember now, his rant in the living room that I ignored. I had heard that rant before, from Cotton, late at night.

Cotton told me that when Hawking dueled with the principle he had to admit that it certainly would appear that the universe was not random. There was a lot of evidence to support Carter's essay. His rebuttal, however, was a very interesting one. Hawking argued that while this universe didn't appear to be random, it would be random if it was one of a gazillion universes—thus making our seemingly deliberate collaboration of physical laws to be nothing more than a random combination of shit together due to the fact that this is just one universe. This universe itself was random versus all the others. All those constants falling together did so by mere chance, while in the other universes, perhaps they did not.

When asked to prove the existence of other universes, he replied that he could not. He could only theorize and argue for it.

Cotton liked to point out, when asked to prove the existence of God, he could not, he could only theorize and argue for it.

Said differently, if you want to believe Hawking, you have to take a leap of faith on whether or not his theory is correct. Ditto upon the opinions of Cotton Mather. Either way, it is faith that is required.

Faith to be religious. Faith to be an atheist. Cotton would suggest that one is harder than the other is.

Cotton liked to argue that the reason why Hawking was so determined to disprove God was that he was so fucking pissed off that God stuck him in that wheelchair to begin with. Trapped that brilliant mind behind such a debilitating disease. He simply thought Hawking had an axe to bury. Perhaps he did.

Don't we all?

It would seem to me that poor Jericho had been losing his mind over all this. I can see how he could. A third alternative, I suppose, is to think of nothing at all. Just watch television and shop for designer jeans. Pay it no mind and the question will not come up. And just what is the question? It is the central question to any man's life. Why am I here?

So why was I here now? Why did I skulk through the city streets to come back? I did not know, truthfully. A power drew me here again, like a moth to the flame.

Yellow police tape surrounded the cemetery. An October moon hung above the Charles; the air was cool. The sound of rustling leaves rushing amongst the gravestones drowned out the soft roar of the city that loomed behind me. I crested the steps and ducked under the tape. It would appear that my newfound celebrity had brought much attention to my dead friends. Beer cans and candy bar wrappers littered the brick path. My feet felt cold upon the brick—I had not yet found myself a pair of shoes and my slippers were worn through. It had been two weeks since I left the asylum. The only shoes I could find so far were too small, a rather dwarfish deadbeat. I shivered; my sweatpants and sweatshirt were not enough to keep me warm in the elements.

The ghosts were quiet.

I made my way towards the back of the cemetery. Tree branches creaked in the wind. Leaves swirled in the air before me. There at the back, I could see the Mather tomb, reduced to a pile of crushed bricks.

The police had torn the top right off the tomb. A second circle of yellow police tape surrounded what was now an open hole down into the crypt. My ladder was gone, replaced with an aluminum painter's ladder instead. I tiptoed to the edge, looking left, and then right to see if anyone was watching.

No one.

The moonlight shimmered off the ladder's side; I climbed down and let my bare feet touch the cold earth.

There was nothing left. The cops cleaned the place free.

Cotton's rotted wooden casket still sat there, though, lonely amongst the dirt walls.

I dug my fingernails under the lid and pulled as hard as I could. The wood creaked and moaned as I pulled. Finally, it broke free in a cloud of dust.

I coughed as I waved the dust from the air. To my surprise, the coffin was empty. Just as Dr. Poland had said it was.

Had I been talking to myself all these years after all? I heard a raspy chuckle echo throughout the graveyard.

I knelt down and reached below the casket. There was one thing the cops did not find. They were probably too nervous to upset the dead. The steel felt cold in my hands. I placed the gun upon my back, hanging from my waistline. I cinched my sweatpants tight.

The grating, gravely laughter met me as I ascended the ladder. There, far off to my right, a shadow sat, perched like an owl, upon Prince Hall's lonely spire.

As I stepped upon the path, the shadow leapt through the air like a toad, landing with a wet smack upon the brick before me. His shadow loomed in the moonlight. A fat, bloated, black turd.

"Dr. Poland…" I said.

He said, "I knew you'd be back here! You had to check the box, didn't you? Couldn't leave well enough alone, could you? Had to see it for yourself! After all you've borne witness to, you still needed to see it with your own eyes." He sauntered towards me, hunched over, moving like a gorilla. As he came into focus, I noticed that he no longer wore a shirt, only torn black slacks. His chest was very hairy, nipples too pointy, a grotesque shade of irritated red. His gut fell over his waistline.

"I had to see if Cotton was there or not."

"Ha! Cotton! There you go again with Cotton. I told you, there never was any Cotton. Just you and Azazel enjoying each other's company all these decades."

The wind howled. Dry leaves kicked up behind his head. I felt the cold steel of a gun barrel against my back.

I clenched my fists. "How many? How many innocent people did you have us kill?"

He sauntered in his gorilla-like walk towards me, knuckles upon the ground. Mucus dripped from his lips. He smiled dagger teeth as he said, "Why, all of course. All were innocent."

I brought my right hand behind my back and firmly grasped the handle of my gun. "Not possible. The Beast knew. He admitted it."

"No, no, no. That was just Azazel. You imagined all that. He was just some poor dope we picked out one night. They were all just poor dopes we picked randomly. You oblivious fool."

I squeezed the handle tight. "Why? TELL ME WHY."

He grinned; a long strand of saliva dangled towards the brick. "There is no why. Never has been, never will be. With time, Azazel will return. Jericho may have sent him away, but he will claw free and we will reunite. It may take years, decades, even a millennium, but he will respawn, and I will be waiting for him. We make quite the dynamic duo."

I took a deep breath and let it out slowly. I could hear the sound of ships rocking upon the Charles River behind me. Off in the distance I could hear a bell buoy knock around the harbor. "Tell me... you know so much... what am I thinking now?"

He cocked his head to the side at a ninety-degree angle; I could hear the bone beneath his flesh crack and splinter. "Excuse me?"

I smiled. A warm tinkling sensation cascaded up my arms. "That's what I thought. Azazel is the one actually in control. You are nothing but *his* lackey. Without him, you cannot read my thoughts. In fact, I doubt you can do much of anything. Tell me, if I send you back to Hell, do you think you'll claw your way out any faster?"

He dug his fists into the brick; blood trickled down his knuckles. He snarled at me and dug his heels in, ready to pounce.

I said, "Let's find out." He rushed me; his arms and legs flailed while saliva and mucus sprayed from his mouth. I pulled the gun from my pants and shot him between the eyes. The smell of gunpowder, my old friend, filled my nostrils.

He lay dead before me, a broken heap of bone, muscles, and mucus.

The bell buoy clanged again as I heard a seagull squawk. It would be light soon.

Upon the distance, I heard sirens scream.

I knelt down, gun at my side, and waited.

It was time I paid for my sins.

Chapter Thirty-Seven

I awoke to the sound of a baton smacking my cell bars. I heard the sounds of shouts, hooting, and yelling. The smell of antiseptic and urine filled my nostrils.

"You have a visitor," a voice said above the howling. Damn inmates. Damn rabid dogs. Always howling for some reason.

My eyes stung from dehydration. I rubbed them raw as the guard came into focus. "Who? Who would visit me? It better not be Kate. I don't want to see her."

The guard stood in the shadows; I could barely see him. The overhead light shown down across his uniform, but his face stayed hidden in the black. "I don't know. I just take the call. They say someone is there to see you and you get two visits a month until your court date. Do you want to go or not?"

I sat up and scratched my knees. The orange prison jumpsuit was itchy. Like sleeping in a bed of sandpaper. I stared ahead at my concrete block wall. There was a brown smear across the surface. God only knows what that was. I could guess but I'd rather not. Who could be here? I wondered if it was my stupid, useless lawyer. Better not be Kate.

"Fine, yes I'll go," I said. As I stood up, I heard my limbs crack. I had barely moved since they stuck me in this box. This four-walled world.

The guard's face came into the light. His skin was as red as a baboon's ass. Drinking problem for sure. Wasn't even trying to hide it. Big, dark circles under his eyes. A tint of yellow. I wondered if he knew his liver was failing. Clear to me. Poor bastard. The drink got him. He just didn't know it yet. "You're not going to give me a problem, are you?"

I shook my head and smiled. "No. No reason. I've done enough already."

He led me down the hall past the cells of the degenerate. Cell after cell of rapists, murderers, and thieves. A den of vipers. They had not allowed me to associate, which was probably best. I'd be a target, given the news. I was popular. I had made the papers. These guys were merely amateurs, jealous of my accomplishments. And I was out of the demon culling business. Retired. Too bad really. Would be a good fight.

As the door opened, my heart leapt in my chest. There, across the glass, was my love. Jennifer. The guard motioned me to sit down. I began to cry; decades of longing came flooding back in mere seconds. Tears streaked my cheeks. I sat down and grasped the yellow phone. My hands trembled.

"Jen… but how?"

She too began to cry; tears fell down her freckled face upon her lips. She sniffled and wiped her nose with her sleeve. Her hair was radiant, matching perfectly with her strawberry-colored blouse.

Her limps trembled as she spoke. "Bobby…"

I wiped the tears from my eyes. "Jen, I don't understand, how can you be here? I've missed you so much." The phone shook in my hand.

She closed her eyes and took a deep breath. "It has been so long."

My entire core quaked. She was as beautiful as the first day I met her. She was as beautiful as the memory burned into my conscience. Breathing and trembling before me. "I love you, Jen." I leaned in close to the glass, huddling in my stall.

"You left me, Bobby. You left me alone. You never came back. I thought you would." She wiped another tear from the corner of her eye. "I thought you would."

"I wanted to, Jen, I really did. But I couldn't. They took me from you."

"But why didn't you seek me? Why didn't you find me?" Her lips trembled.

I held my head in my hands as the phone dug into my ear. "You asked me not to. Remember? You asked me to leave you alone." Never had my head felt so heavy.

"But I thought you would come back... I kept thinking one day I'd see you. That you'd suddenly come back into my life. I looked for you. I always looked for you. Around the corner. At the store. In the park. Wherever I was, I looked. I thought you'd show up, do something crazy. I wanted you to."

I shook my head. "I couldn't. I loved you too much. You asked me not to, remember?" I could smell her strawberry perfume. "You were my world."

She cried, then held her head in her hands, sobbing. "I never thought it would be forever. I thought you loved me..." She looked up at me with the saddest eyes I'd ever seen. "And then you ran away."

I sniffled and held the phone tight. I stared into her eyes. "I do love you. I never stopped loving you. You asked me to leave you be. You didn't want to be my wife anymore. So I left you alone. It was the only thing I had left. The only way I could show you that I still loved you... was to honor you. I loved you more than I loved myself. More than my own selfish wants and desires. All I had left was to not return. To honor your wish of me. It was the only way to show you that I still loved you, by not coming back. You asked me not to. You said you could not be with me."

She shook her head back and forth in disagreement, biting her lip. "I waited, Bobby. I waited for you. For years."

"I wanted to come back, Jen. I did. But I couldn't. I had to honor your wish. And I got lost. I... I got lost."

"I always thought you'd come back!" She held her hand to the glass. She whispered, "I thought you'd come back to me..." I reached out and touched the other side. We stared into each other's eyes. She said, "But then I died, Bobby. I died. And it was too late."

My heart thundered in my chest. "I'm sorry, Jen. I love you so much..." Tears fell like buckets as I tried to contain myself. "I should have been there for you. When I found out, I ran. And I never looked back. I was living a lie, pretending you didn't exist. I tried to live a normal life. I did. But when I found out you died, I could not bear to face the morning. I ran. And then I got lost. Lost for a very long time."

She closed her eyes and pulled her hand back. "And now... after what you've done, you're still lost to me."

"I know, Jen. I know I've let you down."

She sobbed and closed her eyes. "Bobby. I'm so sorry… but I can't see you again. Ever again. They won't let me. This is but one wish. Before you enter the dark."

"I've died before, I know the dark."

"Not like this. This time there is no way back." She sobbed and dropped the phone.

Lightning shot across my eyes as a sharp pain pushed hard behind my retinas.

I felt the heavy hand of the guard upon my shoulder. He squeezed hard, sending a shooting pain up my neck. I turned around to see his gruff, red face. "I guess they're not showing."

"What?"

"They're not showing, you lunatic!"

I turned back around and Jen was gone. No trace of her.

He pulled me up out of the chair and pushed me towards the door. "Fucking lunatic. Sitting there babbling at the air like some freak. No wonder you're in here."

Jen…

Chapter Thirty-Eight

They say that I killed Dr. Poland. They say that I dragged the poor doctor up to Copp's Hill only to execute him. Never mind that he had been missing while I was in the hospital. They blamed me for the whole damn thing. They also claimed that I strung up poor Jericho, that I gutted him with a piece of broken glass that I obtained by somehow smashing the window behind the bars in my room. They do not know how I smashed the window. They do not know how I was able to crucify Jericho despite my weakened condition.

My doctors said it was more than a minor setback. It was obvious to all that I was beyond their clinical help. I was an animal that needed to be put down. I found out soon what happened to my dog tags; the oily, pointy-nosed doctor had taken them. After examination, they claimed that I had stolen them off a dead man in Ohio. An unsolved mystery now solved. They blamed me for his murder and countless others that I did not commit. They extradited me to Ohio. You see, this was in their best interest. For in Ohio, they could put me down like the dangerous dog that I was.

Death penalty.

The papers would claim that I killed an estimated seventy-five people across Ohio, upstate New York, and New England. Their estimates are well short. In particular, New England had over that many alone. I was a very busy boy over the decades. The vast and extensive transportation system around Boston extended my reach. I had the subway, commuter rail, Amtrak, bus lines, stolen cars, and my own two feet at my disposal. You would be surprised how far you can walk when you are determined.

I once walked sixty-seven miles to kill a supposed demon. About fifty miles in, I realized I left my gun and knife behind. No point in turning around then. Sometimes, you have to make do.

I met him at a diner in western Massachusetts. I ordered three flapjacks, some hash browns, and a cup of coffee. After he left, I clutched my maple syrup-soaked fork and followed. You would be surprised how well a perfectly placed fork thrust to the jugular can inflict damage. At just the right angle, you can spray that jugular like a busted garden hose. Only drawback, it is quite messy.

Chapter Thirty-Nine

I decided upon tacos and chili for my last meal. Not that crappy Cincinnati chili, mind you—while I was currently in Ohio, I had not gone insane, at least in my own mind (of course others would disagree). That shit is worse than dog food. And to top it off those people pour it over spaghetti noodles. I can't think of a worse meal. And I have eaten raw hot dogs and beans out of a tin can, mind you. And these people consume this shit willingly and even brag about. It is crap. Yet they eat it over and over again in some weird local pride vain attempt at liking it. Over and over and expecting a different result. The very definition of insanity. And people think I'm nuts.

My goal of course was to leave a mess behind. My last and perhaps greatest accomplishment, a disgusting diarrhea-stained corpse. It was the least I could do, I thought. One small final way to rebel. One last, however insignificant, statement to the world.

I wasn't sad, nor was I even angry. It had been so long. I had lived long enough. They can say I was deluded. They can say that I made it all up in my mind—but I know the truth. They had me questioning myself for a while. But I have my memories, and Jericho was all the proof I required. I wore the years on my soul if not on my body. I was thin on the inside, barely alive within a husk that was still ticking. This would be best.

Had this happened years ago, I am not sure what would have occurred. Perhaps I would have fought the drugs, kicking and screaming for hours, perhaps never succumbing, perhaps becoming a medical mystery. Headline news. Man refuses to die from lethal injection. Now, now that Cotton was gone, now that I had sent the Gateman back to whatever pit he crawled out of—now, I was sure it was my time. But I did not fear, I did not cry. There would be pain, sure, but it would all be over soon.

I had done too much evil. I could claim ignorance. I could claim that it was a set up. I could claim that I was not acting of my own free will. But I knew that deep down I enjoyed what I did. That made me a monster. And monsters should be burned. The world cannot accept them.

I remember the hallway was long, the floor a nondescript white tile with charcoal-colored streaks stained from too many shoes. The overhead lights an unforgiving fluorescent. My wrists hurt; the cuffs were too tight. My shoulders burned, my arms affixed behind my back. A precaution, in their mind of course, but I was not a flight risk. I wanted to die. Seeing Jennifer again murdered me. I was already in Hell. Might as well make it official.

The table was cold, the metal straps frigid upon my wrists. There was a viewing area, a piece of glass. The seats were all empty with two exceptions. There, in the front row, I saw Kate. She wore a black dress and carried with her a black leather purse. As I had always remembered her, she stayed true to character, too much red lipstick and too much rouge. Caked-on eye shadow. Her eyes looked lonely and sad.

With her was a small boy. His hair was a sandy brown; his deep blue eyes I recognized. He did not smile, he didn't frown, and he didn't have tears in his eyes. He looked like me. My son. My boy. Whom I would never know.

As they pumped the drugs into my body, as I felt the icy water fill my veins, all I could think of was why she brought him here. Why did she put him through this? What good could come from it?

I saw the tunnel and started to fall into the black.

That poor kid, being forced to watch a man die. What would it do to him? What psychological repercussions would occur? They say evil begets evil. That poor kid. Perhaps monsters beget monsters as well.

Fucking idiot, Kate. Warping our son.

I was not afraid of where I was going. There are billions more dead people than alive. I was going where we all will go. There is only one certainty in life. It ends. I fell into the tunnel and the light left my eyes.

The black welcomed me like a long-lost friend.

Chapter Forty

She floats before me in the black. Her hair is the color of freshly picked red roses. Her skin appears as smooth as porcelain. Her eyes are green like the leaves of eucalyptus. She is my love. I wish to call to her, but I cannot speak, for I have no mouth. I wish to touch her, to hold her warm body against mine, but I have no arms. I wish to kiss her, taste her strawberry lips, but I have no lips. I am nothing. Nothing at all. A conscious entity, hovering in the abyss, cast away from the world.

This is my hell.

I cannot embrace her. I cannot tell her how much I love her. Yet I can see her there before me. She no longer smiles. Tears streak her cheeks; she cries, her lips tremble. How I long to hear her soft, delicate voice.

It is silent here, purely silent. I cannot hear my own heartbeat, for I have no heart. I do not hear the background roar of the world. To say it is sensory deprivation would be an understatement. I am not deprived—my senses have vanished entirely.

All but one that is… I can see her. She is there. She is concerned, she is tortured. She is hurting. And it is I who am hurting her. She is a memory. Death can take all my senses, but my memory is my own. And I'll never forget her. I'll never forget the moments of sand we spent together. She is my love. Alive in my memory. Here with me, forever. It happened. We happened. And no God, Devil, or hellhound can take that from me.

The End